Straw Hat

Straw Hat

John David Harris M.Ed.

Matador
9 Priory Business Park,
Wistow Road, Kibworth Beauchamp,
Leicestershire. LE8 0RX
Tel: 0116 279 2299
Email: books@troubador.co.uk
Web: www.troubador.co.uk/matador
Twitter: @matadorbooks

ISBN: 978 1789016 222

British Library Cataloguing in Publication Data.
A catalogue record for this book is available from the British Library.

Printed and bound in the UK by TJ International, Padstow, Cornwall
Typeset in 11pt Georgia by Troubador Publishing Ltd, Leicester, UK

Matador is an imprint of Troubador Publishing Ltd

To my sister, Margaret.
’Til the dawn breaks.

Chapter 1

"IT'S SUCH A beautiful building," murmured Susan as she turned to her husband.

He nodded while letting his gaze sweep up over the delicate and lofty vaulting of Chichester Cathedral, all the time being only too aware of the anxious tremor in his companion's voice. This was hardly surprising for they had just left their six-year-old daughter at St Richard's Hospital. She was their only child and needed a series of tests to diagnose the nature of her ongoing ill health, so in an attempt to alleviate Susan's distress, her husband, John, had opted for a sight-seeing trip around the ancient city.

Still barely 9am, the early morning sunlight had transformed the great eastern window and its portrayal of various biblical saints into a sparkling symphony of jewel-like colours, while shafts of light from the clerestory windows set high above in the chancel walls reflected from a brilliant golden cross situated at the centre of the ornate altar.

But, despite all the architectural beauty, nothing seemed able to dispel the worry over their small daughter, and again Susan looked imploringly at the man by her side.

"Oh, John," she whispered. "She will be all right, won't she?"

Her husband, who shared the same concern, nevertheless knew he had to be strong for the woman he loved and chose his words with care.

"Well, she's had these symptoms for some time, you know," he observed gently. "And although they seem to come and go, she never gets very ill, and as I've said before, I think, possibly, that it's all down to an allergy of some sort. So, if we could only strike the right balance with her diet..."

But then, lost for further words, he just placed a comforting arm around his wife's shoulders.

Now in his early fifties, John had married Susan late in life. She was some twenty years his junior, and he viewed the arrival of their daughter, Miriam, as something of a bonus. But, shortly after her third birthday, she had developed distressing and recurring bouts of high temperature accompanied by severe stomach cramps, the result of which had been an endless succession of visits to their local health centre until, finally, he and his wife decided upon a thorough medical assessment of her condition at the private wing of St Richard's Hospital.

Just a shade under six-foot-two and of strong physique, John was by nature a gentle person, although, at the same time, not someone to be crossed lightly – qualities which had originally attracted his wife, and despite their age difference, they had, from the first, been a devoted couple.

John met her shortly after taking early retirement from teaching when increasing demands of the profession had made the job virtually intolerable while Susan, on the other hand, was still commanding a successful career as a housing officer in the Mid Sussex town of Horsham. A woman of style and intelligence, John had immediately been taken with her strong personality but all the while being only too aware of the need to establish a new venture of his own. However, being a retired art teacher and in his mid-forties, he had been at a loss to know just how this could be achieved. But then the new woman in his life had proved invaluable and now they ran a thriving property business, although, sadly, up to the present, mere prosperity had seemed of little help to their young daughter.

Turning away from the delicately carved altar, they slowly made their way down the nave past the elaborate choir stalls and towards the grand twelfth century west door. Gently taking his wife's hand, John paused for a moment to take a last look around the magnificent Norman and early English-style cathedral.

"Nine hundred years old and still absolutely beautiful," he breathed. "You know, when this was built, national values were somewhat different to what they are now. The emphasis in those days was on the quality of workmanship and the finished article rather than time and motion and the size of the pay packet."

Failing to get response, he bent down to look at his more diminutive wife, but from her worried expression he rather doubted if anything he'd said had even registered – a fact amply reinforced when she eventually spoke.

"John, you're quite sure we shouldn't have remained at the hospital? I mean, if anything were to go wrong..."

"Well, you heard what the specialist said, love. There was nothing to be gained by just hanging around in that waiting room the whole morning and drinking endless cups of their free coffee." He pulled a face before adding cynically, "Only, it's not free of course, is it. With their medical fees, it's more like a grand a cup, and those out-dated magazines! God knows how many fingers have thumbed their way through that lot."

"John!" interrupted his wife with a touch of irritation. "Can't you see how worried I am about Miriam?"

He squeezed her hand.

"Of course I can, love," he assured her. "I was only trying to lighten the mood a bit. In any case, we'll be picking her up around mid-day, and you never know there may be some good news. Also, don't forget, if there's even the slightest problem, the nurse promised to contact us on my mobile phone. Although, I must say, when I insisted on it she seemed to think I was being a bit OTT."

Emerging out into the strong spring sunshine, they crossed the spacious lawns surrounding the cathedral and approached West Street where John stopped for a final appraisal of the Norman workmanship.

"The hands that laid those stones have long since gone," he observed philosophically.

"Well, they might have done, but ours are still here," retorted Susan. "So, are we going back to the hospital or what?"

"Well," he replied tentatively. "I thought of visiting 'Barrington's' in Chapel Street. They're an auctioneer firm, and I believe their rooms are open today for a preview of the items in the next sale. They're just round the corner so I wondered if you might like to take a look."

His wife slipped her hand through his arm and looked up with a brief smile.

"All right then. Just to please you."

And so, with her reluctant agreement, they turned into Chapel Street.

Barrington's itself dated back to the fifteen hundreds. Built of Sussex flint, its church-like entrance allowed for access to the ground floor via several steps that led down from the pavement level.

Once inside they found it to be a spacious area lined with trestle tables that groaned under the weight of various antiques ranging from copper bed-warming pans to a myriad of kettles and china tea-sets, while around the perimeter there emanated the solemn rhythm of ticking from various grandfather clocks that stood in stately witness to the multitude of merchandise on display.

Above all though, there was a mustiness that pervaded the entire atmosphere and which John guessed was probably because most of the items originated from elderly people. And he couldn't avoid a certain sadness in knowing that the artefacts echoed the lifetimes of a past era. Wandering through the corridors of trestle tables, he gave vent to his thoughts.

"Well, you can bet your life that whoever owned this lot won't have any further use for them."

At this melancholy observation, his wife stopped dead.

"John, we all know that we don't last forever but there's no need to keep reminding ourselves of the fact. For heaven's sake. Keep harping on about people and hands that aren't here anymore. What's got into you today?" She would have said more but, just at that moment, her attention became drawn to an oil painting above the auctioneer's platform. "Oh. Isn't that absolutely exquisite!" she exclaimed.

And, as John followed her gaze, he found himself looking at the picture of a young boy fishing from a riverbank and he had to agree the beauty of the composition was quite breathtaking. Portraying late autumn, it depicted a low sun which lit up a dazzling array of browns and golds which shone from the leaves of the trees lining the grassy slopes, while in turn the river gradually wound away in the direction of a distant valley set between low-lying hills.

Viewed against the auction room's dark oak panelling, the guilt-framed painting with its azure blue sky reflecting in the gentle waters below seemed a whole different world of light and tranquillity. But what had really captivated John's wife was the boy himself, for sitting with his back against one of the trees and hunched up over a fishing rod, he presented an apparent image of absolute rural bliss.

Probably about eight or nine years old, his bowed head was largely obscured by a loosely woven straw hat whose frayed and ragged brim was edged in gold by the late afternoon sun. And, unable to resist the painting's almost uncanny attraction, Susan moved in for a closer look, but the nearer she got the greater its magnetic pull seemed to become until, finally, it felt as though she were actually walking the river bank towards the boy himself. Shaking off the peculiar sensation, she attempted to look at the subject's face which, although in deep shadow, nevertheless gave an impression of someone lost in sleep.

"It's certainly very beautiful," agreed her husband. "But there's also something strange and compelling about it. I don't know quite what, but it feels almost eerie."

"Oh, John," Susan protested. "You're exaggerating. But seriously, don't you think it would look just perfect above the inglenook fireplace in our hallway? It would give the whole area a totally new dimension." And, without waiting for an answer, she added, "Let's get a copy of the catalogue and check the reserve price."

John had noticed a pile in the entrance area but with no intention of buying anything, hadn't bothered to pick one up. However, after flicking through the pages they came to the section marked 'Pictures'.

"Three thousand pounds!" he exclaimed incredulously. "I don't believe it. It's not worth that money. In any case, the auction's tomorrow which would mean you taking another day off work and that's not to mention the fact that it's nearly an hour's drive to get here." Although this was all very true, however, it appeared Susan had made up her mind. "All right. If you insist," he agreed reluctantly. "But it's a lot of money and it may even reach a higher figure in the auction."

With that, they made their way back to the car park before driving to the hospital for what turned out to be a mixed report on the state of their daughter's health.

After having been ushered into the consulting room, they sat back with the almost-regulation cup of coffee and waited for the doctor to put in an appearance.

"Don't rush that," grinned John at attempted humour as his wife lifted the cup. "At these prices, every sip needs to be savoured."

As he spoke, the door opened to admit the consultant.

"I'm sorry to have kept you waiting," he apologised. "But we had an urgent case come in that took longer than anticipated."

While he was speaking, the doctor switched on a large screen at the side of his desk. A man in his mid-thirties and slightly balding, he exuded an air of absolute professionalism. Smartly dressed and well spoken, he immediately commanded John's attention, which in itself was no mean achievement for he held little respect for any form of officialdom.

"We've conducted several tests on your daughter," he began slowly. "Most of which proved quite satisfactory, but," and at this point he indicated the screen, "this is an x-ray of her liver and it caused us some concern, because if you look closely it shows two small nodules which, for the moment, we've been unable to diagnose."

At this, Susan leaned forward anxiously. "Oh, doctor. You don't think it could be...?"

But the physician maintained his professional calm.

"The fact is, Mrs Grant, we just don't know until we've conducted further tests. They're probably nothing more serious than benign cysts. But, in the meantime, I suggest we keep your daughter in overnight so that by this time tomorrow we'll have a better idea of what's going on."

With that, the consultant rose from his chair and, by implication, terminated the interview.

In the corridor outside with its lingering antiseptic smell, Susan looked up beseechingly at her husband.

"Life's not easy is it, John? We've worked so hard to make a success of the business. We've finally got a lovely home, and now this. Our only daughter may be dying from liver cancer."

"Now, hold on," he protested. "We've no real cause to think that. Miriam's been ill with these symptoms for some time, so if it were anything really serious I'm sure we'd have known about it long before now."

It was the best he could offer and putting a comforting arm round her shoulders he led the way outside to their car.

Home for Susan and her husband lay to the north east of Chichester, just beyond the West Sussex village of Henfield. They had spent several years looking for something suitable in a rural part of the county and had been fortunate to secure a spacious farmhouse several miles from the village centre. It was known as Ley Farm – a name derived from its proximity to an intersection of ley lines. Built of oak timber and Sussex flint, it probably dated from the late fourteen hundreds and enjoyed the added attraction of some twenty acres of land, part of which were heavily wooded with silver birch and pine trees. In short, it had all combined to make the couple's dream come true.

Situated off a quiet lane, the house was approached by a long, unmade drive which sided a large private fishing lake. Built on rising ground, it commanded extensive views across both the lake and the distant South Downs.

However, one of the main features which had so captivated Susan was the huge communal hallway and its almost timeless flagstone flooring. Equally impressive was the massive inglenook fireplace which, like the house, was constructed of Sussex flint. Capable of containing a small table and chairs, it nevertheless housed a dark cast-iron fire-back depicting a phoenix rising from the ashes while the huge metal fire basket was more than adequate for the blazing logs which could spell such a welcome during the winter months.

Above the fireplace, a massive horizontal oak beam decorated with a range of horse-brasses supported the main chimney structure which was where Susan had in mind for the auction room picture. However, after their consultation at St Richard's, pictures somehow seemed of less significance, and as they entered the house, her husband was only too aware of how she must be feeling. Closing the heavy studded oak door behind them, he did his best to offer a little comfort.

"Look, we probably won't be picking up little Miriam until early afternoon, so under the circumstances I'm sure your boss will understand if you took tomorrow off."

As their business became more successful, it had enabled them to engage a nanny in order for Susan to return to work after the birth of their daughter. John's wife was fortunate in that the authority had chosen to keep her position open during the child's early weeks. But it had been a difficult labour, and initially there had been some doubt as to whether the new baby would even survive, with the result that Susan had actually been away from work for over a year. She enjoyed her career, and after such a long break and the council's understanding she felt loath to take any further time off that wasn't absolutely necessary and it caused John's suggestion to make her hesitate.

"Come on," he urged. "You know how you liked that picture at the auction room so why don't we drop in there tomorrow? Even if it's just to find out how much it actually goes for. Then we can pick up little Miriam afterwards."

The bright spring day was now fast approaching its close, with a low western sun streaming in through the front door skylight to illuminate the flint chimney breast which stood in stark contrast to the growing dimness of the hall.

"You know, John. I'm right," rejoined Susan with a sudden flash of renewed enthusiasm. "That really is the right place for that picture, because anyone walking through the front door would find it an immediate attraction."

John just smiled at his wife's exuberance, while indicating the entrance to the kitchen.

"Let's just see what tomorrow brings," he observed with a hint of caution. "But, in the meantime..."

"I know. I know. Don't tell me. Food!" She smiled. "But don't worry, I got the nanny to put something together while we were away." But then, seeing his reaction, she quickly added, "Well, there was precious little else for her to do with Miriam in hospital all day."

Their kitchen was, by any standard, on a huge scale, with the original farmhouse version having been tripled in size to incorporate a panoramic south-facing bay window. Life somehow always seemed to gravitate around this part of the house, so they'd placed a long dining table just in front of the bay to take full advantage of its views across the lake.

Affectionately known as 'Brenny', the nanny's real name was Brenda Hawsworth; an attractive and intelligent young woman in her mid to late twenties who had come from a wealthy landowning family in Hampshire – although John had never been able to quite fathom why anyone from such a prestigious background would want to end up as a nanny to some middle-class family in the rural wilderness of West Sussex. Worse, since her arrival he'd experienced something of a struggle to keep his eyes to himself.

"Well, it smells good," he observed as they entered the kitchen. "Let's see if the taste lives up to expectations."

And with that, he collapsed languidly in one of the carver chairs by the window before proceeding to unfold his long legs and stretch out with a sigh of relief. John found that the encroachment of middle life had been accompanied by the gradual onset of back pain which could make the relief of sitting down almost a pleasure in its own right.

The nanny had left the table ready laid, and with the meal cooked all Susan had to do was dish it up. But in the process, she couldn't help noticing how tired her husband looked. Physically a strong man, she nevertheless knew the day had taken its toll.

Susan met John through a dating website and at first had been very dubious about their age difference, but they soon discovered many things in common for although now a Housing Officer she had originally studied Fine Art at Goldsmiths in London for a number of years. Also like herself, he was the only child of a working-class family who had been determined to make the most of whatever talent he possessed. But perhaps even more importantly, he had proved to be a gentleman who always treated her like a lady; a man who tried to shield her from the slightest difficulty and who never once failed to put her needs before his own – although, in some ways this was ironic because she'd always been a fiercely independent woman who, despite her small stature, was nevertheless a force to be reckoned with; a quality well-suited for her profession. Unlike men in her previous relationships, John had been able to bypass this austere facade and rekindle the protective needs latent in all women while his considerate ways had aroused her sense of femininity, and she loved him for it.

The fading western sun was now all but gone as Susan finally sat down for the evening meal. Glancing through the spacious window, she could see the distant sky now streaked with ribbons of pink and gold as it slowly but reluctantly gave way to the approach of night. And yet, enough light remained to silhouette the tracery-like network of tree branches that lined the edge of their lake while the water reflected a pale image of the dying glory above.

"Such a beautiful evening," she murmured, almost to herself. But then, addressing her husband directly, she added, "You know, my mother always loved this time of year. I remember so well her saying 'Oh to be in England now that April is here'."

"Well, it's a sight better than the winter we've

just been through," he answered quietly. "Some days it hardly seemed to get light at all, and that lake, remember, was right across the drive and almost up to the front door. It felt as though it never stopped raining." But then, changing the subject, he added brightly, "Brenda sure knows how to cook a shepherd's pie and... that gravy..." He clicked his tongue and made a circle of his thumb and middle finger. "Just perfect!"

But, even as he spoke, Susan purposefully downed her knife and fork. "It's no good, John, I've just got to phone the hospital to see if little Miriam has settled down for the night."

Her forehead furrowed as she spoke, and from experience he knew it would be worse than useless to try to dissuade her, while as she reached for her mobile, the lines in her face never relaxed for a moment.

After completing her enquiries with a series of prodigious, "That's fine. That's fine. Thank you very much," she replaced the phone on the table.

"Well?" enquired John. "Is Miriam all right?"

His wife was slow to respond as she picked up her knife and fork to prod listlessly at the remains of her meal.

"Yes, she's okay now, but I think they've had a problem at first because she kept asking if she could go home." His wife slumped in her chair and shrugged expressively. "I suppose that's understandable. She's never been away from home before – oh, I don't know, John. All I've ever wanted for her was to be healthy and happy, but..."

"Well, I don't think you're alone in that," replied her husband gently. "It's what any parent would want for their child."

And so saying, he got up to cross the room and switch on the lights, while with the outside world in virtual darkness the window assumed a reflection of the lighted interior of the kitchen, but with the luxury of not being overlooked John made no attempt to draw the curtains. However, as he re-joined his wife he couldn't fail to notice her continued strained expression.

"What is it, love? I'm sure Miriam will be all right for just one night and she couldn't be in a better place..."

But his wife cut him short with a shake of her head.

"It's not that," she said while taking a deep breath. "It's something quite different. I know," she began slowly after a slight pause, "originally you were not overly enthusiastic about having children. Do you remember? We discussed it several months after we'd first met."

John nodded slowly and thoughtfully.

"Yes. In fact, I remember it quite well. It was a hot summer day and we were sunning ourselves on the lawn behind my old home in Crawley. I couldn't tell you your exact words, but it was to the effect that I'd never even broached the subject."

"And the reasons you gave," she rejoined, "were our age difference and your concern over the genetics of your mother's ill-health."

But John hastened to interrupt.

"I think," he said gently. "If all this is leading up to some sort of regret over having Miriam, then I'm sure you've got it wrong. I mean – there's nothing wrong with me is there?"

"Well. Dare I comment?" she smiled. But then, after shaking her head again, looked very serious before dropping a totally unexpected bombshell. "No. It's nothing like that, John. It's just that I think... in fact, I know... I'm pregnant."

The corners of his mouth twitched as he again stretched out luxuriously with extended arms and hands that reached for the ceiling. But finally contracting back into a sitting position, he looked straight at his wife with a whimsical expression and observed dryly, "You do know, I hope, that this is our kitchen and not the local church confessional."

But his wife was not so easily amused.

"It's not funny," she retorted on the edge of tears. "We've already got one sickly child and that's without my job to consider."

"Would it really be so awful, darling, if we had two children?" he questioned encouragingly. "And would it be so bad for little Miriam to have a playmate? After all, it's no great fun being an only child as we both know. There's also the fact," he added gently, "whatever makes you happy also makes me happy."

"I know," she replied, quietly dabbing at her eyes. "You've always been nothing but loving and considerate."

But even as she spoke, the nanny suddenly put in an unexpected appearance. A woman of undoubted beauty, she wore her thick brunette hair divided into long well-brushed tresses that fell abundantly about her shoulders; of statuesque build, John would have put her about five-foot-seven, while she exuded an indefinable sensuality that most men would have found hard to resist. However, sensing a slight tension in the room, she was quick to apologise.

"Oh, I'm sorry. I didn't mean to intrude but I was just anxious to see how little Miriam got on at the hospital."

At her entry, John had immediately heaved himself into a more upright position.

"No, that's fine," he hastened reassuringly. "It's just that Susan and I are a bit upset at having to leave her in hospital overnight while they conduct further tests."

Having no wish to discuss the intimate details of their family life, it was the best he could come up with on the spur of the moment. But even as he spoke, he sensed that all was not well with their employee while his wife had also picked up on her unease.

"We hadn't expected you back this side of midnight, Brenda. Is everything all right?" At first the nanny hesitated, but then Susan's kindly meant words seemed to burst a dam and she broke down and started to cry. Startled by this unexpected reaction, John's wife raised her eyebrows as they exchanged glances but then immediately got to her feet to comfort the distressed girl. "What is it Brenda? What's the matter?" she enquired urgently. "Are you unwell or something? What's gone wrong?"

"I'm afraid, Mrs Grant," she managed. "I'm really afraid."

Never over-familiar, she always respectfully referred to Susan by her married title, and although not particularly enthusiastic over her employee's sultry appearance, John's wife nevertheless had a high regard for the professional way she executed her duties, not only around the house but also the dedication she invariably showed to little Miriam. But, this evening, the nanny was obviously very distraught, and Susan saw her shiver as she haltingly described her experience at one of the Brighton nightclubs. It appeared that while dancing with several other female acquaintances, she had been approached by a complete stranger who just pushed himself onto the small group. And whereas at first all had seemed pleasant enough, the man gradually became increasingly obnoxious and demanding. Probably the worse for drink and exuding a strong lack of personal hygiene, Brenda had apparently told him in no uncertain terms to leave them alone, but her rejection had triggered a violent reaction as he grabbed her wrist and twisted it high up behind her back. In the dim light of the nightclub and on a crowded floor, it had at first gone unnoticed.

"However, at last," said Brenda, "one of the doormen escorted him out of the club, but as he was going he vowed to get me. And, to my horror, as I left shortly afterwards I found him waiting outside."

"Then what happened?" enquired Susan as she looked to her equally perplexed but increasingly angry husband.

"Oh, I think he said something like, 'Right. I've got you now.' He was so horrible and unshaven looking. Anyway, I managed to dodge him and get to my car, but – and this is what frightens me – his car was parked nearby, and I think he might have followed me here. I could see a set of headlights in the rear-view mirror for most of the way back, but," she added, wiping her eyes, "I'm not sure if it was him or not."

John again stretched luxuriously in his chair. "Well, I shouldn't worry too much, Brenda, if he does follow you here."

"John!" objected his wife as she cleared the table. "You know I don't like your methods of dealing with such situations. If he's foolish enough to turn up and cause any trouble, then we'll simply call the police."

"The police!" he objected derisively. "You must be kidding. We've been here for some four years and I've never even seen one – well, perhaps with the exception of the odd patrol car disappearing round a bend on its way to somewhere else."

At this tirade, his wife exchanged a knowing glance with the nanny.

"Take no notice. He's on his hobby-horse again." But, as she turned from the table she caught sight of car headlights approaching up the drive. "John," she began uncertainly. "We're not expecting any visitors tonight, are we?"

"Not that I'm aware of," he responded, slowly heaving his sixteen-stone frame into a standing position. "Well, not unless we take Brenda's new 'friend' into account."

As the car drew up outside, the whole area immediately became flooded with light from the automatic security system which prompted John to position himself to the side of the bay window. It obscured him from anyone approaching the house but afforded an unobstructed view of the entire forecourt, and seeing the occupant climb from his car he beckoned to Brenda.

"Is that the bloke?" he asked in a slightly mischievous voice. "Well, by the look of him, you sure know how to pick them." But Brenda had just shrunk back in fear and shook her head. "Oh, don't worry," he assured her while striding purposefully towards the hallway. "I'll soon sort this lot out."

Opening the front door, he found himself confronted by one of the most unsavoury-looking individuals it had ever been his misfortune to clap eyes on. Unshaven and with a soiled open-necked blue shirt, the man was endeavouring to mount the front steps, although it was difficult to determine whether his shaky attempt was due to drink or drugs. But, in any case, the cause quickly became irrelevant when the intruder suddenly lost his footing and fell backwards to strike his head with a sickening thud on the unyielding forecourt below.

Horrified, John rushed to the stricken man who lay inert and unconscious with blood streaming from a deep wound in his scalp.

"John, what on earth's happened?" cried Susan who had followed close behind.

"I think it's quite nasty, love. I'll stay here if you could send for an ambulance. Oh, and ask Brenda if she'd mind bringing out a blanket and a pillow. Whatever this person's done, it's our duty to do our best."

Much later that night, Susan turned over in bed to put an arm round John.

"It's been quite a day, hasn't it? And it was so good of you to go in the ambulance with that poor man," she added quietly. "I don't know what he was doing here, but he certainly didn't deserve that. Did they give you any idea of how serious it was?"

"Pretty bad," he admitted, "because the guy's on a life support machine so I don't know what his chances are. Anyway, we've got a long day ahead tomorrow, so I don't know about you," he added, using his playful ploy of tapping his finger on the end of her nose, "but I'm going to sleep."

Quite different from the previous spring-like day, John and Susan approached the auction rooms amidst an absolute downpour with the rain actually bouncing back up from the pavement. Umbrellas abounded everywhere while the besieged curb-side gutters struggled in vain to cope with the sudden volume of water as it surged and gurgled towards the nearest drains.

"Lovely! Absolutely lovely!" he exclaimed while trying to squeeze his outsized frame under the protective custody of his wife's brolly. "Talk about, 'It never rains but it pours'. I sometimes wonder why the hell anyone stays in this country at all."

"Because," retorted his wife, "it gives old moaners like you a perfect excuse to vent their misery on other people." Then, after diving through the auction room entrance, Susan took the brolly and shook it vigorously through the open doorway. "Look at my hair!" she exclaimed in disgust. "After all my efforts this morning. And now it feels like nothing more than a flattened rats' nest."

But, despite everything, her husband was a master of diplomacy. "Darling. You always seem perfect to me."

"You," she replied pointedly with a smile, "are nothing more than an old flannel merchant."

Finally, they found themselves confronted with an entirely different set-up to their first visit. All the trestle tables had been moved aside to be replaced by numerous rows of chairs. And, whereas before there had only been the occasional browser, the place was now packed to capacity and abuzz with expectant chatter.

"John, did you collect a catalogue as we came in?"

"No need," he grinned and reached for his pocket to pull out the dog-eared version he'd picked up the previous day. But then, glancing around the auction rooms, he observed dryly, "By the look of this lot, we'll be lucky to get a seat." However, luck prevailed in the form of two vacant chairs just three rows back from the auctioneer's podium. "Blimey!" he exclaimed after sitting down. "Will you just take a look at that bloke's ears in front?" Obviously in a mischievous mood, John added, "I can well see why ears like that get called 'jug handles'. If he wagged that lot about, he'd probably take off!"

"For goodness sake, keep your voice down or he'll hear you," hissed his wife. "And, in any case,

I'm not the slightest bit interested in the dimensions of men's ears or, for that matter, any other part of their anatomy."

As she was speaking, the auctioneer stepped up onto the dais.

"Ladies and gentlemen. Before I commence, may I first welcome you all to Barrington's Auction Rooms." His bald head gleamed blindingly in the overhead lighting as he continued. "The first item today is an antique musket with a reserve of two thousand five hundred pounds. Thank you, sir. I see that hand. Have I any advance on two thousand five hundred? Thank you, sir. Two thousand seven hundred I'm bid..."

As the auction continued, John leaned over to his wife. "Ours is lot fifteen, so be prepared for a bit of a wait."

In due course, the auctioneer turned his attention to the reason for their visit.

"Ladies and gentlemen," he said with a touch of excitement while indicating the painting. "We now come to lot fifteen; an oil painting of a boy fishing. And, before I ask for any bids, I would first like to point out a little of its history. It was painted by George Blake around the end of the eighteen fifties, and although a little-known artist, I think his style and attention to detail warrants greater recognition than it does. I might also add that he enjoyed a loose association with the Pre-Raphaelite movement which greatly influenced his work, and I believe that in due course his paintings can only increase in value. Now, the picture itself portrays his son on a fishing trip by the upper reaches of the River Arun. In fact, I believe it's still possible to locate the actual spot which formed the basis of his painting. It has a reserve of three thousand, so what am I bid?"

The sale had obviously created a lot of interest and sparked a brisk reaction.

"Three thousand two hundred and fifty I'm bid. Any advance on three thousand two hundred and fifty? Three thousand five hundred I'm bid. Thank you, sir. Four thousand."

And so, the figure crept up towards five thousand – although, by this time, only two contenders remained.

"Going for five thousand once. Going for five thousand twice," called out the auctioneer with his gavel poised for the definitive strike.

"Well," exclaimed John who had held back till the last minute. "Are we, or aren't we?"

His wife responded with a hesitant nod and he raised his hand to take the stakes to five thousand two hundred and fifty; a bid that was followed by a short pause before one determined man at the back of the hall put in a bid for five thousand five hundred.

Thoroughly annoyed, John looked round and gave the individual a cold stare as if daring him to go any higher, while at the same time indicating a bid for six thousand. But it was enough to carry the day and the auctioneer's gavel descended with a resounding crack. And so, the picture Susan had so admired was theirs at last – although, at that point, they could have had little concept of its long-term consequences.

John sat back and folded his arms with a sigh.

"Five hundred pounds down the drain and all because of that berk behind us. Anyway, it's ours now – although whether it's worth that kind of money is another question. One thing I do know," he then added dryly "is that my parents would have been mortified at spending so much money on what they would see as an unnecessary extravagance."

Susan looked askance. "John, I do suppose you know that you're slowly becoming more and more of a moaner. Couldn't you just be pleased for me that we've got it?"

"Yes of course I can," he grinned boyishly while giving her a squeeze. "You know what I always say... If it makes you happy..."

The fact they'd secured their particular lot, of course made no difference to the auction and the frenzy of bids and counter-bids went on unabated.

"Come on," he added, jerking his head in the direction of the entrance. "Let's get the hell out of this racket and find somewhere to have lunch."

Later in the day, and with the painting safely stowed in the car boot, they made their way to St Richard's Hospital where, after numerous circuits of the car park, they finally managed to secure a space, but the whole set-up there had thoroughly annoyed John with its colour-coded bays depicting long-stays and short-stays, consultant and staff spaces. Then, as if that wasn't enough, each colour carried a differing fine for various infringements.

After collecting his parking ticket, John stood for a moment to survey the gleaming rows of cars all neatly arranged according to their order of 'privilege'.

"They must need something better to do," he muttered. "Who the hell on earth managed to dream this lot up?"

"John," objected his wife. "We're here to collect Miriam, remember? Not to grumble about the philosophy behind the parking arrangements."

"I don't know," he retorted. "There're more and more cars, more and more people and more and more red tape to go with them. It's fast getting to the stage where you won't be able to move in the south east at all."

Feeling irritated, Susan just pointed to the hospital entrance.

"Shall we?"

Once again inside the slightly disinfectant atmosphere of the infirmary, they made straight for the reception desk in the private wing where they were greeted by the consultant's nursing assistant.

"Mr Harper will be with you shortly," she smiled. "In the meantime, could I perhaps offer you a little refreshment?"

John had long noticed, perhaps cynically, how the broadest smiles and the greatest courtesy always seemed to eminate from the private sector of medicine.

"No thanks, that's fine for me." He smiled. "But I'm sure my wife would appreciate a cup of something."

Smartly dressed in her starched uniform, the nurse looked every inch a competent member of the profession, although in John's eyes there were far too many inches for the uniform to cover and he lost no time in expressing his opinion to Susan.

"Will you take a look at her backside? Can you imagine how any chair would cope with that lot descending on it?"

But choosing to ignore her husband's crass remarks, Susan just indicated the consultant's door.

"John, can't you see I'm worried about Miriam and not the anatomy of other women? Anyway, I think it's time to go in."

Seated at his desk, the doctor's inscrutable expression at first afforded little relief for her anxiety, but as he again drew their attention to the x-ray screen and quietly described his findings, Susan felt her worst fears begin to fade.

"I'm reasonably confident," explained the consultant, "that the nodules we were looking at yesterday are small abscesses which I'm sure will respond to a course of antibiotics. But," he then added, to their disappointment, "I shall need to keep your daughter here for the next few days in order to monitor her progress."

"But she hasn't got cancer?" stressed her mother.

The doctor shook his head. "Absolutely not. However, I'm still concerned how she contracted the infection in the first place."

Although relieved, it nevertheless left the parents with the unenviable task of telling their daughter they would not be taking her home after all.

Miriam's private room was, by any standards, a bright and cheerful place. Decorated in pale lilac and with numerous illustrations from the world of Disney, it enjoyed far reaching views over the town towards the magnificent Chichester Cathedral. Even so, sitting there on the bed, their little girl cut a lonely and slightly forlorn figure as they entered the room and it tore at Susan's heart.

"Mummy, Mummy," Miriam cried out in delight as her mother raced across the room to gather her in her arms.

"And what have you been doing today, darling?"

But the little girl only started to cry as she brokenly tried to describe how a lady had come into her room and hurt her arm – at which point, seeing a plaster on the inside of their daughter's elbow, Susan assumed that a blood sample had been taken and she tried to reassure Miriam it was only to make her feel better.

But it was a painful time for them all, and Susan felt emotionally exhausted as she and her husband finally came to leave. Dozing fitfully while John drove them back, she only became fully awake when they turned into the bottom of their drive; no traffic congestion; no street lights; just a quiet peace that only the countryside could afford. She stretched luxuriously and turned to her husband.

"Home at last," she breathed thankfully. "Although we should be grateful for the news about Miriam. But I really must go to work tomorrow so perhaps you and the nanny could pop down and see her. She's very fond of Brenda, you know."

"Well, I had promised to visit several of the properties in Brighton," replied John hesitantly. "But yes, I'm sure I can fit it all in."

Finally arriving at the forecourt, he applied the handbrake with a sharp tug. "Now I suppose," he teased, "you'll want me to dig that picture out of the boot and stick it up on the chimney breast."

Her pleading expression precluded any chance of leaving it until the following day.

During their drive home, the rain and heavy overcast skies had cleared to leave a bright spring evening with clean air that was a joy to breathe. Lifting the car boot lid, John reached for the painting which, with its heavy gilt frame, was well in excess of a metre across.

"If you could just open the door for me, love, I'll get it inside because it's no light weight."

By the time John managed to hang it in the

designated position, the western sun had sunk sufficiently low to allow shafts of light across the hall to illuminate its every delicate detail, and as in the auction room, the beauty of its river receding away towards the distant hills seemed like a portal into a brilliant and tranquil scene from another world.

"Perfect!" exclaimed his wife jubilantly. "Perfect. It's just how I imagined." Although whether she would describe it so enthusiastically in the future would prove to be a rather different matter.

By the time they sat down for their meal that evening, it was approaching 8.30pm and they were both tired after a long and demanding day. As John glanced around their vast kitchen with its timber-beamed ceiling, he thought of the numerous generations that must have lived out the rhythms of their lives there – all the mundane chores, in fact, that made up the tapestry of existence – but, he wondered, what did all that amount to now? He recalled some words he'd once read somewhere: 'And the place thereof shall know them no more.'

"What's the matter, John?" asked his perceptive wife. "Don't tell me you've gone into one of your introspective moods again."

"No, no," he lied, concerned to play down the slightly depressive side of his nature. "It's just that it's been one of those days. I mean, there's a series of problems with the properties. Apparently, would you believe, one of the bedroom ceilings in Bernard Road has collapsed. There was a wet patch near the light fitting that nobody reported."

"Well that's the joys of being a landlord," smiled his wife. "I shouldn't grumble though. It pays well enough."

John slowly put down his knife and fork before leaning forward with his elbows on the table and rubbing cupped hands up and down his face.

"I suppose you're right," he replied with a touch of weariness.

But as he went to resume his meal, he noticed his wife's attention had become drawn towards the bay window. And following her gaze he could see why, for the whole of their forecourt and drive had become bathed in brilliant moonlight. The luminous orb hung suspended in a clear star-spangled sky and had completely converted their lake into a sheet of pure silver.

"Wow! That's fantastic," he murmured. But even as he spoke, there appeared the headlights of a car turning in at the entrance to their drive and slowly making its way up towards the house. "I hope this is not going to be a repetition of the other night," John observed testily.

However, as the car pulled up outside he knew he was dealing with an entirely different proposition, for the car was a virtually new Mercedes, and as the headlights dimmed into extinction a smartly dressed woman got out and hesitantly surveyed her surroundings. From what he could see, John would have put her in her late fifties, but with her carefully coiffured grey hair and fashionable clothes she was obviously a woman of charm and poise.

"Well?" he observed, turning to his wife. "A friend of yours?"

But Susan seemed equally perplexed and shook her head. "No, but by the look of it, she's certainly not short of money."

John glanced reluctantly at his half-eaten meal and made a clicking sound with his tongue.

"A mysterious lady in the dead of night." He smiled, rolling his eyes with a touch of amateur dramatics. "So, let us sally forth and see what she's about."

"Oh, come on, John. For goodness sake, get on with it," berated his ever-practical wife.

After striding across the hallway to open the main front door, he found himself face-to-face with probably the most glamorous middle-aged woman he'd ever met.

"I'm sorry to trouble you," began their visitor in a slightly husky cultured voice. "But I'm trying to locate a Mr and Mrs Grant."

Conscious of her close proximity, John replied whimsically. "Well, at least you've got that bit right because I'm John Grant."

The woman responded with a slow and sensual smile that reached the corner of her eyes, while, at the same time, extending a slim hand.

"Then may I introduce myself? I'm Margaret Shawcross and I've come to thank you for your kindness in arranging for my son's hospitalisation."

Seeing her standing there in an immaculately tailored costume and wearing designer knee-high patent leather boots, made it difficult to associate her with the virtual human derelict he'd encountered just two nights previously. The whole situation seemed so bizarre that, at first, he found himself struggling.

"That was no trouble," he began a little uncertainly. "It was the least I could do under the circumstances. But, look, do come in. I'd like to know how the young man's getting on, because when I left the hospital he was in a pretty bad way and on a life support machine."

But then, as the visitor entered she immediately caught sight of their recently acquired picture on the chimney breast and crossed the hallway for a closer look.

"Do you like it?" enquired Susan who had also abandoned her meal.

At first, their unexpected guest failed to respond but just backed away from the painting with a fixed frown, and when she answered it was in a voice filled with uncertainty.

"It's not a question of liking it. It's more..."

But she failed to finish whatever she was about to say, and after a pause enquired where the picture had come from and whether either of them knew anything about its history. In response, John did his best to describe what little they knew and how it had been recently acquired. He then invited her through to the kitchen for a coffee. Upon seeing the table, their mysterious visitor immediately apologised for the interruption to their meal, although Susan hastily dismissed it as a non-problem.

"Just put the plates in the oven, John. We can easily finish the meal later on."

And with that, he and his wife led their guest over to a comfortable sitting area situated at the far side of the kitchen. Furnished by a worn but much loved old three-piece suite from Susan's original family home, it was the location towards which everyone seemed to gravitate, and this despite the alternative of three spacious and well-appointed reception rooms.

"What I can't understand," enquired the woman, after taking a sip from her cup, "is just what my son was doing at your property in the first place."

It was, of course, a potentially very embarrassing question and John moved quickly to play down the facts before his wife had a chance to answer. But, even as he gently tried to outline the events leading up to her son's accident, they saw a look of despair cross the woman's face. Then, carefully putting down her cup on a nearby coffee table, she revealed the kind of family tragedy one would normally associate with the news media. Reaching for a handkerchief from her handbag, she touched at the corner of her eyes before leaning forward and holding it tightly squeezed in her hand.

"You see," she began sadly, "my husband is an extremely wealthy man. He's the son of William Shawcross who founded the famous chain of supermarkets – and yet, despite all that, we seem to be unable to do the one thing we want most, which has been to help our son." She paused as the handkerchief again came into play. "Right from the start," she continued sadly, "he was a difficult child. I won't go into details, but sufficient to say he caused my husband and myself a great deal of grief. We sent him to the best schools, but he always managed to become involved with the wrong sort of people and get expelled."

At this sudden and unexpected outpouring, Susan looked at her husband.

"Children are not always necessarily a blessing." she sympathised. "We have a little daughter of our own and we've experienced nothing but worry over her health since the day she was born."

Susan's remarks drew a fleeting smile as the woman replaced her handkerchief and reached to stir her coffee.

"Are you sure I can't offer you something a bit stronger?" volunteered John.

Again, their visitor smiled briefly. "No, but thank you all the same. I've got to drive back to Brighton, and in any case, I've already taken up far too much of your time as it is." John, however, was still intrigued about her son and, perhaps insensitively, pressed for more details. "Well," she sighed. "To cut a long story short he eventually became a crack addict which made his already unpredictable behaviour far worse. He started to be violent and stole to feed his habit." She sighed again and slumped slightly in her seat as if under some huge but invisible burden. "We sent him to America for treatment in various clinics which worked for a while but then he would always go back to his old ways. Anyway," concluded their visitor. "I understand your employee experienced some of the problem that night in Brighton, and I can only say I'm very sorry."

"There's been no lasting damage done," John hastened to assure her. "Well, only to himself that is. I just hope he recovers all right."

"He's off the life support machine," she replied with a certain cautious optimism. "But I understand he will have to remain in hospital for some time." Then, after a fleeting smile, she added, "If you'd like to give me your mobile number I'll be pleased to let you know how he gets on."

And with that, their guest rose from her seat and prepared to leave. However, while crossing the hallway, she again stopped to gaze up at their prized painting although only to quickly draw back and turn to John. "My mother was what you might describe as a 'sensitive'," she confided unexpectedly. "She was able to pick up on things that most people can't detect and it's a dubious ability that I've inherited." She paused momentarily as if to allow time for her words to register. "I say this because, paradoxically,

I find this apparently quite beautiful and tranquil scene strangely disturbing. And that," she added, "is why I asked you about its history. Admittedly I'm guessing, but by the brushwork and realism, I would say it was painted at about the time of the Pre-Raphaelites."

At this point, Susan's curiosity got the better of her.

"John, what's this business about Pre-Raphaelites?"

Her husband just shook his head and smiled.

"Oh, it's nothing very special, love. It's just that there was a group of artists in the late nineteenth century who seemed to think that nothing done after Raphael was worth talking about. They had a very representational style which, you remember, the auctioneer seemed to think had influenced the artist who painted our picture." John turned back to their guest. "Tell me, just what is it that you find so disturbing?"

"Well," she replied hesitantly. "This is not something I would normally try, but under the circumstances I feel the least I can do is to warn you about anything I might pick up." And then, closing her eyes, she lowered her head. "I somehow detect an overriding sense of sorrow."

After a brief pause, she added brokenly, "It's so sad. So awfully sad. Far off in the distance, I can hear the sound of crying – but no, it's more than just crying. It's the sound of a woman weeping bitterly and there's also a man who seems heartbroken and who's trying to console her. But as I say, it's all a long way off and very faint, and I can't seem to pick up on the cause of their grief. I do know, however, it's associated with this painting, and if you take my advice you'll get rid of it at once. Better still – burn it."

At this outburst, John exchanged glances with his wife and raised his eyebrows.

Finally closing the front door on their extraordinary visitor, he expelled a long thin whistle of relief.

"Burn it," he parroted. "I should say so. Especially when we've just spent six thousand pounds getting it." Then, indicating the kitchen, he added, "Never mind all that – let's get on with our poor neglected meal."

Reheated food never tastes quite the same, and after sitting down for a second attempt at their supper, Susan idly poked about at the contents of her plate before giving up with a sigh of resignation.

"No?" observed her husband. "No good?"

Susan shook her head. "No," she agreed, pushing her plate to one side. "I've lost my appetite. I don't know but that woman's left me feeling distinctly uneasy – obviously I have every sympathy over her son. It must be a terrible problem, but don't you realise, John, she's a psychic."

Her husband, on the other hand, had finished his

supper with some relish and reached across the table to pour her drink.

"That's a nice wine," he said encouragingly. "It's a Chardonnay from the vineyards of Burgundy."

"John," she repeated with a touch of irritation. "Did you hear what I said? That woman's a psychic."

He looked momentarily puzzled at her note of agitation.

"So, she's a psychic?" He shrugged. "Does it really matter?"

"It matters, John, because anything like that runs contrary to our pastor's ministry."

Since moving to the rural part of Sussex, they had enrolled at a local Free Church and had quickly come to respect the minister not only as a man but also as an exponent of biblical truth, and her words caused John to think.

"I must say that hadn't occurred to me," he admitted in a more subdued tone. But then added, "Although it's not as though we were holding a séance, or anything, is it? The woman just advised us as to how she felt. She even said she was loath to practise what she saw as a natural gift."

"I don't care," insisted his wife. "All I know is that I don't want anyone like that here again."

John shrugged wearily before looking out through the bay window, but during the course of the woman's visit the beautiful moonlit scene had undergone a dramatic change; the clear star-speckled sky having become overcast with heavy cloud while the radiant moon had virtually succumbed to what looked like an approaching storm.

"Gone. That beautiful moonlight. All but gone," he observed sombrely while hoping it was not an omen of things to come.

Chapter 2

SOME THREE DAYS later, John and his wife were overjoyed to collect little Miriam from hospital. The storm affecting the night of their strange visitor had long since passed and the afternoon in question was again alive with bright spring sunlight. As the outskirts of Chichester gave way to open countryside, it seemed that Mother Nature had become determined to celebrate the freshness of April in her own inimitable style. Daffodils abounded in great clumps alongside the winding roads and the sun-like brilliance of their greeting was unmistakeable as they swayed gently in the afternoon breeze. Their only competition seemed to be the more diminutive primroses which were equally resolute to herald the arrival of a new beginning.

"You know," observed John as he drove gently through the quiet country lanes, "if we didn't endure months of endless rain and sog, England wouldn't be the green and pleasant land we love so much."

But Susan responded by giving him a funny look. "The trouble is, John," she teased, "you want the best of both worlds, and the fact is..."

"I know, I know." He grinned. "The fact is you can't have it both ways, but," he added, steering carefully round a sharp bend, "there's no harm in wanting it is there?"

But in the midst of this banter, a little voice piped up from the back seat. "Mummy, Mummy. Are we nearly home?"

John's wife immediately turned further round in her seat.

"Yes, darling," she assured their precious six-year-old. "We're nearly home. It won't be much longer and then you can see Mummy and Daddy's new picture."

"And will Brenny be there?" enquired the youngster eagerly, with an enthusiasm peculiar to small children.

"Yes, darling. She's at home getting your room ready."

"Good. I like Brenny," Miriam responded gleefully.

By the time they pulled up outside their farmhouse, it was approaching 5pm, but the evenings were fast drawing out, and as they vacated the car, John suddenly stopped and held up his hand.

"Listen. Just listen to those birds." And from the trees emanated a chorus of twittering, some of which was quite shrill while others sounded mellow and subdued. Nevertheless, each species made their own individual contribution to the overall orchestral harmony. “Wow!” he breathed. “What a welcome home. Even the birds are telling us it’s springtime.

“Aren’t you glad now that we moved to the countryside, John?” responded his wife before asking him to bring in the shopping.

However, just as he grasped the heavy plastic bags from the car boot, his mobile phone decided to sound off.

“Sue. Can you get that, love? It’s in my right-hand trouser pocket. You’ll have to be quick because it only gives three rings before cutting out.”

His wife’s expression precluded the need for words as she struggled to retrieve the offending item from the depths of her husband’s trousers.

“Hello!” she said sharply.

She sounded intentionally abrupt but then recognised the speaker at the other end and immediately clapped a hand over the instrument.

“John,” she hissed irritably. “It’s that woman again. You remember – the one that was here the other night. For heaven’s sake, get rid of her.”

Dumping his burden on the forecourt, her husband reluctantly reached for his phone.

“Mrs Shawcross? It’s John Grant.” But then, as the reason for her call unfolded, he felt his heart sink. “I’m so sorry to hear that. I’m really sorry.”

And then, after a further period of listening, he gently bade the woman goodbye. All through the conversation, his wife had been frantically gesturing for him to terminate the call.

"What did she want?"

But, from her husband's sombre expression, Susan wondered momentarily if her uncharitable attitude had been quite appropriate.

"I think," observed John, "it would be better if we discussed the matter after Miriam has gone to bed."

Once indoors, their little daughter flew straight into the nanny's arms for a welcome home cuddle.

"Love you, Brenny," she cried touchingly.

"And I love you too," came the equally touching response. "It's great to have you back home. I've got your room all ready and guess what? I've a new book for you that's full of lovely bedtime stories."

The warm display of mutual affection caused John to raise his eyebrows and nod approvingly at his wife. But, once again, he felt uneasy stirrings at the sight of their employee for she had obviously gone to a great deal of effort over her appearance. Freshly washed hair hung in thick, shining tresses to her shoulders while a close-fitting jumper accentuated an enviable figure. John had learned to live with her presence, but it had never got easier and her exemplary efficiency had always excluded any reason for dismissal.

But even as such thoughts flashed through his mind, Miriam suddenly caught sight of the new picture and pointed towards the chimney breast.

"Mummy. There's a boy fishing!" she exclaimed excitedly.

In response to the child's enthusiasm, Brenda carried her across the hallway for a better look, where, despite her tender years, Miriam proved surprisingly perceptive. "Brenny?" she asked brightly. "Is the boy asleep?"

Her nanny studied the subject's face beneath the shadow of the straw hat. "It certainly looks like it," she agreed quickly.

"But... but..." her charge struggled, "how will he know if he catches any fish?"

The child-like logic brought a smile to their faces as Brenda did her best to come up with an answer.

"That's a very good question, Miriam. I can only think, perhaps, that if he did catch anything then it would jerk the fishing rod and wake him up. Anyway," she added cheerfully, "we've got about an hour left for play before your supper so let's see if there's anything new in the nursery."

It was a suggestion motivated in part by a feeling of unease at being in such close proximity to the painting, and it was also not the first time Brenda had experienced the sensation. When John originally put the picture up she had been drawn to its sheer light and beauty but then only to immediately experience a sense of discomfort which she had quickly dismissed. Today, however, it had not been so easy.

Finally, with little Miriam being happily entertained in the nursery and with the shopping safely stowed away, John and his wife retired to the comfortable area of the kitchen. It was a routine half hour of relaxation prior to their supper, but as her husband placed the two customary glasses of wine on the coffee table he sensed that Susan had something on her mind.

"Come on. What is it?" he enquired while languidly draping his elongated frame over the nearest armchair. "No. Don't tell me," he added, turning his eyes towards the ceiling. "Don't tell me. It's about that phone call?"

"Well," she replied taking the first sip of wine before carefully replacing her glass on the table. "What was she on about? And don't you dare roll your eyes up at me!"

He should have known better than to hint at any disrespect and he was quick to make amends.

"I'm sorry, love. I didn't mean any harm, but I just can't help feeling sorry for the poor woman." And seeing his wife about to interject, he hastened to continue, "You see," he explained, in a sombre voice, "her son died in hospital late last night. She didn't go into details, but I understand he was their only child. So, you never know, do you? You just never know."

"Oh, John, I didn't realise. You say she gave no indication as to the cause of his death?"

John solemnly shook his head while remaining sprawled out with his arms folded across his chest. "It must have been brain damage. If you'd heard his head striking the concrete forecourt... I'm really not surprised. Oh, and there's one other thing. You know, even though that woman was absolutely heartbroken, she was still big enough to be concerned about that painting of ours and pleaded again for me to get rid of it."

At this, Susan reached for her handbag and withdrew a packet of cigarettes, but as she was about to light up her husband asked pointedly if she'd bothered to read the health warnings liberally splashed across the carton.

"Oh, don't keep on at me about it," she objected irritably. "You knew I was a smoker when we got married. So, there's no point in moaning about it now. In any case," she added tartly, "I'm completely free to smoke in my own home if I want to."

John managed to pull himself up into a more elegant sitting position. "I'm not questioning your rights, love. I'm just concerned about your health because I want you around as long as possible."

"I know I shouldn't smoke," she admitted lamely. "But that woman having the audacity to tell us what to do with our own possessions."

He went to reply, but knowing his wife's temperament, perhaps wisely, refrained from any further comment – which was probably just as well, because at that moment Brenda entered the kitchen.

"We've had our supper in the nursery and now Miriam wants her bedtime story," pronounced the nanny. "So, I just wondered if either of you might like to do the honours seeing as it's her first night back from the hospital. Oh, and, by the way, she won't settle for anything other than 'The Tiger Who Came to Tea'."

John did his favourite trick and raised his eyebrows. "I do believe you. I must have read that thing a hundred times. In fact, I don't even need the book. I could recite it off by heart."

The nanny responded with a smile that left Susan feeling distinctly uneasy.

"I'll leave it to you then, John," added Brenda before leaving with a seductive sway of her hips.

Sometime later and with his duties done, John re-joined his wife for supper.

"Three times," he smiled. "Three times before I could manage to escape."

"Sorry?" she replied putting his plate on the table. "Three times what?"

"The story! You know, 'The Tiger Who Came to Tea'. She insisted on a third reading."

But, from the way Susan ran her fingers through her hair, it was obvious her mind was elsewhere.

"Oh, yes. I'm sorry," replied his wife. "Did she go down all right?"

"Like a lamb. But I can tell you this – the next time she hears about the tiger emptying the fridge and then never coming back, it's going to be from you."

"That's fair enough," she agreed vaguely while asking him to pass the gravy boat. And then, as the hot appetising brown fluid seeped its way round the vegetables on her plate, she looked directly at her husband. "John," she said, starting her meal, "I'm not happy about the nanny."

"Ah," he nodded. "I thought you seemed a bit pre-occupied. Is there anything in particular she's done to upset you?"

"John!" she said flatly. "The girl's a flirt. She dresses provocatively and flaunts herself about – especially," she added acidly, "in front of you." His attempt at a facial expression of innocence only served to aggravate the situation. "Oh, don't pretend you don't know what I'm talking about." she snapped. "And like most men, you lap it up. What's more, she's far too familiar. It's 'John' this and 'John' that. For heaven's sake man! You're her employer not someone in the first stages of an infatuated relationship. Where's your dignity? And mine for that matter!"

By the slight tremor in his wife's hands John realised she was obviously very upset, and he immediately got up and moved round the table to take her hand.

"Come on, love," he said gently. "You know I always count myself lucky to have you and I'm not the slightest bit interested in anyone else."

She looked up with a visible tear at the corner of her eye. "John!" she almost shouted. "I've seen the way you look at her and the way she gives you the odd sly smile. And don't deny it – because I've watched you."

"It's true," he admitted whilst gently stroking the back of her neck. "Men find attractive women... well... attractive. And they often look without even realising it. That's the nature of the beast, and any man who says otherwise is either a liar or... well, you know what... But if Brenda's presence here is causing you unhappiness," he added finally, "then she'll have to go. Although, it's a pity because Miriam's obviously very fond of her."

"Oh, I don't know," replied his wife taking her plate of unfinished food to the sink. "I don't know. You'll just have to do whatever you think is best. In any case, I'm fed up and going to bed."

"But Susan," he called after her, "we can always get an older woman who would be just as good."

His wife, however, had made her way out of the kitchen without another word, to leave John wondering what he could do to restore the harmony of their relationship. He made to follow her and try to reason things out, but only to quickly realise it would be futile.

Reaching the kitchen entrance, he was barely in time to see her disappearing round the bend of their ornate oak stairwell. He pondered on the cause of his wife's unhappiness and it made him wonder whether the human species wasn't over-endowed with the sex drive for its actual purpose. Certainly, it caused its fair share of domestic and social difficulties – not to mention downright criminal acts such as rape.

He turned to re-enter the kitchen and clear up after their disastrous supper, hoping, perhaps, that it might earn a little domestic collateral. But as he did so his eye caught their picture of the fisher boy and he recalled his earlier telephone conversation with Mrs Shawcross. He was not superstitious, although after the night's unpleasantness, he began to wonder, for rows with his wife were virtually unknown. Whenever business problems became particularly difficult, John had a habit of retiring to the peace of his study or his 'retreat' as he sometimes called it. The modest-sized room housed a number of treasured artefacts from his boyhood which included his father's roll-topped desk and a large framed photograph of his parents on their wedding day. But perhaps his most precious possession was his grandmother's inlaid Victorian workbox. All in all, the room offered a portal of escape back to the security of his childhood. Situated at the side of the desk was his rather worn but very comfortable armchair, and he sank down with a sigh while glancing round the room of memories: memories of a different age when, under the protective shelter of his parents' 'umbrella', life had seemed so much simpler.

Finally, after switching on his favourite country & western CD, he laid back with his long legs stretched out and tried to relax, while with little desire to join his wife in her present mood he found himself gradually drifting off into an uneasy sleep.

"And what happened to you last night?"

The sudden irritable sound of his wife's voice came, piercing the clogging veil of John's slumber, and caused him to sit up with a jerk. Having had no blanket, the early morning chill had seeped into his bones and he shivered involuntarily.

"Well, tell me. Why didn't you come up to bed?" she persisted.

"I'm sorry," he struggled to apologise. "I just came in here to listen to some music and that's the last thing I remember. I woke up around 4am but was hesitant to come up and disturb you."

He felt slightly humiliated at having to explain his behaviour like some naughty child, but that was the effect his wife's tone was beginning to have. They'd been married for some ten years, and although he'd always respected her outspoken ways he could never recall the unpleasantness that he was now experiencing. He also noticed his wife was not only still in her dressing gown and with her hair unbrushed but that she was also smoking. All of which were unprecedented for such an early hour. His watch told him it was approaching 7.30am. Normally, she would have been putting the finishing touches to her make-up before setting off for her Horsham office.

"Susan," he said gently. "If you'd like to get ready for work I'll rustle up some breakfast."

But his conciliatory gesture only met with an immediate rebuff. "Oh, don't bother. I'm not hungry. Just get your own breakfast."

And again, leaving John's emotions in turmoil, she abruptly turned away.

Utterly bewildered, he sat there not knowing what to do, for his wife's inexplicable attitude had left him at a complete loss. It almost felt as though she had undergone some sort of personality disturbance. Brenda had been with them for over eighteen months and had never caused this sort of reaction before. He remained in his chair for a long time before hearing the front door slam and the sound of her car receding down the drive. No 'Goodbye, love, hope you have a good day with the business.' Nothing. Absolutely nothing.

Slowly and reluctantly, he heaved himself up and crossed the small inner hall that led off to the dining and reception areas. Situated at the rear of the house, these rooms enjoyed extensive views across the larger part of their grounds. Reaching the main hallway, he looked over at the front door which had been so firmly shut. Doors, he knew only too well, could be either closed or shut, for in his experience being shut carried painful implications of being shut out, and his mind drifted back to an earlier marriage when money had been desperately short and when he and his then wife had been compelled to take in lodgers to make ends meet.

However, it had proved a calamitous decision, for to his horror she had become infatuated with one of their guests just three months after moving into their new home. Tired out after teaching at both day and night school, he had often retired to bed early but then only to listen to the chink of wine glasses and the sound of jazz music from downstairs as the lodger and his wife enjoyed the early stages of their relationship. One night, as the sound of their laughter drifted up from the lounge below, he determined to have it out with her once and for all. How vividly he recalled her reaction and the resultant humiliation.

"Don't tell me what I should and shouldn't do. I'm an adult!" she had shouted back while the lodger, standing close behind her, just laughed as she slammed the door in his face. And, since that day, John had, on principle, never completely closed an internal door not wishing to impose the abject feelings of rejection he had experienced that fateful night.

He drew a deep breath before expending a long drawn out sigh as he tried to shake off the bitter memories; memories which he knew could never be entirely eradicated. The whole episode had left him cautious and it had been a number of years before he again contemplated any thought of marriage. But there had been nothing flippant about Susan and he felt instinctively that her forthright, dependable personality and the love he had to offer, would be enough to ensure success. But now...

He could appreciate, perhaps, his wife's discomfort at having an attractive woman like Brenda about the house, but standing in the hallway while staring fixatedly at the front door, he found it difficult to believe that the odd smile he'd exchanged with the nanny could really have justified such an extreme reaction. After all, he reasoned, Brenda had been his wife's choice out of a number of suitable applicants. He glanced across at the fisher boy and wondered. John was essentially a man of logic who believed in the physical laws of cause and effect. Therefore, the dire warnings of Mrs Shawcross had made little impact because, in his mind, that sort of thinking belonged to a bygone age when superstition had filled the void caused by a lack of knowledge. And yet...

He moved over to confront the enigmatic painting with its clear blue summer sky and the lush green vegetation of its river banks. Standing there with his hands clasped behind his back, he focussed on the slumbering youth as he dozed with his back to a tree and where the river curved away into the distance. An artist himself, he could well appreciate how the painter had arranged the composition and the consummate, time-consuming skill applied to its detail. In all, it was a harmonious and beautiful piece of work that would have graced any home.

He shook his head unable to believe that something so apparently peaceful could possibly affect the tranquility of his home. But his sombre ruminations were suddenly interrupted by little Miriam's slightly reed-like voice.

"Daddy."

And there, crossing the hallway, was his beloved little daughter fiercely clutching the nanny's hand, but it was Brenda who really caught his attention. She looked stunning, having parted her generous auburn hair and allowed it to cascade down the right side of her face while a revealing white blouse was only seductively matched by tight-fitting black jeans.

"Hello, John."

Her greeting was accompanied by a slightly coy smile and the sultry flicker of heavily mascaraed eyelashes which, despite himself, caused Susan's husband to involuntarily catch his breath. Sometimes it was not easy being a man and he fought for control in the face of this blatant 'come on'.

"Hi," he responded guardedly. "Is Miriam all ready for school?

But, before she could answer, his little girl piped up anxiously, "Where's Mummy?"

In response, John immediately crouched down to her level.

"Oh," he explained gently. "Mummy's had to leave early for work, but she'll be back this evening, and remember it's her turn to read your bedtime story."

"You're so good with her, John," observed the nanny admiringly before turning her attention to the little girl.

"Darling. Would you just pop into the nursery for a few minutes because I would like to speak to your daddy?" And then, as the youngster disappeared from the hallway, Brenda blew her a kiss which was just the sort of affectionate gesture that made it so difficult for John to terminate her appointment.

Once satisfied the youngster was out of earshot, she turned to her employer. "John. I know this might sound silly," she confessed while indicating the painting. "But, last night I had a very strange experience. I dreamt of an overwhelming compulsion to come down in the early hours and speak to that boy, and I can tell you the urge was so strong it was almost as though something or someone had taken over control of my mind." She paused briefly as if expecting a reaction, whereas, in fact, all she got was a brief smile and the invitation to continue. However, her expression precluded any room for humour. "Anyway," she stressed, "as I reached the hallway, that boy!" And she emphasised the point by tapping the canvas. "I swear that boy slowly straightened up and turned to look at me from under the edge of that straw hat. And his eyes, John," she almost cried. "His eyes were full of hate and anger." Pausing to catch her breath, she added tearfully, "It was horrific and I could hear myself screaming and screaming until I finally woke up drenched in sweat."

"Nasty," he admitted. "Not nice at all." But then added, perhaps a little insensitively, "Well, if it's any consolation, it was only a dream and we can get up to all sorts of things in our dreams. Can't we just!"

However, his seemingly frivolous attitude only served to distress her further.

"It really upset me, John," she insisted. "And what's more, I'm not entirely sure it was a dream. It all felt so real. I can vividly recall steadying myself against the oak panelling as I came down the stairs and the sensation of wood under my hand. If I'm really honest, John, I don't feel safe being in the same house as that painting. Anyway," she added, "I must get Miriam ready for school."

And, before he could formulate a response, the nanny had turned and made her way towards the nursery. Her experience was yet another episode in the past twelve hours that had proved abnormal. But worse was to follow later in the day when his wife failed to return home from work.

As 5pm arrived and went, he became increasingly concerned, for Susan always tried to get back early and spend as much time as possible with little Miriam before her bedtime.

Initially John avoided trying to contact her mobile phone, mindful of how she'd behaved earlier in the day. However, little Miriam was becoming very distressed so, finally, he gave in and dialled her number. Although, in the event, all he got was a metallic-like female voice informing him that the person he wished to speak to was unavailable and would he like to leave a message.

"Great," he breathed. "Very helpful I'm sure." But as he replaced the handset, Brenda appeared at the doorway of the nursery.

"Problems, John?"

He responded with a negative shrug. "Susan's late and she's not picking up her phone. I'm not quite sure what to do. I'm hesitant to just go charging off up to Horsham and demand to know what's keeping her. You can imagine how that would go down, can't you?"

Brenda closed the nursery door to prevent Miriam hearing any unpleasantness.

"Forgive me for saying so, John," she began quietly, "but I was tidying up the nursery last night and couldn't avoid overhearing some of what was being said. I didn't listen deliberately, you understand, but I got the distinct impression your wife's far from happy with my being here. And then this morning I heard the front door go with a hell of a bang, so I guessed she was still very upset." The forthright and embarrassing observation left him searching for words. "Look, John," she continued. "I'll get straight to the point. If my being here is causing trouble, then I have no option but to resign." She shrugged. "I am what I am, and I can't change that. So...?"

She'd put her cards on the table and stood there waiting for his reaction.

"Well, at least you're honest," he began reluctantly. "I'm just sorry it's come to this." He shrugged helplessly. “I’d like you to stay because I think you do an excellent job.” He would have said more, however, as her employer, he could hardly admit to finding her sexually very attractive and, for his wife’s sake ask would she be kind enough to tone it down a bit. So, instead, he decided on a more moderate approach. “I don’t know how much you heard last night, but it was so unlike Susan.” He glanced across at the fisher boy. “You know, it may be a coincidence, but it seems to me that from the moment I first clapped eyes on that picture we’ve had nothing but trouble. There was your unpleasant experience at that nightclub. Oh, and, incidentally, did you know that man died in hospital the night before last.”

On hearing this, the nanny blanched slightly. “I knew he’d been taken to hospital but...”

“Well, he’s dead,” reiterated John. “There’s also something else you might like to know. His mother’s a self-confessed psychic and she warned me of the consequences if I continued to keep that picture in the house.” He rubbed a forefinger thoughtfully across the cleft above his chin. “She was here a few nights back and, come to think of it, Susan wasn’t very pleased about that.”

The nanny paused before excusing herself to look after Miriam, while John just stuck his hands in his jeans pockets and made for the kitchen where he slumped down on the sofa in front of a glass of wine. It was fast approaching 6pm with still no sign of Susan, and he leaned forward with a sigh while resting his elbows on his knees. Lifting his head, he could see the bright spring evening through the bay window. However, his thoughts were anything but bright as he again tried his wife's phone, with the same result.

A further two hours passed and still he sat there while the beautiful day seeped away over the western horizon. Suddenly, however, his thoughts were shattered as someone switched on the lights and blinking against their unexpected brilliance, he turned to see Brenda.

"John, are you all right?" she enquired, obviously concerned to see him sitting in semi-darkness.

"Yes, I'm fine," he responded, but it was an automatic response that held a hollow ring. "I just don't know what's become of Susan," he added despairingly. "I keep trying her mobile phone with no result."

The nanny, who had changed into a short dark blue skirt, took a seat opposite and crossed her shapely legs.

"I can't help feeling," she confessed, "this is all my fault."

But John shook his head.

"It's not your fault, Brenda," he assured her. "It's something else. The problem is I just don't know what." He again felt himself struggling with conflicting emotions and getting up crossed to the bay window where he stood looking vacantly out at the darkness beyond. Finally, he turned. "You know," he said solemnly, "I'm beginning to have severe doubts about the influence of that picture." But even as he spoke, he noticed the headlights of an approaching car begin to reflect on the kitchen ceiling as it made its way towards the house. "Oh!" he exclaimed with relief. "I just hope this is Susan." He paused uncertainly before adding, "I think perhaps, under the circumstances..."

But the nanny pre-empted him.

"It's all right. I fully understand. I'll just go up and see if Miriam's asleep."

However, whether he heard was debateable, because by the time she'd finished he was half way across the hall on his way to the front door, and as he snatched it open there was his wife on the floodlit forecourt locking her car.

"Susan!" he shouted.

And heedless of the tragedy they had so recently incurred, he took the front steps in a single bound while the sheer intensity of his relief precluded the need for any words as he gathered her fiercely in his arms.

"Careful," she whispered. "I can hardly breathe." Her reaction could have been mistaken for an anti-climax, but he knew 'he'd got her back'; and, while still in the protective custody of his arms, she asked anxiously about little Miriam. "Oh, John," she began apologetically. "I know the trouble and worry I must have caused, but I've felt so depressed and fearful over the last few days. I don't know why. It may be my hormones. Remember the problems I had when I was expecting Miriam? Well, this time it's been so much worse."

John could see she was close to tears and immediately bridled his own concerns and instead took her hand and led the way to the front door.

"Right, young lady. It's the doctor for you first thing tomorrow morning," he announced emphatically. "But, tonight I'm going to prescribe a large dose of red wine."

Seated on the kitchen sofa, his wife began to pour out the tribulations of her day.

"I felt absolutely awful this morning, John. My mind was a complete mess. I can't begin to describe how bad I felt. Everything seemed so totally out of proportion." But, as her husband laid his arm along the back of the seat and gently caressed her shoulder, she suddenly sat upright and looked him straight in the eye. "John, you know perfectly well I'm not the jealous kind and I can't think what possessed me to carry on like I did last night." The very word 'possessed' immediately triggered thoughts of Mrs Shawcross – although he instantly dismissed them. "One of the reasons I married you, John," she continued earnestly, "was because I knew I could trust you."

A slight mistiness appeared in her eyes. "Oh, you don't think Brenda heard me, do you? Oh, I hope not. How embarrassing." He'd never believed in lying but knew instinctively this was one of those rare occasions when an exception was called for. Finally, however, he enquired if she'd had anything to eat. "Yes, I'm fine thanks," she replied quietly, nestling back against his supporting arm. "I know I should have come straight home tonight," she confessed, "but I really was in an awful state. I'd had the most terrible day at work. I just couldn't seem to do anything right. On top of which, I had a dreadful row with my deputy, so in the end I decided to go round and see my old friend Wendy. You remember her? We were at school together and she's always been so supportive."

"Oh," he smiled briefly. "You mean 'Wino Wendy'. The one I sometimes refer to as the 'Bottle Girl'."

"That 'Bottle Girl' as you call her," she objected, "happens to be a good friend of mine, and after years of abuse at the hands of a violent womanising husband it's not surprising she turned to alcohol."

"I know, I know. I was just kidding, but honestly, I was really worried about you. Especially when you didn't answer your phone."

"And there's a very good reason for that," she explained promptly. "I managed to leave it at work," she shrugged apologetically. "All in all, it's been a pretty disastrous twenty-four hours, hasn't it?"

"I've known better," he admitted, glancing at his watch. "But as it's now approaching 9pm, how about calling it a day and having an early night?"

And so, with their harmony apparently restored, he took her hand and they made their way towards the foot of the stairs.

Several weeks were to pass without further incident as the rhythm of life at the farmhouse gave an appearance of returning to normal. Visitors took time to admire the new attraction on the chimney breast, but that was as far as it went until early one Saturday morning, John woke to find his wife propped up against her pillow and with one arm behind the back of her head. Obviously deep in thought, she turned to him with a hesitant expression.

"John, I've just had the strangest dream."

"Then I'll bet it was about me." He grinned while playfully tapping the end of her nose with his forefinger. "I can't think of anything stranger than that..."

But she cut him short. "John, I'm being serious."

"Well then, love. Tell me. What happened in your dream?" he asked sympathetically while shuffling round on his side to face her.

At first, she didn't answer. Gradually, however, she began to describe her peculiar experience.

"I was walking along by a stretch of water on a beautiful sunlit day. I didn't know where it was, and I didn't know where you were, but the sense of peace was absolute. The lush green of the trees and grass defied description, and the air, John, it was just so pure and sweet. You know how clean it can smell when it's just rained? It was like that." She paused and looked away as though momentarily back in her dream. "It was as though," she added wistfully, "I was the last person on earth. Only the sound of grasshoppers disturbed the silence, and yet, no," she hesitated "'disturbed' would be the wrong word, because if anything they complemented the tranquillity." She moved her arm to stare straight into his eyes. "John, it was almost as if I'd died and gone to heaven."

"Well, I'm not sure about the dying bit but the rest of it doesn't sound too bad." He grinned.

"But then," she continued in a subdued voice, "and this was the disturbing bit – my dream seemed to change. You know," she added, "how dreams can change? Anyway, the lake suddenly became the river in that picture downstairs."

"Go on."

"I found myself walking along the riverbank towards that boy, but in my dream he was not alone. There was a tall woman in a long Victorian dress standing side of him and gently caressing the back of his neck. But her hair," she suddenly emphasised. "She had the most luxurious copper-coloured hair I've ever seen. It reached way down past her waist. Somehow," Susan continued, "the woman sensed my approach and looked up, but you should have seen her eyes. She'd obviously been crying dreadfully and when she saw me she tried to speak, but although I did my best I couldn't make out a word, and, you know, she seemed to realise it because I could see from her frustrated expression how desperately she wanted to communicate with me." At this point, his wife paused as if struck by a sudden thought. "But, wait a minute. Didn't that Shawcross woman say something about detecting the sounds of a woman weeping?"

John's expression became serious.

"Remember how the auctioneer described the artist's affiliation with the Pre-Raphaelites? It may be a coincidence, but they had a strong preference for women with red hair. There's a painting entitled '*Ophelia*' by John Millais which depicts a woman drowning in a river. She had abundant red hair." He compressed his lips in a flinty expression. "Do you know? Well, you probably wouldn't know, that he got his girlfriend to pose in a bath of water and she died of pneumonia as a result." His wife began to look strained. "Death, weeping, a river and a woman with copper-coloured hair. It's becoming almost uncanny," he added, swinging his legs over the edge of the bed. "In fact, although I don't like to sound overly dramatic, it almost feels as though some drama from the past is trying to force its way through into the present, and I'm beginning to suspect that picture downstairs could be the mediation for it." He sat hunched on the side of the bed with his elbows resting on his knees. "I didn't tell you at the time, but several weeks ago, Brenda also had a disturbing dream and it was not dissimilar to the one you've just described." He turned around and grinned briefly. "I think it was the same night you were in the middle of your 'two and eight'."

She frowned slightly.

"My what?"

"Oh, it's cockney slang," he explained, "for being in a stressed state."

"John," she retorted. "There's no need to bring that up."

He rolled back on the bed and gently tapped the end of her nose.

"No," he agreed, "but isn't it strange how you both had nightmares about virtually the same thing? Anyway," he suddenly added brightly, "let's hope today turns out to be what I call a day of nothing. You know? I just love days of nothing. No problems with the business. No water leaks. No collapsed ceilings." But, as he rose to collect his dressing gown off the bedroom door, he thought he detected a slight giggle from his wife. "What?"

"It's your legs, John. They're absolutely the hairiest pair of male legs I've ever seen."

"Well," he laughed, "that would depend on just how many hairy male legs you've encountered. And no, don't tell me, because I really don't want to know."

Her answer took the form of a flying pillow, so he wisely decided to postpone any further comment until behind the relative safety of their partially open bedroom door.

"By the way," he ventured gingerly, peering round the edge, "don't forget Pastor Tim is supposed to be coming to see us around 2pm, so you won't be able to lie there all day." And without waiting for a reply, he quickly closed the door and fled for the stairs.

Apart from these light-hearted altercations and Susan's first bout of early morning sickness, the first part of the day slipped away without further incident. However, at about 2pm their expected visitor phoned to say he wouldn't be round until sometime after six. Susan had taken the call, and when John heard the news his relief was patent.

"I don't know why you're taking that attitude," she observed sharply. "Tim's always been a good friend to us. Remember how supportive he was when your mother died? You seem to forget that."

Admonished, he went on the defensive. "The point is, Tim's all right but you must admit, he's a bit... well, you know, short on conversation, and I sometimes find it hard work – oh, I know he's got the gift for preaching and all that, but it never seems to get much beyond the pulpit. Anyway," he sighed gratefully, "I've now got a whole afternoon of nothing."

And so, with Miriam and Brenda at the cinema, they prepared for a quiet afternoon in the comfortable area of the kitchen. This entailed John being spread-eagled across the sofa and trawling

The Mail on Saturday supplement in search of the ensuing week's preview of *Coronation Street*, while his wife made do with one of the armchairs as she settled down to enjoy her current copy of *Woman's Own* magazine. The sound of contented quiet slowly ticked by until...

"Listen!" proclaimed John suddenly and unexpectedly.

"What? Listen to what?" exclaimed his wife, aggravated by the interruption to her reading.

"The quiet, of course." He grinned mischievously. "Listen to the quiet."

"Look. If you've nothing better to do than to irritate me, then for goodness sake go and find something useful," she retorted. "For a start, I can barely open the front windows with all that ivy. Try taking a pair of shears to that lot. The exercise will do you good."

"Yes, I might do that," he added lazily while replacing the supplement on the nearby coffee table and wiggling down into a more comfortable position. "I might just do that."

Needless to say, his idle speculation never materialised into any actual physical activity and he was still ensconced on the sofa when Pastor Tim arrived around 6pm when it fell to his wife to answer the door.

"Hello, Susan. Sorry to have made it so late," apologised their visitor, "but I had a call from Mary.

Apparently, her father's quite poorly and probably won't make it through the night."

"Oh, I'm sorry," replied Susan. "She's such a lovely person and wasn't he a church elder at one time?"

Tim nodded as he made his way into the hall area.

Of slight build, he barely stood much above five-foot-five inches and at no time ever wore the traditional dog-collar; a quiet and inconspicuous man in his late fifties, he was nevertheless always immaculately groomed with iron-grey hair that never saw a strand out of place.

"You know, Susan," he said almost enviously, "you really do have a beautiful home here. That blossom of yours along the drive is absolutely breathtaking."

"Yes, it's a lovely time of the year," she agreed. "Everything's at its best. I don't think I can remember when I last saw so much colour. The pink and white of the magnolia trees has just been incredible. Although, it never lasts very long, and before you know it all that gorgeous blossom just ends up lying on the drive."

The sun was slowly dipping down towards the west and sending bright streams of light across the hallway to illuminate their enigmatic painting.

"I haven't seen this before," he observed with undisguised admiration. "But I must say I like your taste. Is it John's work by any chance?"

"No. I'm afraid I can't lay claim to that," admitted her husband who had just joined them from his 'bed' in the kitchen. "Mind you," he added, "it would be a miracle if I had because it was probably painted somewhere around the early eighteen fifties."

"Do you happen to know who the artist was?" enquired their guest, intrigued by the picture's intense sense of reality.

"As far as we understand," answered John, "it was done by a man called George Blake and I believe that's his son with the fishing rod. But look, come on through to the kitchen. There's something I'd like to discuss with you."

However, Tim was not to be so easily distracted.

"The grass," he enthused. "You could almost touch it. Every blade has been so meticulously done. Can you begin to imagine the patience it must have taken?"

It was an uncharacteristic outpouring for the pastor, and John glanced over his head to exchange a meaningful look with his wife.

"Er, Tim. Can we perhaps offer you a cup of coffee?" she volunteered while heading towards the living area. "I seem to remember you like it black with no sugar."

Finally, with their visitor comfortably seated and duly equipped with the promised beverage, John again sprawled himself across the entire length of the sofa, although catching his wife's expression, he immediately assumed a more dignified position.

"You're not an octopus, John," she complained.

"Where am I supposed to sit? I wonder about your manners sometimes." But, all unrepentant, he just grinned.

"There was something you wanted to talk to me about, John?" Tim enquired.

In response, Miriam's father indicated the hallway. "I'm not a superstitious man as you probably know, but from the time we acquired that picture we seem to have had nothing but trouble." He then went on to describe his wife's strange dream, and the tragic death of Mrs Shawcross' son. But, what really caught the pastor's attention was the woman's dire warning.

"You say this lady detected sounds of a woman crying and your wife actually saw the same woman in her dream?"

"Well, I've no means of knowing whether it was actually the same person," observed his host. "But I suppose it's a possibility – I hadn't even thought of that."

The pastor's expression became grim.

"John," he said slowly and solemnly. "You are aware that we struggle with dark forces in this world – and when we have contacts with psychics, we don't know what we're dealing with? I cannot warn you strongly enough to have nothing to do with them."

"Well, Tim," John replied defensively, "I didn't actually invite the woman to conduct a séance. In fact, I had no idea she was a psychic. She simply visited us to apologise for her son's behaviour and then just upped and out with how she felt." He leaned forward in his seat. “Let me put it to you bluntly, Tim. In your experience as a man of God, do you believe that an artefact, such as a painting, could be capable of mediating the horror of some past tragedy into a future time, like now?”

At this point, it was the pastor’s turn to lean forward, and with his elbows resting on his knees he joined the tips of his fingers in a tent-like formation. Obviously deep in thought, he pursed his lips before replying.

“John, an honest answer to that is, I just don’t know.”

But his host was determined to press the case. “Tell me this then, Tim. In the light of what I’ve told you, would you still keep it in the house?”

At this, however, there was no hesitation.

“No!” he exclaimed adamantly. “I certainly wouldn’t. I’d be very much against having something I suspected of being of a doubtful supernatural nature.”

“Fresh coffee, Tim?” suggested Susan, more as a gesture to lighten the atmosphere than as an act of hospitality.

“Oh, yes thanks, Susan. Just half a cup will do.” He turned back to his host, although John was busy ensuring he didn’t miss out on his wife’s offer.

“Sorry, Tim,” he smiled mischievously, “but I have to keep an eye on things or I’d miss out wouldn’t I, darling.”

“I was going to ask,” observed their visitor, “whether you’ve any knowledge of the artist; George

Blake I think you said his name was. I know you used to teach Art History, so I wondered if you'd ever occasioned the name before?"

But John shook his head.

"No," he replied adamantly. "I've never heard of him. Really all I know is what we learned at the auction, and that is he worked on the fringe of the Pre-Raphaelite movement during the eighteen fifties and sixties.

His wife, now duly equipped with her own coffee, had just about managed to squeeze back onto the sofa and wasted no time in expressing her own opinion.

"I do hope you gentlemen aren't consigning our painting to oblivion without my consent. And, John," she added pointedly with a judicious use of her elbows, "could you please move over. Honestly, you're like a jelly before it sets. You sit down and spread out over everything."

Their slightly sombre visitor smiled briefly.

"It's nothing like that, Susan," he assured her. "In fact, I was about to suggest..."

But, whatever it was he was about to suggest became lost to the ether as the nanny poked her head round the edge of the kitchen entrance.

"John, there's a woman at the front door who insists on speaking to you."

"Thanks, Brenda," he called back, reluctantly hauling himself up while apologising to the pastor. "Sorry, Tim. I'll be back in a moment."

Susan was quick to put in her own tuppence worth. "I do hope, John, that it's not that psychic woman again."

But their visitor was to prove anyone but the maligned Mrs Shawcross, because as John reached the front entrance, he found himself face-to-face with none other than the woman who had slammed the door in his face all those years earlier. Stunned beyond belief, he found it impossible to articulate as his mind flashed back to that humiliating night and the following day when, upon returning home from teaching, he had found the house picked clean with no sign of either his wife or her lover. Slowly however, he began to notice how the intervening years had taken their toll. The once-slim figure now looked stocky and overweight while the long dark hair he remembered appeared little more than an unsightly and ill-kept bob. But then something far more disturbing caught his attention, for although she was obviously trying to conceal it with the upturned collar of her coat, light from the hallway nevertheless revealed a vivid scarlet abrasion to the left side of her face, and upon closer inspection he could see a dark bruising round her left eye.

"John," she said hesitantly in a broken voice. "John, I don't know how to say this, but I need your help."

Totally nonplussed by this bizarre turn of events, he was reduced to saying the first thing that came into his head. "How on earth did you manage to find me, and where's your car? I mean, we're right out in the sticks."

"I took a bus to Cowfold village with the last of my money, and then walked," she admitted lamely.

In some respects, she was not dissimilar to his present wife, for they both shared the same sort of fortitude and he could never once remember seeing her cry during the whole time they had been together. But now she looked utterly crushed and desolate, with moisture beginning to seep from the corners of her eyes.

Suddenly, on impulse, he spun round to stare across the hallway, but whether a combination of the fast-fading daylight and the artificial hall lighting combined to affect his sight he couldn't be sure because, for a split second, he could have sworn the fisher boy had turned to gloat. He shuddered involuntarily while blinking to clear his vision. The eye, however, had deceived the mind, for as he looked again the boy still slumbered in the shadow of his ragged straw hat.

"Are you all right, John?" enquired his unexpected visitor.

"Yes, yes. I'm fine," he retorted dismissively as the initial shock of seeing her began to wear off and be replaced by bitter thoughts of her betrayal. Indeed, he felt sorely tempted to ask what the dickens she was doing here in the first place and where the hell was 'laughing boy', for the sound of that lodger's derisive sniggering still rang in his ears.

However, he faced a moral dilemma, for although his gut instinct was to slam the door in his ex's face, Tim's teaching made him hesitate and he stood there engaged in a bitter mental struggle; a struggle which was suddenly interrupted by his wife.

"John, what's going on?" And then, catching sight of her husband's ex, she asked pointedly, "And who might this be?"

Overcome with curiosity and tired of waiting, Susan had left Tim in the kitchen to find out what was taking so long. But her sudden intervention only added another ingredient to the cauldron of his churning emotions. Susan was, of course, well aware that her husband had been divorced, but he'd never gone into the sordid details of how it had come about.

It was an almost impossible situation, but finally he decided that truth was his only option.

"This lady," he sighed resignedly, "is none other than my ex and she seems to be in some sort of trouble."

"But why...?" began Susan. "Has she...?"

He shrugged. "I'm afraid we haven't got that far."

Mindful of her recent unpredictable behaviour, he was extremely concerned how she might react. His wife, however, was not only a perceptive woman but also a compassionate one and she quickly recognised the wretched state of their visitor.

"What on earth's happened to your face?" she asked.

Ensuing events, however, left John feeling not only totally mystified but also slightly irrelevant as a strange dynamic seemed to develop between the two women, for to his surprise, Susan unexpectedly stepped forward to put an arm round his stricken ex and invite her in. To say that he felt distinctly uneasy would have been an understatement for he had a nasty feeling the whole situation could blow up in his face at any moment.

"John, for heaven's sake will you stop dithering about!" exclaimed his wife. "Go and attend to Tim. You can see quite well I've got my hands full. And, while you're at it, ask Brenda to bring two strong cups of coffee to the drawing room."

Susan was obviously in full flow, and whereas he'd never considered himself a wuss, he did sometimes wonder if he wasn't already well on the way.

Finalising his coffee instructions, he returned to the kitchen.

"Trouble?" enquired their pastor quizzically.

"Don't ask, Tim. Just don't ask," replied John, stretching out across the settee. Then, with arms clasped behind the back of his head he added, "No warning! Nothing! After some fifteen years, my ex just turns up on the doorstep. For the life of me I can't imagine what she hopes to achieve, but then again, I didn't get the chance to find out because Susan more or less took over and ordered me out of the way. But... think of it... My wife and my ex face-to-face. Lovely situation! And then, Susan goes and invites her into the house. I mean, they don't even know each other's name." He suddenly swung his feet back to the floor and sat upright. "But her face, Tim. You should have seen the left side of her face," he exclaimed. "It was red raw, and she had dark bruising round her eye. It looked to me as though she'd been attacked." He shook his head in disbelief. "But, I ask you, who would do something like that? Certainly not the weasel she left me for." Seeing the pastor's change of expression, he hastened to apologise. "Oh, sorry, Tim. I mustn't bore you with the ins and outs of my past."

"No, no. That's fine, John," he smiled. "I already knew this was your second marriage. It was just your choice of phrase that amused me. That's all."

"You know, Tim," John observed. "Taken on its own, I wouldn't have given it too much thought. Sure, it's something I could have well done without, but when I think of the other unpleasant experiences we've been through lately it does make me wonder."

"You mean," rejoined the pastor, "it makes you wonder if there's some connection to that painting."

Finally, Tim got to his feet. "Thanks for having me, John. Do give my kind regards to Susan. I'm just sorry I didn't see more of her." But, as he made for the hallway, he suddenly paused. "Look, I'm off for the next two weeks attending a theological lecture in London, so while I'm up there I'll try to drop into the British Library and see if I can find out anything about this George Blake. I might also be able to pick up some information from the British Museum." Then, moving across the hallway towards the front door, he turned momentarily to gaze at the boy by the river. "I can see why you bought it, John. It has an almost transcendental quality."

As John bade him goodbye and closed the door, he heard his wife's voice coming from the drawing room.

"John, can you spare a moment?" Compliant as ever, he entered their main reception room to find the two women sharing a bottle of wine. "Has Tim gone?" she enquired. "Because really I would have appreciated his advice." As her husband nodded, he noticed that his ex had removed her coat which made her facial injuries all the more apparent. He went to make belated introductions which Susan quickly waved aside. "It's all right. We know each other's names. But the point is, Jeanette is in a serious situation and virtually homeless." At which point she indicated the drawing room entrance and, taking her cue, John left the room. Obviously anxious to shield the injured woman from what she was about to say, his wife drew the door to before joining him in the hallway. "Your ex," she began in a terse and subdued voice, "should really be in hospital and I'm going to phone for an ambulance. The top of her chest is black and blue. In fact, I wouldn't be surprised if some of her ribs are broken."

"Well, what do you think could have caused that?" he began. But she cut him short.

"I'm making that phone call first," stressed Susan. "Then I'll tell you what I found out."

Assured that medical help was on the way, she made for the kitchen and reached into the 'medicinal cupboard'. Then, with two generous glasses of whisky duly ensconced on the coffee table, she began to explain.

"That poor woman in the drawing room has been involved in an abusive and violent relationship for months."

"You mean we've got another 'bottle woman' on our hands?" he observed pointedly.

"No," countered his wife. "I've no reason to think we've 'another bottle woman on our hands' as you put it. Really, you can sound so sarcastic at times."

Although not unsympathetic, his cruel experience had warped his attitude, and he took a draught of the whisky which made him whince as he swirled it around in his mouth. "Well, any problem my ex-wife's got can't be related to that worm she left me for," he retorted with a certain satisfaction.

"John!" she exclaimed disgustedly. "That's just not worthy of you. Quite apart from which, I've absolutely no interest in the squalid details of your bygone married life."

He shrugged and pulled a face. "That's why I've never bothered to discuss them with you," he replied defensively.

"Never mind all that," she retorted. "We need

to consider what can be done for that poor woman in the reception room; because she is terrified. And whatever happened in the past in no way alleviates a moral responsibility for helping her now."

"Well," he observed tersely, "as far as I can see, her only recourse is a sheltered home for abused women." But, alarmed by Susan's reaction, he continued, "I don't know exactly what you've got in mind, but she's certainly not staying here; no way! Can you imagine it? My wife and my ex under the same roof. I'd end up on a one-way trip to the funny farm." And with that, he downed the remainder of his whisky. "In any case, where's her family? I know for a fact she had two sisters. Mind you, they were a couple of funny birds, if there ever were any."

"John," protested his wife, "she's totally alone. Her elder sister died unexpectedly, and her half-sister lives in New Zealand. We've six bedrooms here and would hardly ever see her. It's just," she pleaded, "until she gets back on her feet. I'm sure Tim would do the same thing in such a situation."

"What? My ex up at the manse. I'll believe that when I see it."

Finally, however, it was agreed that at least in the short-term Jeanette could stay at the farm after her return from hospital; although, only time would tell what the 'short-term' would actually prove to be.

Chapter 3

DESPITE THEIR PASTOR'S promise, it would, in fact, be many weeks before they saw him again, by which time high summer was fast approaching – a time when the vivid tree blossoms and daffodils had long since given way to the graceful sway of lupins and the abundant generosity of wisteria. It was a time when the pale mauve lilacs spoke of nothing but romance, for the heavy rains of winter had at last brought their reward.

And the particularly verdant summer would be one John long remembered. Overall, he would think of it as a very happy family period, for although his property business demanded a great deal of his energy he, nevertheless, always endeavoured to spend as much quality time as possible with Susan and little Miriam. Set in the heart of the Sussex countryside, nothing pleased him more than to share a picnic with them in one of their own fields. It had been a long haul from the terraced house of his origin and he was determined to make the most of it. Moreover, since her illness earlier in the year, their little daughter had seemed to go from strength to strength, while despite continued early morning sickness, Susan's pregnancy also appeared to be progressing well. Normally they would holiday abroad, and never far from the Mediterranean, because they all enjoyed swimming, but with the expectant addition to the family they had decided to remain at home and make the most of their immediate environment. As John often pointed out, the summer's a long time in coming and far too short when it arrives.

However, there were exceptions to this otherwise tranquil period, and the first of these took the form of a phone call from Pastor Tim. Unfortunately, it came on a Saturday morning when John was sprawled half asleep across the kitchen sofa.

"It's for you," exclaimed his wife, passing the mobile. "I do hope I didn't disturb you," she added pointedly before returning to the sink to finish their breakfast things.

But, failing to come up with any suitable repartee, her husband turned his attention to the phone.

"Hello," he stated abruptly.

"John, it's the pastor," came the more mellow reply.

"Sorry, Tim," he apologised. "I didn't realise it was you."

"I guessed," replied the caller with a smile in his voice.

"Anyway, Tim. What can I do for you? We'd expected you back weeks ago."

"Yes, I'm sorry. I won't go into the details but things up here are far more complicated than I realised. There's been serious disagreement amongst the governing body of our church." In his semi-comatose state, this was something John really didn't want to know about and his caller was quick to pick it up. "Look, John. I'm sorry but I feel it my duty to warn both you and Susan of the spiritual danger I believe you face if you continue to harbour that painting in the hallway."

"Spiritual danger? What spiritual danger...? I don't understand."

"I haven't completed my enquiries, but I'm seriously concerned about what I've found out so far."

"And...?"

"I'll explain when I see you, but, in the meantime, I can't advise you strongly enough to get rid of it."

Now fully alert, John terminated the call.

"Was that Tim?" asked Susan.

John responded by flinging the mobile to the end of the sofa.

"Yes," he sighed wearily. "That was Tim."

"Well?"

"Basically," he breathed resignedly, "it was Mrs Shawcross all over again."

But Susan found it far from humorous, and as

she began to put up the ironing board she dropped a bombshell of her own.

"I was speaking to Brenda last night and she indicated her intention to leave. Now, I know in the past," she added, "I've expressed reservations about her behaviour, but nevertheless I shall be sorry to see her go and I know Miriam will be dreadfully upset. I think a number of factors have influenced her decision and that picture might well have been one of them, but anyway the point is... she's leaving."

"That picture. That picture," John almost shouted as he resumed his monopoly of the sofa. "How the hell can something which is just oil paint and canvas cause so much bother?"

"I agree," observed his wife while lifting a basket of laundry onto a nearby worktop. "But it makes me wonder whether it's the oil paint and canvas or what goes on in people's minds. Like for example, my funny dream."

It was an interesting speculation as to whether the problem was projected onto the painting or vice versa, but time would tell that the latter was only too terrifyingly the case.

Later that evening, while looking for little Miriam, John wandered into the nursery and found the nanny busily tidying away the toys. Brenda looked up and smiled in the way he always found so enticing.

"You know, it's sad somehow," she observed nostalgically while gazing around the cluttered playroom, "but Miriam won't need a nursery much longer. What is she next month? Seven?"

"Yes, it slips away before you know it," he agreed. "And, yes, she's seven on the fourth."

The nanny moved across the room to stand by the dapple-grey rocking horse.

"It's funny," she mused. "This used to be her favourite toy. When I started working here, it was always the first thing she made for, but now she hardly ever uses it." And so saying, Brenda gave the wooden horse a gentle push, where it continued to rock silently on its moorings before finally slowing to a halt. She looked wistfully at her employer. "Tell me, John. Why do things always have to change? Why can't they just stay the same?"

His expression reflected her mood as he slowly shook his head.

"I wonder how many people have asked that question," he answered quietly. "Or when a loved one dies, how often such thoughts have been on their mind. The reality is, there are no answers." Brenda gently stroked the horse's mane in response. "You see," he pointed out, "we live in a reality of irreversible events; a constant one-way stream that's laid down by certain physical laws which I believe were instigated by God." But then, realising how heavy all that must have sounded, he added with a smile, "Well, you did ask." He then pointed to the rocking horse. "That used to be mine, you know, when I was a little boy. In fact, I can never remember a time when it wasn't around. I was so small my dad had to pick me up and put me on its back – and I can still recall how he always kept his arm around me as he pushed it to and fro. But now..."

Sombrely, John allowed his eyes to wander over the room: a place full of memories where every artefact told its own story; the huge teddy bear leaning against the wall with its legs spread-eagled out amongst an assortment of picture bricks which had been Miriam's third birthday present. Then there was the scooter lying abandoned on its side not far from the rocking horse; a fourth birthday present, it had initially been her pride and joy but now... Even the walls echoed his original enthusiasm over the nursery with its brightly coloured paper depicting the Mr Men. The nanny was so right, he thought. Everything slowly but imperceptibly slips into the past and now it looks as though this would include Brenda herself.

"My wife tells me you're thinking of leaving," he observed suddenly.

For a moment, she stopped what she was doing.

"Believe me, John. I don't want to leave. I've been very happy here. Miriam's a lovely little girl and I know I'd go a long way before I found such a beautiful location."

"But?"

She looked away as if embarrassed. “I don’t know quite how to put this, John, but the fact is...” However, the nanny didn’t need to finish.

“I see,” he exclaimed. “I see. But even if I were available, you do realise I suppose that I’m heading for sixty.”

“There are other reasons as well, John,” she continued. “For a start it’s not fair to your wife and then there’s my father. He lives all alone and is beginning to develop dementia.”

She paused as though loath to say any more, but John was quick to pick up on her hesitancy and shrugged encouragingly. “And...?”

“I don’t like to sound overly dramatic,” she confessed slowly, “but you remember the dream I told you about? Well, recently I had another unnerving experience.”

“Such as...?”

“On two separate occasions, I dreamed I could hear someone crying. Or perhaps it would be better to describe it as the sound of a woman wailing. Oh, I don’t know,” she continued. “But it usually happens in the early hours around 3am or 4am. But strangely, although it seems to start as a dream I can still hear it briefly even after I wake up.”

John’s attention was immediate as he recalled the reactions of Mrs Shawcross and how she’d ‘tuned in’ to similar sounds.

“You know,” he suggested cautiously, “that we’ve got my ex-wife staying here and she’s been through some pretty rough times lately. You're quite sure it wasn't her?"

But Brenda dismissed the idea immediately. "No. Jeanette's in one of the downstairs back bedrooms and I'm up on the second floor. There's also something else," she added. "Once or twice I'm sure I could detect a man's name mingled in with the crying."

"A name? What sort of name?"

The nanny looked thoughtful for a moment.

"Well, it sounded a bit like Alf or Ralph, but I couldn't really be sure because it was long and drawn out. At least, that's the best way I can describe it."

On hearing this, John led the way out of the nursery and across the hallway where he stood in front of the cryptic painting.

"It may be coincidence, but several weeks ago my wife dreamed she could see a woman standing side of that boy." He tapped the exact spot on the canvas. "Apparently," he continued, "she was dressed in long Victorian costume and seemed to be gently caressing his shoulder. But the point is, she also appeared to be cyring."

The nanny had heard enough.

"I'm sorry, John, but it's just too uncanny. I don't know what's going on but whatever it is I'm not staying to find out."

At this stage, the nanny looked at him with a touch of longing finality.

"I just hope that you don't live to regret buying it." Then, going right out on a limb, she added, "I'm only sad that things couldn't have been different."

She hadn't actually said the words, but by implication he knew how she wished things could have been different between them. And the thought left him with a bitter, yet sweet sadness, for here was someone in her early prime; old enough to know her mind; and probably one of the most beautiful women he'd ever met, but who was willing and daring enough to declare her feelings for him; a man almost twice her age. From the dim and primeval past, he felt an overwhelming urge to just gather her in his arms. But he knew he could not for the sake of little Miriam; for the sake of his wife and their unborn child, and for everything that was decent and honourable. Instead, he just contented himself by looking tenderly down into her eyes with the fervent hope she'd understand.

For a brief moment, time stood still, and then she whispered in a barely audible voice, "Goodbye, John."

And with that, she turned to slowly make her way towards the foot of the stairs, and with a heavy heart he watched her go before she reached the first landing and disappeared from sight.

It would prove to be the last meaningful time he'd ever see her, for during the night and into the following Sunday she slipped away by taxi without a further word. But he never forgot the pleasure of seeing her about the house with little Miriam, nor the sound of her voice. And, despite the tumultuous events that were to follow, she'd left a void in his life that could never be filled.

For a long time, he didn't move but finally crossed the hallway to again confront the boy and his fishing rod. Having studied art, he was well aware of how a painter could rearrange a composition during the course of its execution. Had the woman his wife dreamed about originally been part of the scene but later painted out, he wondered. John stepped closer and ran his finger over the space she might once have occupied. Normally, art connoisseurs would have relied upon x-rays to settle such speculation whereas all he had was the sensitivity of his index finger, but sure enough he could detect faint vertical ridges in the paintwork near the boy which almost certainly indicated that something, or someone, had been eradicated.

In the light of his wife's dream, it raised serious queries as to why such an action should have been deemed necessary. And if it had been the image of a woman, he wondered whether she was the same person who had tried so vainly to communicate with his wife or the woman that Brenda had heard crying in the early hours. Common sense, however, warned him that it was all mere unsubstantiated coincidence, and yet...

Suddenly, however, he was jarred back to reality by a thunderous knocking at the main entrance. Irritated by the interruption to his thinking, he made to cross the hallway.

"John," Susan urged from the kitchen. "For goodness sake, attend to the front door before someone has it off its hinges".

Reaching the door, he angrily wrenched it open, but then only to immediately recognise trouble, for standing there was a man with his fist poised to resume the onslaught; stockily built and with upper arms that spoke of long hours in the gym, he was obviously someone not to be trifled with. Standing beyond him on the forecourt was a four-wheel drive Land Rover with a second man leaning idly against the bonnet with his arms casually folded.

John took all this in at a glance, but before he had a chance to speak the stranger placed a meaty hand on the door.

"You've got my wife here!"

It resonated as a statement that combined fact with threat, but someone of John's build didn't threaten easily, and he slowly and deliberately let his gaze move up from the man's feet until he was looking him straight in the face.

"As I don't know you," he retorted, "it's highly unlikely then that I'd know your wife now, isn't it?"

His words were sufficient to ignite the powder keg and the stranger's raw-boned face twisted into a mask of fury. Taking his hand from the door he grabbed the front of John's shirt in an attempt to lift him forward. But it was a bitter mistake for his 'victim' had the advantage of being on a higher step, and keeping his elbows well in, John drove his right fist straight into the visitor's solar plexus with every ounce of strength he possessed. It was a central area of nerves just below the breast bone, and the aggressor staggered back gagging for breath.

But John had no intention of allowing such a vicious piece of work any chance to recover, and combining his fists swung them like a hammer from knee level straight into the offender's face. The resulting crack was audible, and the recipient collapsed backwards down the steps onto the forecourt where he lay in an inert heap near the Land Rover. Leaping down from the doorway, John wasted no time in confronting the man's indolent-looking companion.

"Friend of yours?" he snapped, indicating the crumpled figure.

"My brother."

"My sympathies," John echoed sarcastically. "Now, get him on board and get the hell off my land."

"He'll be back," warned the man's sibling. "You can depend on it. He won't let you get away with this easily."

But at that moment, Susan came racing down the front steps.

"John, what's going on?" she exclaimed, catching sight of the man's prostrate form.

In turning to answer, he saw his ex-wife's terrified face at the kitchen window.

"This," he almost snarled, "is the low-life that caused Jeanette's injuries, and if there's one thing I can't stand it's a man who uses violence against a woman."

Even as he spoke, however, their belligerent visitor was attempting to haul himself up by hanging on to the Land Rover's wheel arch. But then, to Susan's horror, she saw her husband do something totally out of character; something she would never have dreamed him capable of; for with his adversary still partly on the ground and with his face almost unrecognisable with fury, John repeatedly kicked the man's chest and body. Unable to believe her eyes, Susan rushed forward in a desperate attempt to drag him away. Grabbing and shaking his arms, she screamed repeatedly.

"John! John! What are you doing? For heaven's sake, you'll kill him."

The rigidity in her husband's body was incredible, and only after constantly shouting his name did she see the unnatural glare in his eyes begin to fade. Shaken and weak, he tried to focus on his wife.

"John!" she exclaimed angrily. "Come on indoors, now!" And with that she guided him up the steps and into the hallway where he collapsed limply onto the monk's seat situated just inside the front door. Apparently totally devoid of energy, he just sat with his head rolled back bereft even of the strength to hold it upright.

"Oh, Mrs Grant. He looks ghastly," observed Jeanette who had witnessed the entire encounter from the vantage of the kitchen window."

"Jeanette?" Susan requested anxiously. "Would you be kind enough to fetch some whisky from the 'medicine cabinet' in the kitchen? It's just next to the microwave."

When his ex-wife had said John looked ghastly it was no exaggeration, for it seemed as though his entire life-force had been mysteriously drained away and he was as white as a sheet.

"John, John, what's the matter with you?" begged his wife. "You didn't get hurt, did you?"

"No," he finally whispered slowly and with great effort. "I just feel so weak I can hardly move."

"Jeanette, have you got that whisky?" Susan called out with renewed urgency, while in the meantime her husband just lay sprawled across the monk's seat with arms that hung lifelessly by his sides.

However, as Susan helped him drink from the whisky bottle, he gradually felt the unnatural exhaustion begin to fade, and slowly pulling himself upright he endeavoured to speak.

"I don't understand it," he said. "It was as though something took me over out there and I suddenly possessed unbelievable strength. But," he added weakly, "it left me barely able to stand." Suddenly, the experience reminded him how Brenda had felt a compulsion in her dream to descend the stairs – as though something had taken over her mind. He paused and pointed feebly to the picture on the chimney breast opposite. "Susan!" he exclaimed slowly. "Remember you dreamed there was a woman standing by that boy?"

"Don't remind me."

"Well, I believe," he continued, "there was such a woman, but for whatever reason it was decided to paint her out." He shook his head. "I hate to say it, love, because, as you know, I've always relied on reason and the laws governing physical reality, but I'm beginning to wonder if there's something sinister going on here that we just don't understand and it's starting to affect all our lives."

But then, as he finished speaking and tried to get up, Susan rushed to assist him.

"John, never mind all that. Come into the kitchen. It's more comfortable there and I'll call out our doctor."

Thus, with his wife helping on one side and his ex-wife supporting his other arm, the oddly assorted trio made their way across the hall.

"Those wooden monks' benches are not exactly made for comfort," John managed with a wan smile. “And, as far as I’m concerned, the monks are welcome to them.”

Finally, with him settled on ‘his sofa’, Jeanette faded away to another part of the house. Indeed, since her unorthodox arrival, she’d made a point of being as unobtrusive as possible, while, strangely, his current wife got on with her very well and was always quite happy to spend time in her company. Susan was also very impressed with the way she had developed a relationship with their little daughter.

“Can you see what’s going on outside?” asked John as he took another swig at the whisky.

“You!” stated Susan firmly. “Have had enough of that.” And, grabbing the bottle, she wasted no time in restoring it to the ‘medicine cabinet’ before glancing out through the kitchen window. “I think they must have gone,” she called back. “There’s no sign of them anywhere. I just hope that man’s all right.”

By now, John was more or less recovered. “I hope so too,” he agreed. “Mind you, he was a trouble-maker of the first order and I can’t imagine how my ex could have got caught up with such a brute. Oh, and by the way, you’re right. Brenda has decided to leave.”

“Well, I’m not altogether sorry,” she replied, “because she always fancied you something rotten.”

He stretched and yawned.

“I can’t imagine why,” he retorted modestly. “I’m old enough to be her father. But that’s not really the point, because I believe one of the main reasons for her leaving is fear of that canvas we've got in the hall. In fact, I've a good mind to get back in touch with that Mrs Shawcross and ask her opinion."

"You'll do no such thing," retorted Susan testily. "I've already heard enough of her opinions. I dread to think what Pastor Tim would say if he knew you were inviting a psychic back into the house."

John sighed resignedly. "I've even wondered perhaps if I contacted Barrington's we might learn a bit more about what we're dealing with. I mean, whoever originally owned it must have sold it for a reason."

"Six thousand of them to be precise," observed his wife dryly before adding in the same breath, "Cup of tea?"

John was to quickly find out that the emotional fallout of Brenda's loss would not be confined to himself, when during the following evening his ex burst into the kitchen.

"I think," she began uncertainly, "you need to come and speak to Miriam because she's crying bitterly and keeps asking about Brenda."

But, as Susan got up, John shook his head.

"I'll deal with it," he offered gently. And, after following Jeanette into the nursery, he immediately became touched to see his little girl's flushed face awash with tears, and crouching down he took her small hand. "What is it, darling?" he asked kindly. "Tell me – what's the matter?"

"Where's Brenny?" Miriam asked almost pathetically. "I can't find her anywhere. She always plays with me before bedtime and then reads me a story." Her words tore at his heart, for how could he explain the situation to such a young child? "Tell me, Daddy," his little girl sobbed, "has she gone? I mean, gone forever?" John looked up to exchange a hopeless glance with his ex who seemed equally affected by the child's sadness. "But I didn't do anything wrong, did I, Daddy?" little Miriam murmured. At which John took her in his arms.

"No, darling. Of course you didn't," he said soothingly.

"But, Daddy, doesn't she love me anymore?" asked his small daughter tearfully.

"Of course she does," he reassured her. "It's just that... you see... like you, she also has a daddy who lives all on his own with no-one to look after him. So really Brenny had no choice. She's gone to take care of her daddy. You know, just like you would if I was alone and ill."

For a moment, the little girl seemed slightly mollified but then again burst out, "But Daddy. She didn't even say goodbye."

He looked at his ex again, for in reality he knew there was no answer to his daughter's unhappiness.

A week later saw John trying to explain the result of his enquiries concerning the picture's original owner. It was a Saturday afternoon and he and his wife were relaxing in the kitchen area while their daughter played happily in the grounds with Jeanette. His ex-wife, it seemed, had gradually assumed Brenda's role.

"According to Barrington's," he began, "our picture was submitted for auction by no less than one Charles George Stratford-Hugo."

Sitting opposite and deeply engrossed in a book, his wife merely raised her eyebrows.

"Well, I suppose he can't be blamed for that," she observed absently without even looking up.

"Anyway," John persisted, "apparently, he doesn't live far from here. It's at a place called Farnham Manor. In fact, we've often passed it on the way to Horsham. The point being, that's if I could get your attention for a minute! We've been invited up there next Saturday."

She nodded with the same lack of enthusiasm. "Next Saturday it is then. Although, what it will achieve...?"

"Well, it might..." But with her blatant disinterest, he decided to abandon the conversation and leave her to the 'joys' of her book.

Later that evening, he was quietly relaxing to the country music of Johnny Cash when there came a gentle tap on the door of his retreat. Surprised that anyone should feel the necessity to knock, he went to get up, but in doing so caught sight of his ex peering hesitantly into the room.

"All right if I come in?" she enquired cautiously.

"Yes, yes. Come in," he invited reluctantly while indicating an ancient armchair whose only virtue appeared to be its dilapidated comfortable appearance.

Since her unexpected arrival, John had made a determined effort to see as little of her as possible, which had made the situation just about tolerable. Even so, her continued presence was something he could well have done without.

"What can I do for you?" he asked disinterestedly.

"John, it's just that I want to thank you for all you've done – especially in light of..."

Her already softly spoken words began to fail and he reached to turn down the music.

"To be honest, Jeanette, I don't know quite what to say to you. Except that I've no patience with men who abuse women... As regards anything else..." He shrugged.

For a moment she just sat with a lowered head.

"I know. I fully understand," she began slowly. "I treated you abominably. None of which you deserved, and if it's any consolation – I've always regretted it."

Anxious to terminate the exchange, he again enquired as to the purpose of her visit. However, as she looked up, he couldn't help but notice how much better she looked compared to the night of her arrival. The stay with them had obviously proved beneficial, yet the smooth forehead he remembered was now furrowed with stress while the firmness of her cheeks had given way to a more harrowed appearance which was accentuated by the marionette lines emanating from the corners of her mouth.

"John," she began awkwardly, "I've just been through the most terrible years of my life." And, as she spoke, she clutched at a screwed-up handkerchief in her left hand; an action reminiscent of Mrs Shawcross. "Anyway," she continued with a touch of desperation, "there's no way I can return home. I just can't stand my husband's violence any longer."

"That man in the Land Rover?" She nodded miserably. "Well," continued John emphatically, "I do hope you realise that none of this is any of my business."

At which she rose despondently to leave. "I had thought, perhaps..." she ventured resignedly. "But it doesn't matter."

However, the sight of her despair again began to bring his conscience into direct confrontation with the bitter resentment he'd harboured through the years, and his mind slipped back to a happier time when her open and cheerful manner had so enamoured him. He recalled how they would often meet up after teaching evening classes, and later share a bag of fish and chips in the local car park. Life had seemed so much simpler in those far-off days: days when they had dreamed of a whole bright future together as man and wife. But then...

However, beneath all the hurt and disappointment he slowly began to wonder whether there was a sense in which true affection never completely dies.

"Hang on a minute. Don't go," he heard himself say. She wavered uncertainly for a moment. "What was it you wanted to discuss?" he asked more sympathetically.

"John," she began, on the edge of tears. "As I told you, I effectively have no home and no money. That brute drained every penny from our account and wasted it on liquor and I dread to think what else." She slowly sat down again. "I had wondered," she began hesitantly, "now that Brenda has left, if it might be possible for me to take over her duties. You remember, I had lots of experience as a nanny with a family in Germany before we met, and I get on so well with your little Miriam."

"I've noticed," nodded John noncommittally, although there was no way he could have known that he was about to make a decision for which he would be only too thankful in the years to come. He rubbed the groove just above his chin – his classic move when deep in thought. "I've also noticed," he observed, "how surprisingly well you get on with Susan, although I suppose you do realise what you're suggesting would be an inordinately strange arrangement. However, that's not to say I'm completely against it. It's just that I wonder if I could live with such a set-up. But, all right," he concluded finally. "If Susan's in agreement, I'll go along with it. You'll obviously have to see her first because she will need to make the final decision."

Her relief was tangible as she rose to leave. "John, you'll never know how grateful I am," she whispered. "And I promise you'll never regret it."

He raised his eyebrows. "I hope you're right!" he exclaimed. "But I guess only time will tell." Even so, her smile together with a deep instinct told him it was the right decision. He sat back tapping his fingers on the chair arm and realised it was the first time he'd seen her smile since the night of her arrival. The mind is a strange thing, because somehow it left him with a feeling of warmth. Perhaps, he thought, Pastor Tim was right: one should return good for evil.

Upon reaching the door, she stopped and turned slowly. "Brenda was a very beautiful woman, wasn't she?" observed his ex unexpectedly. Her sudden remark seemed somehow out of place and John certainly had no intention of discussing such a personal and sensitive subject with his ex. So, he merely nodded. "Strange," she continued, "your Susan said she left without even saying goodbye."

Again, he just nodded to terminate the exchange, although he remembered only too well his little daughter's distress at finding how her faithful nanny had left without a word.

After his visitor had gone, John sat for a long time in his shabby old chair. Deep in thought, he listened to the soothing sound of music, for if he were honest he desperately missed the nanny; a poignant fact he would never be able to share with anyone. His mind drifted back to how she used to laugh and play with little Miriam and the endearing way she would blow her a kiss. Above all, he remembered her exceptional beauty; strange, he thought, how he realised the fact even more now she was no longer there. She'd made it plain on that last occasion how she was his if he wanted her. Could he, he agonised, really have deserted his expectant wife and little daughter for what was, after all, an uncertain future with a younger woman? He gazed reflectively round at the memorabilia of his retreat. Any life with Brenda, he knew, would have to remain forever one of life's enigmas; one that could never be truly resolved, and with a heavy heart he hauled himself up and made for the door.

The following Saturday saw John and his wife driving along the 281 on their way to Farnham Manor. With the year now approaching high summer, the bright sunlight was creating intense patterns of light on the road as it streamed through an archway of branches overhead.

"It's really so beautiful," observed Susan while keeping a careful lookout for their destination. She turned sideways to face her husband. "I know I've said it before, but it's strange how Brenda just upped and left without a 'by your leave'. You'd have at least thought she would have said goodbye to Miriam. It goes to show you can never tell with some people," she added pointedly. "Can you think of any reason why she should have just left like that?"

John could, but wisely contented himself by shaking his head.

"I suppose," concluded his wife, "we should just be grateful for having your ex to help out." But, to that John offered no response at all – although it didn't matter, because just then Susan spotted their objective. "I think," she exclaimed, "that's the place we're looking for. Over there on the right."

And, sure enough, as he glanced across the road, John caught sight of massive wrought-iron gates set between two imposing-looking pillars – each of which were adorned by a sculptured eagle.

"Hmm, very nice," he murmured as he pulled over. "But, it looks to me as though it's been some time since that metal last felt the caress of a paintbrush." It was a typical John remark which she chose to ignore, but it was an observation of neglect more than amplified as they progressed up a drive in desperate need of resurfacing. "Pity the springs," he muttered, estimating the distance between the entrance and the house to be something less than a mile.

But the lack of maintenance was obviously not confined to the gates and the drive, for, everywhere they looked, overgrown fields stretched away almost as far as the eye could see; a state of dilapidation reinforced by broken fencing that lay largely concealed in dense weeds and stinging nettles. In fact, there were places where even the drive itself seemed under threat by the encroachment of nature.

"Lack of money or intent?" observed John cynically.

By now, however, they were pulling up in front of an imposing Georgian mansion, or at least the part that had escaped being enveloped by the undergrowth.

"Well, this is it," he exclaimed, stepping out onto odd patches of tarmac that had once formed part of a grand forecourt.

But, even as he spoke, the sound of an approaching vehicle caused him to turn.

"Ah! John Wrant," came a sudden deep and imperialistic-sounding voice.

"Grant. John Grant, actually," asserted Susan's husband while, at the same time, catching sight of one of the fattest men he'd ever seen and who was in the process of laboriously climbing down from a powerful-looking quad bike. "Hmm. The neglect is obviously not limited to the premises," John observed while imagining him to be somewhere in the region of twenty stone – a fact which had stretched his trouser fabric to breaking point as it strained to contain his massive midriff. Worse, some of the buttons on a rather grubby-looking shirt front had finally given up the struggle to reveal an equally unwholesome-looking vest.

"Sorry, old boy," apologised the new arrival. "Just been going round the old estate. Got to keep an eye on things and all that, you know?" Then, switching off the engine, he added in the same public-school tones, "Nothing's like it used to be. What?" Exactly what he was alluding to escaped John but looking at the man's distended girth he couldn't help but think he'd got a point. However, from the way he spoke, John took him to be the owner. "Just put this old girl away," he exclaimed. "Then perhaps we can share a tot or two while we discuss... What was it you wanted to find out about? Some antique or other?"

"It was a picture," asserted Susan's husband. "A picture you recently auctioned at Barrington's." Then, as the man pushed the quad bike into a nearby derelict-looking lean-to, John turned to Susan. "Too much education and too much interbreeding if you ask me," he whispered out of the corner of his mouth. "Also, by the look of those spider-veins on his cheeks, I'd say too many tots of whatever he imbibes – brandy, at a guess."

"John," she retorted. "You're so critical. You

don't know anything about this man at all. Or what's made him like he is."

But her husband couldn't desist. "Yes, I do." He grinned. "I've just told you – too many tots." He'd said it very quietly because their extraordinary host was just about to re-join them, and what was more, he had a way with the ladies.

"Ah. Am I to take it that this beautiful young lady is your wife?"

"Correct," responded John shortly.

The landowner nodded his approval. "Anyway, old boy. Do come in and I'll see what I can recollect about this... What was it again? A picture, you say?"

Then, as he led them through into the main hall, John again whispered to his wife, "Imagine, you could have married that. Whereas, instead, you lucky thing, you got me."

Increasingly out of patience, however, Susan just chose to ignore his silliness – not least, because of the mansion's sheer breathtaking interior, for whereas the front of the building had been graced by the pure lines of Georgian architecture, Greco Roman influence held sway on every side. Directly in front of them, a magnificent in-laid marble floor stretched away towards an equally stunningly elegant stairway with steps overlaid in the same marble design. Then, flanking the expansive hall, a series of Corinthian-topped fluted columns supported the first-floor balcony. And, as John gazed about in wonder, his attention became drawn to the building's crowning glory, for set high in the ceiling was a vast glass dome through which rays of light streamed in to illuminate all the classic splendour. In addition, situated either side of the foot of the stairway, two life-size statues of Roman deities stared out across the hall – one of which he immediately recognised as Mars, the god of war. Yet, this initial impact was almost immediately spoiled by an impression of abject neglect, for everyday litter lay scattered across the beautiful floor while thick layers of dust and cobwebs further served to dim the innate architectural grandeur. However, before either of them had a chance to react their host indicated one of the numerous Romanesque-style doorways set at the edge of the hall.

"Come into the library, old boy," invited the obese owner. "Oh. And by the way, I should have introduced myself. I'm Charles. Charles George Stratford-Hugo, to be exact."

John made an almost inaudible sucking noise between his tongue and his teeth as he looked at his wife.

"Don't you dare say a word," she whispered back.

Like the grand hallway, the library proved equally impressive, but it also spoke of total neglect. Lined on three sides with well-stocked Mahogany bookshelves, the huge imposing room was lit by rectangular Georgian-style windows that afforded extensive views over the surrounding countryside; most of which, John assumed, formed part of the

Farnham estate. But, the magnificent drapes that had once graced the windows were now no more than ragged shadows of their former glory. In fact, everywhere he looked spoke of a ruined bygone perfection. The huge central table with its ornate carved legs, which had probably once been the preserve of study, now served as a repository for an endless assortment of vodka and whisky bottles scattered amongst empty crisp packets and the remains of half-consumed cigars.

Sensing their reaction, their host quickly moved to apologise. "Sorry about the state of the place, old chap," he exclaimed, slightly breathlessly. "Just can't seem to get the servants these days, would you know? And that's presupposing one could even afford them. Bloody Government takes all the money. As far as I'm concerned, I'd put that Tasbourne fella in the tower along with the rest of the bloody sharks at Whitehall. And throw away the key!"

It was a sentiment expressed with some feeling and one with which John could readily concur, for he'd seen his own property business brought under severe financial pressure by the same chancellor. However, he also realised that the seediness of their surroundings was getting to his wife and he wasted no time in again broaching the subject of their visit. But their host seemed determined to press on with his dissatisfaction.

"Would you believe," he stressed in his thick public-school accent, "that there were some twenty housemaids and groundsmen in my great-grandfather's day? Whereas, now, there's only myself." For a brief moment, the slightly grotesque Charles looked soulful. "Do you know, when I was a very young boy I can remember the clamour and excitement of my grandparents as they prepared the place for one of their 'festivities' as they called them. Servants would dash about making sure everything was just so, while the constant chatter and disagreements... But now..." And with that he held up his hand. "Listen. Nothing. Only unutterable silence. Where's it all gone I sometimes ask myself. But gone it has. And gone forever."

It was a poignancy reminiscent of Brenda's remarks concerning the nursery, and John recalled some lines he'd read somewhere: 'Time, like a rolling stream, bears all its sons away.'

But, even so, he couldn't help comparing such privilege with his own origins and was sorely tempted to say how his great-grandfather could barely afford the necessities of life. But, catching Susan's eye, he decided to keep such family gems to himself. Meanwhile, their somewhat unsavoury host had become busily engaged rummaging amongst the bottles on the table, and with a sudden gleam in his eye snatched up one which still contained a small amount of spirit.

"Tot, old boy?" he asked, proffering the bottle. But Susan's husband graciously declined with a wave of his hand.

"No thanks but you go right ahead." And with that, the obviously practiced imbiber finished off the bottle in a single go. But then, much to John's wife's disgust, he proceeded to wipe the back of his hand across his mouth before belching appreciatively.

After this performance, John's patience began to wear thin. "I'm sorry, but is there any chance of discussing the picture you recently auctioned?"

"Ah. Yes. I hadn't forgotten," he admitted, "but, you see, I've had to sell so much lately just to keep going."

Or just to keep totting, thought John.

"Damn shame and all that," their host continued, "but perhaps you could tell me a little bit more about the thing you've got in mind."

After John finished describing the purpose of their visit, the landowner nodded. "Ah, yes. The fisher boy!" He waved to a Chesterfield couch strewn with yellowing old newspapers and magazines which he hastily shoved to one side while inviting his visitors to take a seat; although, catching the expression on his wife's face, John was surprised she even deigned to sit down. "Now, from what I understand," began Charles as he sank into the armchair opposite, "the picture in question used to hang in the smoking room during my great-grandfather's time. Huh. In those days men had to do their smoking well away from the ladies – funny custom if you ask me but apparently that's the way things were."

Unable to contain himself, John observed acidly,

"That's the way things should always have been."

"Well, yes. Every man to their own," agreed the landowner while at the same time fumbling through his pockets before coming up with the sorry-looking remains of a cigar.

"Do you happen to know how your family first acquired the picture?" asked John.

"All I know," replied their host as he resumed the fumbling, "is that my great-grandfather was an acquaintance of the artist; some fella by the name of Blake, I believe. Yes. That was it. George Blake." And as he triumphantly came up with the name, his groping was also rewarded by the retrieval of a cigarette lighter. "Anyway," he continued while proceeding to light up the grubby stub, "just before he died, Blake sold it to my ancestor. Now, I'm not sure of the details, but I seem to think there was some sort of tragedy associated with the deal. I believe I'm right in saying that not long before he died, this Blake fella's wife was suspected of committing suicide." He drew heavily on his cigar, but then continued gravely that the disaster hadn't ended there.

"What do you mean?" John demanded.

"You must realise," responded the landowner, "that I'm telling you about events which happened long before I was born and only what I've been told."

"Well?" persisted John.

"My father informed me that his grandmother –

that's my great-grandmother – also died by her own hand. Apparently, they found her early one morning hanging from the first floor landing. Just out there in the hallway. It seems she must have jumped from the balcony."

"Oh, how awful," gasped Susan. "Was there any reason why…?"

But their host just shrugged.

"I'm afraid," he confessed, "my great-grandfather's wife was something less than she might have been. I say this in the strictest confidence of course, but the fact is she owed her existence to incest; the result of a sister and brother liaison."

John turned and looked knowingly at his wife who, in turn, just glared back.

"Don't you…" she whispered.

"So," continued Charles, "although to all intents and purposes she appeared normal, and I might add an apparently very attractive woman, she nevertheless obviously suffered from some sort of underlying psychological problem. Now, the question is," he emphasised suddenly as he struggled to sit upright, "was it her genetic make-up that destroyed her or something here in the house?"

"You mean," queried John, "something like that painting?"

The fat man wriggled uncomfortably while looking at the end of his defunct cigar. He then made an observation that carried a familiar ring.

"You see," he explained, "before she died, my

great-grandmother had apparently described seeing a strange woman standing just in front of the painting. It seems she came downstairs in the early hours and there she was. Why on earth my ancestor should have been up and about at such a god-forsaken hour, is an open question. But whatever she saw or thought she saw was never established as actual fact. However, I understand she reported having the experience on more than one occasion." John, again, looked at his wife before asking the landowner if he had any knowledge of the 'strange' visitor's appearance. "Well, one thing I can tell you is that she purportedly had extremely long red hair."

"One of the 'Stunners'!" exclaimed John to his wife. "One of the copper-haired women so favoured by the Pre-Raphaelites."

"Ah! I see you know your art history," rejoined their informant.

"My husband was an art teacher for years," explained John's wife.

"Really, old chap? How interesting. I must show you some of the work we've still got here at Farnham." But, ignoring this suggestion, John pressed for more details about the enigmatic woman. "I'll tell you what," offered their host while struggling to extract himself from the armchair, "I'll show you the letter my great-grandmother left for her husband just prior to her death, because that will tell you all there is to know." Then, having got himself upright, he waddled across to one of the ornate bookshelves and lifted down a heavy and dusty-looking leather bound volume. "The family 'bible'," he announced in answer to their unspoken question.

It was obviously quite weighty, and John rushed forward to help whereupon, once in position, Charles carefully opened the thick cover with a slightly unsteady hand to reveal a variety of faded papers resting on the back flyleaf. After carefully sifting them apart, he picked out a yellowing envelope on the front of which John could just make out three beautifully written words:

'My darling Albert,'

"My great-grandfather, old boy," explained their host, whereupon he proceeded to extract a folded sheet from inside before looking straight at his guests. "I'll read it out to you:

'My dearest Albert,

By the time you get this letter I will have left this earthly existence for good, but please, please, my darling, do not blame yourself for you are and have always been the dearest, sweetest man it's been my joy to know and I will forever love you with all my heart.

But, the mental anguish I constantly endure has finally become more than I can bear. I've tried to tell you about my encounters with the lady by the painting – the lady with the long copper-coloured hair – but I don't think you or anyone took me seriously. It was serious though, dear Albert. Serious to me, for while I couldn't hear what the woman was trying to say, I nevertheless knew instinctively that she was trying to warn me of some pending disaster and I just couldn't stand the added fear.

I know that you will take the very best care of Jennifer and Frieda, and that one day we'll all meet again. So, my darling, until then, goodbye for now.

Your loving wife,
Susanne
xxxx'"

As their host looked up, John could see the tears in his eyes.

"Sorry, old boy," he apologised reverently re-folding the fragile piece of paper. "But every time I read that letter it makes me want to cry. Obviously," he added nostalgically, "I never knew the poor woman personally, and yet in some strange way I feel I do, and I'd just love to be able to go back in time and put my arms around her and comfort her."

"That I can well understand," sympathised his listener. "But I find it disturbing that my wife had a similar experience with the picture, only in her case the woman was actually part of the composition, and pertinently she also had long red hair. Now, I'm a sceptic of the first order, believe me. But, if there is some sort of spiritual activity going on then I wonder if the woman you describe and the one my wife encountered are the same person. And, if so, who is she?"

Charles looked thoughtful for a moment as he lovingly replaced the letter in its envelope before restoring the 'bible' to its place on the bookshelf.

"That, old boy, is something we'll probably never know. Although, I suspect that may well be the case. Also, don't you think it strange how only the fair sex seem able to pick up on this sort of phenomenon? Oh, and by the way," he added, returning to his armchair, "it may be of no significance, but before my great-grandmother was laid to rest they discovered she had been expecting a male child." He gave a slight sigh while clasping both hands over his prodigious stomach. "Anyway, the upshot of it all was that my great-grandfather, consigned the painting to the cellar where it remained until I sold it. Apparently," he added, "they were a devoted couple and he couldn't bear anything that might have contributed to her loss."

By this stage, although sympathetic, John's practical working-class background was making him increasingly irritated with the man's public-school demeanour. Getting up from his seat, he made his way over to one of the windows.

"You've a lot of land here."

"Far too much for me to handle," exclaimed the self-indulgent owner. "Do you know, there are over a thousand acres out there which was all very well during my grandfather's time. But, when he passed away, the resultant inheritance tax virtually crippled my father, and although he did his best to hang on, I remember it was always a struggle for him."

"And, by the look of it, when it came to your turn," pre-empted John, "the situation became virtually impossible."

A look of sadness crossed their host's face.

"Farnham Manor has been the family seat for more generations than I can recall. Certainly," he added, "it goes back to the early eighteen hundreds, but now..." He shrugged the shoulders of his massive torso. "When I go it will just become a juicy lump of real estate to be fought over by the Tax Man and the National Trust."

"So, you've not married or had any children?" observed John, perhaps a little impertinently.

"Can't vouch about the children, old chap. A fella can never be quite sure about things like that." He winked. "Been round the block a few times though, eh? What? But marriage?" he added, tapping his prodigious girth. "Can you imagine any woman...?"

At this, John refrained from comment and instead turned to his wife. "Darling, I think I've learned about enough..."

"I think so too, John," she agreed.

On the way home, they were quiet for a while, each being busy with their own thoughts. Eventually, however, John broke the silence. "Strange set-up back there."

"I know," Susan replied.

"On the surface, that man seems to have so much, and yet in reality he's drinking himself into oblivion. I'm just surprised he doesn't sell up and start a new life," observed John. "I think he's probably so used to that way of life he just can't let go. Entrenched mindsets are almost impossible to change. You've only got to ask any psychologist."

Susan turned to gaze out at the rolling green countryside as they sped on their way back to the farmhouse.

"Very sad," she answered. "But changing the subject, John, this year seems to be racing away. The trees have already lost that light, green freshness of springtime."

Indeed, evidence of the month seemed to call out from all sides with endless regiments of tall, white milkmaids lining the edge of the road, while, intermingled with these 'weeds', the long grass was gradually turning a pale ochre as if awaiting the attention of some harvester's sickle.

Later that night after they'd gone to bed, a totally different aspect of their visit made itself felt, for, unable to sleep, Susan's mind kept regurgitating what they'd heard earlier in the day. Although her husband was already deeply asleep, she finally felt compelled to wake him up.

"John! John!" she whispered urgently, shaking him by the shoulder.

"Uh. Uh? What's the matter?" he eventually grunted. "And what's the lamp on for?"

"Well, for a start," she retorted, dragging back the duvet, "I wouldn't mind my share of the bed." Then, referring to her pregnancy, she added pointedly, "There's hardly enough room for my bump let alone the rest of me. I mean. Look at you. You're sprawled diagonally right across the mattress."

"Oh, sorry," he muttered, still half asleep, while at the same time reluctantly relinquishing his illicit takeover of their sleeping arrangements.

"Honestly, John, you'd think you'd got a dozen legs instead of just the standard two."

"All right. All right," he mumbled incoherently. "I've got the drift. Now, can we just go back to sleep?"

"That's my problem," she responded, clinging tenaciously to the duvet. "I can't sleep because I'm too worried."

"Worried about what, for heaven's sake? Can't it wait till the morning?"

"No, it can't wait till the morning!" And sitting upright with her elbows resting on the pillow, she repeated angrily, "No it can't."

Finally, with the haze of sleep beyond hope

of recall, he sat up and reluctantly listened to her woes.

"What is it, love?" he asked more sympathetically, now fully awake.

"It's the things that old boy said at Farnham Manor."

In search of a little consolation for the loss of his sleep, John reached across to the bedside cabinet where he kept a bottle of wine and, grabbing it by the neck, took a swig.

"Well," he observed, "Charles, or whatever his name was, said a lot of strange and rather sad things. What was it in particular that you found so disturbing?"

"John," she complained, choosing to ignore his question. "You've really got some very slovenly habits."

"I know," he grinned. "But you still love me, so I know I can always get away with it."

"Don't count on it," she warned as a slight frown crossed her forehead. "Anyway, did you happen to notice how his great-grandmother was called Susanne?"

"So?" He shrugged. "It was probably a popular name in her day."

"Well, whatever," she replied. "But I thought it was one of a number of coincidences that seemed uncomfortably close to home." Although, having said that, her face suddenly and unexpectedly lit up. "Oh, go on then. Give me the bottle. I might as well be as vulgar as you are."

"Hypocrite," he grinned, passing over the offending article.

"But, John," she stressed after taking a long draught and before turning on her side to lean on one elbow. "Remember how I saw that woman in the painting? Well, now I come to think about it I wonder if she was pleading with me or trying to warn me about something. Because I'm pregnant too, just like that poor woman at Farnham who hung herself."

"Now, hang on a minute," objected her husband. "Didn't you say originally that she was merely trying to communicate with you? Nothing about any warnings. It's no good letting your imagination run riot." However, the frown lines on his wife's forehead only deepened.

"Oh, I don't know. But to be honest, I'm beginning to find the whole thing quite frightening. John!" she exclaimed finally. "I originally intended to wait for our baby to be born before knowing its gender, but after hearing about that woman I want to find out if we too are expecting a boy."

And seeing how upset she was, he reached out and took her in his arms before playfully tapping the tip of her nose with his finger.

"Darling, you've got to stop thinking like this because there's absolutely no connection between you and that woman whatsoever." But his words somehow seemed to hold a hollow ring even to himself.

“John,” she responded tearfully. “It’s just something I’ve got to know.”

And despite his well-meant advice, she went ahead with the relevant tests which confirmed that by January the following year she would give birth to a son.

Chapter 4

WITH HIGH SUMMER drawing to a close, John and his wife had almost given up hope of ever seeing Pastor Tim again. But then, late one September evening while relaxing in the kitchen, they received a phone call.

"Fancy that!" exclaimed the ex-teacher while replacing the receiver.

"Why? Who was it?" asked his wife.

"Tim," he replied. "He wants to drop in and see us both next Saturday evening, and by the sound of it he's got a lot he wants to discuss."

"Well, that'll make a change," retorted Susan. "Because, as you say, he's usually got barely two words to rub together."

"Let's not be too critical," replied John. "He's a good minister, and, frankly, I've missed him at church." Then, with that, John finished his coffee before getting up and moving over to the bay window. "I tell you what," he observed, "I don't think Tim will be best pleased with us still having that picture in the hallway."

He stood for a moment and looked out over the lake in the fading light. The russet colours of autumn were slowly beginning to make themselves apparent while early discarded leaves gently drifted across the surface of the water in ever-changing and diverse patterns. Glancing up, he was in time to catch a v-formation of geese flying just above the treetops and obviously on their way to... But to where? John wondered, for winged creatures recognised no boundaries. He looked back at his wife who was busily engaged with her packet of cigarettes. "Time's moving on," he observed with a hint of pathos.

"I'd noticed," she responded, tapping her ever-expanding bump.

The following Saturday found Susan opening the front door to welcome the pastor.

"Hello Tim," she greeted him. "It's good to see you again. We were beginning to think we'd lost you forever."

He smiled a rare smile.

"You can't get rid of me that easily." But as they crossed the hallway, he was quick to point out, critically, "I see you've not taken my advice about that painting."

"No, Tim," she apologised with a slightly shamed face. "But you know, John. He's not one to be easily deterred. Although we have been having some serious thoughts over it. Anyway, I'm sure he'll tell you all about what's been going on in due course."

Comfortably seated in the kitchen, Tim continued solemnly.

"As you know, I've been away on church business which turned out to take far longer than I originally envisaged."

"Coffee, Tim?" suggested John's wife with her usual impeccable timing.

His original brief smile momentarily reasserted itself.

"Thank you, Susan. That would be very pleasant," he replied gracefully while reaching down to retrieve his slim briefcase. Then, after zipping it open, he took out a loose-leaf folder. "One of the few advantages of my stay in London, was that it gave me the opportunity to do some research on George Blake."

"Actually," interrupted John, a trifle rudely, "we've been doing a little research of our own."

"John!" his wife objected. "Don't be so ill-mannered when Tim's speaking."

But her husband carried on regardless.

"Apparently," he explained, "the wife of the man who originally owned that painting committed suicide, and to cut a long story short, the tragedy was largely attributed to having that canvas in the house. In fact," he added, "it happened just up the road at a place called Farnham Manor."

"And yet," protested their visitor, "you still insist on keeping the wretched thing here in your own home." John pulled a guilty look and shrugged. "Well," continued Tim. "Let's see if you're still as keen after you've heard what I've discovered."

"You already know," he began, "that the artist in question was quite familiar with several of the Pre-Raphaelites, although he was never an actual member of the brotherhood. However, it appeared that he did know Holman Hunt." Their visitor reached forward for his coffee. "Sorry, Susan," he apologised, "but may I have some sugar? Just one spoonful please. Ah, that's lovely," he thanked her as she even stirred his drink.

"It's difficult," continued the cleric, "to pinpoint just when the story of your picture actually begins, but from what I've discovered I'd say it was from the day Blake met his wife, Suzette; she was part French, and incidentally a distant relative of Hunt; that's probably how they first became acquainted. He describes her in his diary as an elegant, graceful woman with the most beautiful luxuriant chestnut hair. In fact, I understand that in the early days he asked her to pose for him – which she did – and it's a quite well-known portrait in a private collection somewhere. Blake might not have enjoyed the fame of some of his contemporaries, but he was nevertheless a very competent artist. Anyway, be that as it may," he observed, "it's my belief the seeds of their later trauma lay in the fact that she was in her late thirties while he was even older."

"Ring a bell, John?" queried Susan.

"Well," he grinned back. "It may ring a bell, but the question is, which one? A bell for my coffee perhaps, eh? Maybe?"

"All right, all right. I've got the drift," she retorted, reaching for the pot.

"Shall I carry on?" ventured their guest tentatively.

"Yes, yes. Please do, Tim." encouraged Susan after catering for her husband's demands.

"It turned out," explained Tim, "that Suzette was desperate to have a family, and with her biological clock running out it became a major issue. However, finally, she managed to conceive and had a son around about the time the brotherhood was formed."

On hearing this, John was struck by a sudden and uneasy thought. "Did you happen to find out what the boy was called?"

Tim looked at his notes. "Ralph. Ralph John Blake, to give him his full name."

For a brief moment, Susan's husband looked as solemn-faced as their guest.

"She's left now," continued John, "but I wonder what you'll make of it when I tell you that Miriam's nanny dreamt on several occasions of a woman crying out that name here in the house. It was a dream," he stressed, "and to my knowledge, she was the only one who ever experienced it."

"You've never mentioned that before," interjected Susan sharply.

Her husband just raised his arms in a gesture of mock guilt.

"What can I say, darling? With Brenda leaving and all, I probably just forgot."

But if his wife was mollified she showed no sign of it, although this might have been due to Jeanette's sudden appearance in the doorway.

"Sorry. I didn't mean to intrude," she said hesitantly. "It's just to tell you I'm taking Miriam across the main field to see the neighbour's new pony. Apparently, it's the same colour as her rocking horse and she's been dying to see it for days."

"That's fine, Jeanette." Susan smiled. "Take some carrots along with you."

"Is that the new nanny?" enquired their guest.

"Sort of," responded John but without being specific.

"I must admit," confessed Tim with an uncharacteristic touch of mischief, "I think I prefer the original model."

To which John, perhaps wisely, kept his mouth shut. However, his wife obviously felt less inhibited.

"Well," she observed with a hint of sarcasm, "you're a man, aren't you? So that's not very surprising is it, Pastor?"

A brief but pregnant pause ensued as Tim passed a hand nervously through his hair before continuing. "I've known you both for some time," he said gently. "And, as a friend, I feel duty-bound to warn you that you are playing with fire."

"Oh dear," exclaimed Susan as she refilled her

husband's cup. "You do make it sound dreadfully gloomy."

"Anyway," continued Tim, "Ralph was the only child Suzette and Blake ever had. She virtually worshipped him. And, for a number of years it seems the family was very happy."

However, at this point, Tim was interrupted yet again.

"Tell me," asked John, "how did you manage to find out about all this?"

"It's not difficult," replied their guest, "because Blake left behind a series of personal diaries which are currently held at the British Library. They're digitally stored, and you can read them on screen. But, the point is," he continued, "about the time their son reached ten he'd contracted typhoid fever – or typhus as it was sometimes called. Contagious diseases like that, as you probably know, were the scourge of the age and often the result of water-borne bacteria. You have to remember that this was well before the time of Pasteur and his 'invisible armies' as he liked to call his newly discovered germs."

"I've got a horrible feeling," declared John, "that I know where you're going with all this."

"You mean," intervened Susan as she reached for her packet of cigarettes, "the boy died."

Tim just nodded.

"Tragically," he concluded, "the only child that woman had so desperately longed for died despite all their care and attention. Blake's description of their suffering at the time," he added, "is an agony to read, and it's something I wouldn't recommend to anyone."

"Hmm. All very cheerful stuff I'm sure," voiced Miriam's father while lounging back on the sofa.

"John! Don't be so offhand," reproved his wife while drawing heavily on her cigarette. "Tim has obviously gone to a lot of trouble to help us."

But the pastor, who was well acquainted with John's foibles, just smiled briefly.

"Oh, that's fine, Susan. Don't worry." He then added, "With the boy's death, events took a very bleak turn. Now, I don't know if you're aware that with the advent of photography it became fashionable with certain elements of Victorian society to dress deceased relatives and prop them up in a chair as though they were still alive, and then take a picture. They would even gather round and support the departed in a standing position in order to produce a group photograph."

"Oh, how macabre!" exclaimed a disgusted Susan. "I think I need something a bit stronger than coffee." And crushing her cigarette into a twisted mess, she made for the 'medicinal cabinet'. "Tell me, Tim," she asked after returning to her seat with a suitably charged glass, "is all that really relevant to our picture in the hall?"

The pastor sighed and shifted uncomfortably in his seat.

"I'm afraid it's only too relevant, Susan, because

when Blake saw his wife's desolation at the loss of their son, he took an extreme course of action. You see, the family lived just outside Arundel, and quite near to the Arun River, so he decided to take his son's body and lean him up against a tree by the waterway. Apparently, it was the boy's favourite spot and they'd often gone there together on various fishing expeditions. Anyway, he placed a fishing rod in his hand. But instead of using a camera, he had the ability, of course, to paint the scene in full colour and the result is now hanging in your hallway."

"So, you're telling us," cried a horrified Susan, "that our beautiful picture is nothing more than the painting of a corpse?"

Tim nodded. "I'm afraid so. Yes. I know the boy looks as though he's just dozed off in the sunshine, but in reality, he was dead. What's more, Blake had to work quickly, because, as you can see from the painting, all this took place in high summer, and as he explained in his diaries, decomposition soon became a pressing problem. In fact, he even describes how..."

"Oh, Tim. Please spare us the details!" implored Susan.

"Sorry," he apologised, "but I only tell you this to try to protect you both. To put it bluntly, I believe that if you persist in keeping what after all is a symbol of tragedy, then you may well be heading for real problems. Particularly if I tell you..." But, again he was interrupted.

"Is there much more then?" enquired John who was fast becoming concerned about the effects of these revelations on his wife.

"I'm afraid so," responded Tim reluctantly, "but if you think..."

"No, no. That's fine," John replied. "But, now might be a good time to take a break. We've got benches and a table at the far end of the big field, and a Portakabin where we can make some fresh coffee. It would also give us a chance to see this pony my daughter's on about."

The quickest way to their destination lay via the back of the property which was the oldest part by far. The previous owners had chosen to leave it untouched and it constituted something of a time capsule. Originally just two small rooms that were lower than the main house, it was necessary to step down to the original floor level.

"Wow!" exclaimed Tim in awe. "This really is a piece of history."

His eyes wandered over towards the ancient stone sink which stood on brick supports just below a tiny window and owed its water supply to a wrought iron pump operated by a curved lever.

And seeing the pastor's fascination, John indicated a low doorway that led to the second room.

"I think the whole of the farmhouse started life as just a crofter's cottage. I also suspect that the early inhabitants had to make do with an earth floor, because there's no sign of any foundations under the present flagstones." He indicated a primitive hearth on the far side of the room. "And that is probably where any cooking was done."

"And no gas, no electricity and no phone," observed Tim. "Plus, you're so isolated. Can you even begin to imagine how lonely it must have felt at night?" He paused reflectively. "Have you any idea how old it is?"

"Well," replied Susan, "we don't know for certain but reckon it was probably here in the late fourteenth or early fifteenth century."

"But so lonely though," repeated their visitor. "The nearest village would have been Henfield, but that's miles away – and how many houses would there have been in those days?"

John shrugged. "Who knows? Not more than half a dozen or so grouped round a crossing of farm tracks. And incidentally, they're still there if you know what to look for amongst the more recent stuff. But I think, you know people were hardier in those days. They had to be just to survive, and if they weren't..." He shrugged again.

"Although, it's not just the loneliness," stressed Susan with a slight shiver. "I often feel very vulnerable if I'm here by myself – particularly in the winter with no street lights and, as you say, miles from anywhere. I've often told John how uneasy I feel during the dark evenings when I get back from work and he's still out on business."

Her husband, however, hastened to reassure her.

"You know I've already promised to be back before dark in the future, darling. Oh, mind your head there, Tim," he warned suddenly as the cleric made for the back door. "It's a bit on the low side, and, I should know from the times I've hit my head on that lintel."

Their visitor ran his fingers over the offending timber.

"I believe you, John." Tim grinned. "I can feel the dents."

Out in the fresh air, the small group made their way across the grass to where Jeanette and Miriam were admiring a small dapple-grey pony who was busily poking its muzzle over the wooden fencing.

"I believe," observed Jeanette, "that you might have a problem." And indicating her young charge, she added, "Her Ladyship here would like one of her own thanks very much."

It amazed John the ease with which his ex had settled into her new life and how she felt able to blend in with the family.

"Daddy!" exclaimed his little girl. "Isn't the pony lovely?"

Lovely, he thought, but only provided the animal remained on the other side of someone else's fence.

"Couldn't we have a pony, Daddy?" entreated Miriam earnestly, her eyes alight with excitement. "We've got a big field."

He smiled as he briefly savoured the warmth of

her enthusiasm, but then his ex decided to intervene.

"It wouldn't be impossible would it, John? You had a lot of experience with horses in your early days."

While that was true, he nevertheless felt like shouting back, "Mind your own business. This family's got nothing to do with you." And, choosing to ignore her, he spoke directly to his little girl.

"Tell me, darling. If you look over the fence what can you see?"

Puzzled, the child gazed out across the neighbour's field. "I don't know, Daddy. Just lots of grass I suppose."

"But," he smiled, "there's also lots of something else and it's called horse dung." Then, looking down into her bright eyes, he added gently, "Somebody has to clear all that up or the grass wouldn't be fit for the pony to eat. Horses can be a lot of hard work, and although your bucket and spade might be great with sandcastles, I doubt whether they'd make much impression on a pony's whoopsies!" Kneeling down to her level, however, he suggested encouragingly, "It might be an idea, you know, to familiarise yourself with one of the horses at the local riding school and even take some lessons, because afterwards you can simply hand back the reins and let the proprietor do all the saddle-soaping and other chores that go with keeping a horse."

"John!" came his wife's voice suddenly. "Tim hasn't got all day."

"Sorry," he called back. "Just coming." Then,

turning to Jeanette, he proposed she explain not only the joys but also some of the dangers associated with horse riding.

"Sorry, Tim," he repeated as he joined them at the garden table. "Oh, and thanks, love," he added taking a very welcome cup of coffee from his wife before settling down to give the pastor his full attention. "What else was there that you wanted to share with us, Tim?"

"You see," he continued, "when Blake's son died, his wife was totally beyond consolation, and to make matters worse she was the love of his life: a beautiful woman who he idolised. He describes being at his wits' end as to what to do." He paused for a moment at the prevailing smell of caffeine and looked round in the hope of a fresh cup.

"All right, Tim. I've got the idea," smiled Susan while reaching towards the coffee pot.

For a brief moment, all was still that late summer afternoon, until Tim finally spoke again.

"You've heard me say on many occasions," he warned solemnly, "how the Bible warns us against evil. It's a war, John, and we need to be on our guard. Yet, despite this, Blake, initially decided to call on the powers of darkness for help." With this revelation, the atmosphere became almost electric and their visitor turned to ensure that John's ex and little Miriam were well out of earshot. "The fact is," stated Tim categorically, "one cannot make a pact with evil in the hope that good will come of it, and realising the magnitude of his error, Blake quickly revised his decision."

"So." John frowned. "What did he do?"

Susan, who had been busily clearing away the coffee cups, stopped abruptly in order to hear Tim's response.

"Well," replied the pastor, "basically he did what he should have done in the first place. He turned to God. But by then it was probably too late. Anyway, let me read this out to you. The assistant at the library was kind enough to print a section of William's diary for me, and it vividly illustrates his agonised state of mind. See what you make of it:

'I have done everything humanly possible to ease my wife's pain after the death of our son. I have even tried to preserve his memory by portraying him and Suzette along by the River Arun where the three of us enjoyed so many happy hours together fishing. Unfortunately, it meant ferrying his body there every day and being during the height of summer I was under a great deal of pressure...'"

"Well, we've already touched on that bit," murmured Tim. "Anyway, he goes on to say...

'... and all I've received in return is a wall of silence. Suzette now neither speaks to me nor shares our bed. In fact, I believe she is in contact with her

French relatives, and in all probability will desert me entirely; and I have to ask myself, why?'"

"I should think so too!" exclaimed Susan. "Why on earth would she want to treat him like that?"

"Well, the next part might help to explain," answered Tim. "It's also the most crucial bit, because as he says here...

'... I have even asked God to take my life in the place of my son, and yet this is all the thanks I get. My wife is a devout woman and I can only assume that, in her eyes, I have committed some unforgiveable sin – and in a sense I suppose I have, but I can honestly say that I've always loved my wife and son dearly. They've meant the world to me. However, now I have nothing to look forward to but a life of emptiness, and in the void of my anguish, I have eliminated my wife's image from the painting that I had so lovingly and painstakingly completed solely for her benefit.'"

"I was right," asserted John with a ring of triumph. "I suspected someone had been originally portrayed standing by the boy but for whatever reason had later been painted out. And now I know why."

"But, how desperately sad," cried Susan quietly.

"Indeed, it was," agreed their friend. "And it didn't end there, because shortly after Blake wrote this account, his wife passed away, which is strange, for apparently she hadn't been ill. In fact, it was suspected she might have committed suicide

– although there was no physical evidence to that effect. It's possible, of course," he speculated, "that she was so overcome with grief and despair that she just took some sort of poison to end it all."

"We did hear something along those lines at Farnham," observed John. "But, as my wife said, it all sounds very sad."

By this time, the late afternoon sun had dipped down towards the trees that lined part of the field, while at the same time a slightly cold breeze suddenly seemed to sweep in across the open landscape; a chill which somehow echoed the depressive nature of what Tim had just said. Jeanette and Miriam had already disappeared indoors, and with a slight shiver, Susan suggested they follow suit.

"Before you go," entreated the churchman, "let me just finish the last bit, because I've got to rush off to a meeting."

"All right. Provided you make it quick," agreed Susan while pulling her cardigan tightly round her shoulders.

His expression again became very solemn.

"It appears that some years later when Blake was sorting out his late wife's possessions, he came across an old notebook that indicated a strong belief in reincarnation; which is strange, because such views are so at odds with our faith, and as Blake pointed out his wife had always been a devout woman."

"Interesting," observed John brusquely. "But, so what?"

Tim reached forward to close his folder which had been lying on the table.

"Well, John. It's only an extrapolation, but I think it's possible that after her husband's attempted deal, she became afraid; afraid that if her son was reincarnated at some time in the future, then she would have no authority over him nor be able to protect him from the influence of evil. People had some funny ideas in those days you know." He shrugged. "At least, that's my take on it," he added getting to his feet. "Oh, and there's one other thing. You remember asking me whether I thought a past drama could mediate its way into the present via some artefact like that painting? From what you've told me about the fate of its first owner's wife, I'll leave you to decide... But, whatever your conclusions, John," he stressed "for goodness sake, get rid of the wretched thing before it's too late."

Back in the house, John and his wife made for one of the main reception rooms where, after the Tim episode, they decided to lighten the early evening with a little comedy television, but then only to discover they'd been pre-empted by their daughter and Jeanette who were up to their eyes in the latest episode of Peppa Pig.

John looked at Susan and rolled his eyes.

"Back to the kitchen," he grumbled resignedly, whereupon having secured herself a modest portion of the sofa, he noticed Susan's slightly strained expression.

"Be an angel, John, and get me a glass of wine."

"You mean," he smiled jumping up, "if we can't laugh away our miseries, we can at least try to drown them." Then, opening the 'medicinal cupboard', he added over his shoulder, "We could always get a TV in the kitchen, you know."

"Oh, I'm not so sure," she replied while placing a cigarette between her lips. "This bit of the house always seems a final retreat from the razzamatazz of the outside world."

"I know what you mean," he agreed as he filled her glass. "That's why I've got my own mini-retreat from the world of razzamatazz inside the house, let alone the outside bit."

"John," she said suddenly, "I didn't mention it, what with one thing and another, but I felt our baby move for the first time recently."

"That's good news," he smiled while leaning forward to take a sip of his wine.

"Yes. On its own, of course it is," she responded. "But when you take it in conjunction with something your ex told me the other day, I'm not quite so sure."

"Oh. And what was that?" he asked curiously while replacing his glass on the coffee table.

"You were away in Brighton at the time and I think I must have been doing something on the top floor, but, apparently, as Miriam was about to go out for a walk, your ex said she stopped by that painting and insisted the boy had changed the position of his right leg. I just hope she hasn't started getting feverish again."

"I take it you're making some sort of unwarranted paranormal connection between our child and that boy in the picture, but it's absolute rubbish," he insisted. "Painted images don't just move about under their own steam." His wife lit her cigarette and drew heavily on its smoke. "You should stop that straight away," he said reproachfully, "because it will do our baby no good at all."

"John, can you remember the exact position of that boy's legs?" Susan asked anxiously, ignoring his objection.

He drained the last of his wine.

"As far as I can remember, the boy's legs were in alignment so, hang on a minute, let me go and see if there's been any change." From his tone he was obviously not taking it very seriously.

"Well?" she demanded upon his return.

In response, he crossed to the settee and leaned forward thoughtfully with his hands clasped between his knees.

"It's difficult to be sure," he ventured slowly, "because I'd never really studied his leg position in the first place."

"But?"

"The fact is," he replied cautiously, "the far leg does seem a bit forward, but then again it may well have been like that all along. In any case, love," he stressed while pulling her towards him, "the difference is so slight it's not worth worrying about – and that's supposing there is a difference."

"John," she responded emphatically as she violently stubbed out her cigarette. "I want that picture gone! And I mean, gone. And out of the house forever." But then, with a broken and tearful voice, she added, "I only hope it's not too late."

"Why do you say that?" he enquired gently.

"It's obvious, isn't it?" she managed between tears. "Can't you see that the artist's wife, Suzette, or whatever Tim said her name was, lived in fear that after her husband's pact with the devil, her son might be reincarnated and all the terror that might involve." Susan reached unsteadily for another cigarette. "Even from beyond the grave," she stressed, "the woman tried to warn Susanne of the danger; remember how Charles' great-grandmother, who was pregnant at the time, believed she saw her standing in front of the painting?"

"Now, steady on," he protested. "You're making an awful lot of assumptions; because, even if the figure she thought she saw was some sort of apparition, there were no independent witnesses to substantiate it."

"But I saw her in the painting as well," Susan insisted. "And I know she was trying to contact me about something."

"Look," reasoned John, "even if these visitations

are true, why, of all the hundreds of thousands of pregnant women in England, should just you and Susanne be chosen for attention?"

And, at this, his distraught wife almost shouted, "It's because we've both owned that damned picture." She then lit her cigarette but only to invoke a violent bout of coughing which caused her husband to look away with an expression of despair.

Gazing out over the lake, he noticed how the evenings were gradually closing in ever earlier, but as he turned to remark on the fact, his wife observed, "Don't you think it ironic, John, how there have been three women involved and how they all seem to have virtually the same name? There's Suzette, Susanne and myself, Susan."

"What I think," he retorted, "is that we've wasted enough of our time and energy on what, after all, are no more than a series of unsubstantiated coincidences." But, these were just words and words he would have cause to remember. "However, I agree with you – the picture should go. Even if it's to shut Tim up. So, in the meantime, I'll shove it in the storage space under the Portakabin."

Following Tim's Saturday visit, John decided to take the Monday off work. The autumn term had just started and Miriam was back at school. Jeanette was exploring the nearby village while Susan was seeing out the last of her duties in Horsham before the start of her maternity leave. So, with the place to himself he headed for his own highly personalised little retreat.

Settling down in his old worn armchair, he gazed about at the memorabilia that spoke to him from every direction. Had he done the right thing, he wondered, in leaving his parents' home to marry Jeanette? Certainly, the emotional upheaval at the time of her betrayal had been enormous, and that without the huge financial divorce settlement which he'd always viewed as a form of legal theft.

A dedicated coffee drinker, he reached for the cup he'd brought in from the kitchen and breathed a sigh of appreciation as he savoured the bite of his first sip. But, even as he did so, he heard the clacking sound of the front door letterbox followed by the flopping noise of letters as they hit the hall floor.

"More bills," he muttered.

And, sure enough, as he glanced across the hall there they were – a pile of buff-coloured envelopes each with its own window displaying a neatly printed version of his address. But, as he stopped to gather them up, he spotted a notable exception, for half concealed amongst all the demands for money was a white letter, and turning it over he saw his name in a neat clear handwriting which somehow seemed familiar.

Tossing the 'browns' onto the monk's seat, he headed for the kitchen and, with his cup fully recharged, cast himself indolently down across the sofa. Personal correspondence was few and far between, and he tore at the missive with a certain curiosity before lifting out a folded sheet of paper. Written on one side only, he opened it out, but then, seeing the initial words, immediately abandoned any thought of his coffee.

'Hello, John,'

And sensing the writer's identity, he impatiently glanced at the bottom of the page where it simply read:

> 'If you ever need me, John, I'll always be there for you.
>
> With all my affection.
>
> Brenda'

Then, with a slight mistiness gathering in his eyes, he slowly read the remaining lines:

> 'I felt I had to write and explain why I left in such a hurry and without saying goodbye to little Miriam. But more especially, to you. I know that is what I should have done but I couldn't. I just couldn't. I think you know how I felt and I suspect you feel the same about me. Even when we first met, and I took the job as nanny, I knew it would be difficult, and I was right. Finally, the emotional pain became too much knowing we could never

> share a future together. But, I'll never forget you, John. Ever.
>
> You've probably found it by now, but I left a little something of myself for you in my room. You'll remember, I'm sure, how I wore it on that beautiful Easter day at the Henfield funfair. A memory I'll always treasure.
>
> Please say goodbye to little Miriam for me and tell her I still love her. Also...'

And the letter concluded with what he'd already read.

With a heavy heart, he lowered the paper to his lap and gazed blankly out across the kitchen towards the bay window as he recalled that particular bank holiday. His wife had been poorly at the time but insisted that he and the nanny take little Miriam to the fair. Brenda had worn an attractive floral print summer dress and a wide-brimmed sunhat for the occasion. How well he recalled the way she smiled up at him from beneath its shade and how she'd worn her long auburn hair in braids that reached down to her narrow waist.

In his mind's eye, he could still see her smiling and holding her hat against the breeze as she and his daughter had whirled past him on the same brightly painted carousel horse. Brenda always radiated happiness and laughter, which combined with her natural beauty made her irresistible. And yet, resist her, he had. Sometimes he'd pondered on the if onlys of life, and wondered why he couldn't have been a few years younger and why couldn't their paths have crossed under different circumstances. But, as he left the kitchen and made for the foot of the stairs, he knew only too well there were no answers, because it seemed sometimes that fate often connived to make life nothing more than a cruel joke.

John was on a pilgrimage as he wound his way up to the top floor and Brenda's old room; a pilgrimage that, in the past, had been prohibited by nostalgia. But now, in the light of her letter the need had become overwhelming, and as the door of her room swung back, it was all there: the colourful floral duvet on the neatly made up divan; the matching bedside table lamp and the carefully drawn-back curtains; everything, it seemed, combinined to make a sense of Brenda's persona almost tangible.

But then he caught sight of something which eclipsed all else, for there hanging on the corner of her bed was the beautiful wide-brimmed hat she'd worn on that summer-like Easter day at the Henfield fair, and he knew instinctively this was the piece of herself she'd left behind as a symbol of their time together and how things might have been.

Reverently he reached to lift it from its resting place, and in doing so was momentarily transported back to the fairground; back to the place where she'd smiled up at him with her appealing eyes. He recalled how excitedly she'd wanted him to share a ride with her on the carousel and how priggishly he'd turned her down, fearful perhaps that it might get back to his wife. Now, however, he so bitterly regretted having missed that elicit moment of pleasure while at the same time hating himself as he thought of how Brenda must have felt.

The hat consisted of a white synthetic material, and as he tenderly ran his fingers round its delicate thin red edging he vividly recalled how lovely she'd looked. He gazed at the tiny red rose which formed its single embellishment and remembered wondering whether it was a real flower. But now, as he gently touched the petals, he knew that unlike its live counterpart it would never have to fade.

Gently replacing the symbol, he moved across the room before stooping to gaze out from the small dormer window: situated on the second floor and at the front of the house, it afforded extensive views not only to the Downs but also the Channel beyond. Ominously, to the west, heavy cloud formations were beginning to gather over the distant horizon and seemed somehow to reflect his own sombre mood.

Turning back to glance round the room, he caught sight of himself in the wardrobe mirror, and, for a moment, paused as he thought of the many times it must have reflected Brenda's image.

As he left the room and quietly closed the door, the last thing he saw was the token of her affection.

Once outside, he stood for a long time before making towards the head of the stairs. Should he contact her, he agonised. Would he at some later moment in the future regret missing this opportunity? Though he wrestled with the excruciating dilemma, it refused to go away and would remain with him, to a greater or lesser extent, for the rest of his life. Certain he was, though, the link with her love that he'd just left behind together with the letter, would never leave his possession. And, feeling more deeply moved than he could remember, he re-entered his tiny retreat and slowly slumped down on his chair, totally lost in remorse.

Desperate to expend his emotions, he eventually heaved himself up and crossed the room where he lifted a small notepad from his desk drawer. Then, returning to his seat, he endeavoured to pen something of how he felt.

'It is but once we travel this life
Although fate dictates the path we tread
But whether it's the way we choose
Is often quite another thing'

Tearing the sheet from its pad, he folded the message carefully before placing it in Brenda's envelope along with her letter. At the time, he fully intended to send her the little poem in the hope that it might help her understand the impossibility of ever realising his feelings for her. But, in the rush of life's demands, it was one of those intentions destined never to be fulfilled.

Chapter 5

OVER THE NEXT months, the russet browns and golds of autumn surrendered to the approach of winter, and, before the family knew it, Christmas was upon them.

John's ex had stayed on to assist with little Miriam – an arrangement he'd come to accept, mainly because of the support it gave to Susan and the help she would need after the arrival of their new baby. But, the longer she remained the more he wondered what the hell he'd ever seen in her in the first place. Especially when he thought of Brenda...

Miriam, John knew only too well, had hoped for a pony that Christmas, but wary of the work involved he'd settled to buy her an aquarium, which if he were honest was partly for his own amusement. Located in a corner of the kitchen's comfy area, it was an instant conversation piece. This was particularly true as the winter nights got longer and the illuminated tank became a whole separate world of light and movement as its colourful inhabitants darted about their spacious environment.

As the year plunged down into the depths of the following January, bitter arctic weather began to set in. Vicious east winds howled across the flat countryside as Siberia opened up its jaws and roared out its freezing fury. It tore at the surface of their fishing lake and transformed the normally tranquil water into a solid sheet of opaque ice. In addition, the initial heavy rain suddenly turned into a raging blizzard of driving snow which quickly formed a deep, white blanket over the whole area. Movement in such conditions, at first difficult, rapidly became out of the question and left John seriously worried on two accounts, because, firstly, any day now his wife was due to start her confinement, and, secondly, they depended entirely for heating and hot water on a liquid gas container situated at the rear of the house. Miles from any mains supply, the cylinder required regular refilling, but if the supplier failed to get through then he could well see their new-born baby dying of cold in an icy house.

However, in the event his wife's delivery was a week late, by which time the weather had eased its stranglehold. Although enjoying the benefits of a private clinic, Susan nevertheless experienced a hard time with their son's birth. From the moment her waters broke, it was some eighteen hours before the boy deigned to put in an appearance, and it left her utterly exhausted. Moreover, John, who had stayed throughout the ordeal, also felt emotionally drained and it didn't end there, for no sooner had he retired to the waiting area to relax with a coffee than one of the white-coated doctors appeared in the doorway.

"Mr Grant?" he enquired with a smooth professional voice.

Resignedly, John put down his plastic beaker. "Yeah, that's me," he responded in his best working-class accent.

The medic sat down while attempting to fold his arms with his stethoscope still in place – a difficult procedure at best, John would have thought – while the starched white coat seemed to creak at his every move.

"Understandably," the medic began, "your wife's very tired. In fact, it's been the most protracted arrival I've ever experienced. However," he added reassuringly, "she'll be fine with plenty of rest – I take it there's help on the home front?" John nodded, mutely. "Anyway," continued the doctor while attempting to disentangle his arms from the stethoscope, "although your son appears quite healthy, and I don't wish to alarm you, he does display several features that seem a bit unusual."

A faint sense of unease stirred in the depths of John's mind.

"What do you mean?" he replied abruptly. "A bit unusual?"

The man was a young clean-cut-looking individual who, John estimated, would not have long completed his internship.

"Well, normally," came the reply, "the lungs of a new-born baby are filled with embryonic fluid, which is a liquid the young child floats in during pregnancy, and when these waters break it's a sign that the birth is imminent."

"So?" interrupted John irritably. "I've got that bit already."

"Well," continued the medic, "usually, new-born babies cry to clear their lungs, whereas your son hasn't made a sound, and it looks as though his chest was already fully functional when he first appeared. But," the man added, "there's also something else, which, frankly, I found a little disturbing."

"Such as?"

"When I examined him," frowned the doctor, "I could almost sense a sort of resentment."

"Resentment? For heaven's sake man, we're talking about a new baby."

"I know, I know," he insisted seemingly unphased by John's attitude. "But, the fact is, that's how it felt. Have a look at his eyes. They're piercing green, and when I went to turn him over they seemed to glare right into me, and what's more, the nurse noticed the same thing."

For a moment, and in the light of Tim's recent visit, John sat quietly looking down at the floor as a myriad of distressing thoughts flashed through his mind; not least being the horror of reincarnation, and seeing his stricken expression the young doctor hastened to enquire if he was quite all right.

"Yes, yes, I'm fine," asserted John. "It's just that no father likes to hear that his child is peculiar in some way."

"No. I fully understand." The 'white coat' would have said more, but in the event clearly decided that silence was the better option. Finally, however, he contented himself with more routine information. "Bearing in mind your wife's difficult birth," he advised, "the paediatric team and I felt it better that she and your son should stay overnight in order for us to monitor their progress."

"Fair enough," replied John as he reached for his now cold beaker of coffee – although he found the thought of spending the next twenty-four hours in the sole company of his ex-wife something less than appealing.

The following morning saw him promptly back at the clinic around 10am, but upon entering his wife's room he immediately detected something wrong. Although it all looked quite normal on the surface with her breast-feeding the baby, her face nevertheless betrayed a desperate anxiety, and sitting down on the edge of the bed, he gently enquired whether everything was all right.

"I can't hide anything from you, can I, John?"

"Not much," he replied with a grin. "But, come on, tell me. What's the matter?" However, as he reached over to gently stroke the new baby's head, the infant immediately flinched and turned to stare at him with unwavering emerald eyes which reinforced yesterday's feeling of disquiet.

"It's just that Peter doesn't cry," explained Susan. "He never cries, and it's not natural."

"Oh, it's Peter is it?" He nodded.

"Well, I just thought it was a nice name," replied the new mother defensively. "But it's a joint decision, of course."

"That's fine, love," he smiled with a gentle squeeze of her arm. "If it's Peter you like, then Peter it is."

But even while speaking, she had been busily undoing the press-studs of the new child's baby grow, and, pulling the top half down, she showed John a strange birthmark high up on the infant's left shoulder. "Tell me. What do you make of that?"

The shape caused him to wince internally. He was widely read, not only in the history of art but also history in general, and possessed a sound knowledge of the classical world. So, he was immediately able to recognise the configuration as being similar to a letter from the runes alphabet; an ancient form of Germanic communication which sometimes involved the unknown.

"Well?" Susan persisted.

Striving to contain the shock, he just shrugged dismissively.

"Well, it's obviously just some sort of birthmark. It happens to be a funny shape that's all. At least it's easily concealed. Some unfortunate people have to live with a defect like that on their face."

But his perceptive wife was not so easily fooled.

"I just hope you're right, and that it's nothing more sinister. Anyway," she added while adjusting little Peter's outfit, "changing the subject, how did you manage last night with that ex of yours? She always seems to have plenty to say for herself, although I must admit I find her good company."

John leaned forward and rubbed cupped hands wearily up and down his face.

"I'd noticed, and you're not the only one. Everyone used to be taken in by her yap."

"I didn't ask you for a lecture on her attributes," protested the new mum while indicating for him to put little Peter back in his cot.

"No. I know," he relented gently taking his son. "Last night was okay. She took care of Miriam which was the main thing, and then kept very much to herself."

Peter's homecoming was made nothing short of rapturous by John's excited ex and little Miriam's enthusiasm. Up to that point, she had been an only child and heard friends at school talk about their brothers and sisters. But now it was her turn, and she couldn't wait to hold Peter as Susan carried him in through the front door.

"There we are, darling, but please be careful

because he's quite delicate and breaks easily," she smiled while still holding the baby's main weight.

Jeanette, who had been hovering in the background, found it impossible to contain herself any longer.

"Susan!" she exclaimed. "I've got one of the downstairs bedrooms all ready and I've completely done out little Miriam's old cot."

Unseen, John responded to what he saw as an odd form of familiarity and rolled his eyes. However, despite the overall warmth of their reception, it was in sharp contrast to what had been left outside; for after experiencing a brief thaw, arctic conditions had once more returned with a vengeance. In fact, John was only too grateful to get back safely because driving snow had reduced his visibility to a few yards.

"Jeanette," he said abruptly. "Much as I hate to interrupt all this maternal euphoria, can you tell me if there's been a delivery of liquid gas while I've been away?"

"I'm sorry," she confessed dragging her attention away from the new attraction, "but not to my knowledge."

Although he didn't pursue the matter, he was again seriously concerned about their fuel reserves.

Later that same evening, Susan took the opportunity to relax on the kitchen sofa, while John was busy doing accounts in his little retreat. So, she had the place to herself for a change. And, with her feet up she settled back to enjoy a cigarette with a cup of her favourite coffee. But even as she reached for her lighter, she noticed her husband's ex appear in the doorway.

"Come in, Jeanette. Please do help yourself to a drink."

"Oh, Susan," eulogised the new 'nanny'. "He's such a lovely baby and his skin's like a fresh peach."

"I know. It's just a pity that it doesn't last very long," rejoined the new mother. "It's something the very young seem blessed with at birth." Jeanette reached to pour herself a coffee. "If you want sugar, you'll have to get it from the cupboard," she smiled.

Then, as John's ex lifted out the packet, she continued, "And he's so heavy. It must have been a difficult time for you. I mean, what does he weigh? About ten and a half pounds?"

"Spot on," agreed Susan while taking the first draught of another cigarette down onto her lungs. "And even though I was fortunate enough to have an epidural I still needed a number of stitches, so I've got to take it easy for a bit. But I tell you what," she added emphatically. "That's the last time. If John wants any more babies, he can jolly well have them himself."

"Now, that would be an achievement." Her companion smiled.

"You've never mentioned any children of your own," observed the new mother with a certain idle curiosity.

"No. No, I haven't."

"Did you and John...? I mean, he's never said anything about children."

But her recent friend slowly shook her head with a touch of sadness. "No... John and I never had any children."

She fell quiet for a minute.

"That's not to say I wouldn't have liked a family. I would, but it just didn't happen. You see," she confessed, "I don't think John saw me as, well, you know, sexually attractive – although he was always very good, and if I'm honest I behaved abominably. But it was sex, or lack of it, that caused the problem." She stopped again briefly and shrugged. "Anyway, I don't know why I'm telling you this, because you've probably heard it all before."

"No," replied Susan as she again drew on her cigarette. "John's never discussed his previous marriage."

A slightly awkward silence fell between the two women before Jeanette spoke again.

"I've got one daughter though," she exclaimed quietly. "But I've never seen her because she was adopted at birth." A brief look of sadness again crossed her face. "It was all a long time ago – before I met John. She must be in her early twenties by now, but I do sometimes wonder how she's getting on, although I suppose it's just one of those things in life that you can't change."

"Why? Have you never thought of contacting her?"

"No," she sighed. "I've always considered it better if I let her get on with her life without the emotional upheaval of my interference. I mean..." She shrugged. "She may not even know she was adopted."

"I do see your point," agreed Susan.

"Oh, don't mind me." Jeanette smiled. "It's just that your Peter's made me feel all broody again. You know, he really is a very beautiful baby and I don't think I've ever seen such deep green eyes."

"Well, we can share him," volunteered Susan while offering her companion a cigarette.

"I'll pass on that," she responded gently. "And you shouldn't be smoking either with a new baby and all." Then, frowning briefly, she observed, "It's strange but I haven't heard him cry at all since you brought him home."

Susan didn't respond immediately because her friend's observation had touched a nerve.

"I know," she confided. "And it worries me. There's also something else. You were saying what lovely eyes he's got, but the funny thing is they never seem to blink. Anyway," she smiled, getting to her feet, "I've had enough for one day, so if I could leave the coffee things to you I'm off to bed."

"Oh, just before you go," enquired Jeanette. "I've been wondering what's happened to that lovely picture that used to hang in the hall. It seems quite bare out there now it's gone."

"You might well ask," retorted a thoroughly tired Susan. "It's a long story and I'll tell you about it one day, but in the meantime, I'll just say goodnight."

"Goodnight, Susan," rejoined the new 'family member'. "Oh, and by the way, thanks for having me," she added gratefully. But all her benefactor could manage was a wave of acknowledgement before disappearing beyond the kitchen entrance.

Long after Susan's departure, Jeanette just sat in the empty silence of the vast room while letting her mind wander back over her own life and tried to think how she could have got everything so terribly wrong. Certainly, at first, she and John had been very close. He had, like men before him, obviously enjoyed her companionship, while, in turn, she had admired him not only physically but also for his mischievous sense of humour and very obvious talent as an artist.

And yet, she thought bitterly, it had not been enough, for early on in their marriage it had become clear that she failed to attract him in ways that really mattered and after months of deprivation she had turned to their rather nondescript lodger. But this had proved a slippery slope and seen her go from one disaster to another until the final and fatal error of her marriage to a real brute; a man who had more than met his match in John.

John, who appeared to have achieved so much... while her own life...? Could she have done any differently? Somehow, she doubted it. And, slowly getting up from her seat she wandered over to the huge bay window, but if she'd hoped to find any solace out there she was doomed to disappointment, for the great white wilderness she'd expected had become swallowed up by the intense blackness of a starless night.

Early the next day, heavy dark and snow-laden clouds permitted just enough light for John to see the full extent of a prolific overnight fall – a fall which had made it virtually impossible to identify even everyday objects such as their five-bar gate. The whole landscape, in fact, slumbered under an all-pervasive white camouflage and somehow had the effect of reducing everything to a common yet peaceful denominator. However, as he stood watching from the kitchen window, John quickly realised it was deceptively tranquil as sudden bitter east winds howled across the lake and buffeted the stout farmhouse. Tearing over the open fields in violent bursts of fury, it lifted up the fallen snow into great shifting flurries which formed deep drifts wherever they came up against anything solid. Everywhere he looked, in fact, was evidence of a terrifying blizzard with the east side of trees and field walls virtually obliterated by white.

A glance down at his watch told him it was fast approaching 8am, and he again wondered briefly why there'd been no sound of the new baby crying. But, with other worries on his mind, he made his way towards the rear of the house because his overriding concern was the fuel and he was anxious to take stock of the situation.

Passing through the rear of the property, he wrenched open the back door, but only to be faced by a white wilderness and a wall of snow that stretched more than half way up the doorframe. The gas tank, which was only yards away, had become little more than an inaccessible mound of snow.

"F..." he mumbled.

Later during the day, John and Susan sat down in the kitchen to discuss the seriousness of their situation. Her husband leaned forward and agitatedly tapped the tips of his fingers together. "Anyway, I managed to plough my way through to the gas tank, but I reckon even with careful conservation, there's only between three and four days left. After that..."

"What do you mean, 'after that'?" she echoed. "What are we going to do after that? We're completely snowbound with a new-born baby. And, John, I've seen the forecast. There's no hint of a let up. This weather from Russia is set to continue for the next week, or even ten days."

Although he looked grim, John, perhaps unwisely, tried a touch of humour.

"Well, I suppose we could stay in bed all day with hot water bottles and get you to change them every time they got cold."

"It's no joke," she cried almost tearfully. "And there's also the food situation, because if nothing can get through we've only got what's left in the fridge and freezer."

"Look, if we keep our cool," he replied, but then grinned as he suddenly realised what he'd said.

"I do wish you'd take the problem seriously, John, because I'm worried enough about little Peter. And remember there are five mouths to feed now."

"Four," he corrected her. "We can starve the ex." However, catching her expression he decided it was time to stop the silliness. "But tell me," he said seriously, "what makes you so worried about Peter? I mean, he takes his bottle and that, doesn't he?"

Susan took a deep breath. "John," she reminded him, "he doesn't cry. They noticed it at the hospital. He just never cries. I've had experience with very young children, apart from our Miriam, and I can tell you it's unnatural." She paused to rummage in her handbag for the comfort of a cigarette, and lighting it up she added fearfully, "Supposing, John, just supposing, he got very hungry. Would he still not cry? Would he just let himself die of hunger...? Oh, I don't know," she added and shivered slightly at her own thoughts.

He reached forward and drew her close. "But that's just a hypothetical fear over nothing," he objected gently. "And it's not going to happen because you're always there to feed him."

However, her expression and body language betrayed a very real unease.

"John," she stressed. "Have you noticed his eyes?" She faltered for a moment and drew on her cigarette. "What I can't understand is how he came by their colouring, because all my family have grey eyes and yours are a deep blue. And then there's the way he stares. It's almost like an adult. He just stares and stares into space as if desperately trying to remember something." Again, her husband found himself trying to suppress the one word that came into his mind. And he was not alone. "You don't think do you," she almost sobbed, "that our lovely little son somehow suspects he might be the boy in that painting?"

And it was at that point John decided to approach an old friend for help and advice. To advance his career, he had originally taken a year's secondment to study for a Master's Degree at Sussex University where he had met and befriended one of the lecturers – a man who specialised in history and ancient languages – someone, in fact, who might be able to decipher his son's strange birthmark. However, in the meantime, John determined to comfort his distressed wife in every way possible.

"Darling," he said gently. "If you're not careful, you'll allow a series of minor and unrelated instances to take control, and that's all they are. Minor instances – and you've got to try to stop it." He leaned forward and removed the cigarette from her hand before firmly squashing it out in a nearby ashtray. "Now, we know the baby's got green eyes – but so what? So have tens of thousands of other people. There have probably been a number of our ancestors who've had the same colouring. It's just taken a few generations for that particular gene to surface." He paused, almost tempted to have a cigarette himself as Susan reached for yet another of her comfort sticks. But, no sooner than she'd taken down the first draught than she began to cough; a deep hacking cough – something John had noticed was fast becoming more pronounced.

"Smoker's cough," she admitted guiltily, catching sight of his concerned expression.

"If you're not careful," he warned, "you'll end up with some form of COPD, and you won't be able to get your breath; worse – you could even get..." But he refrained from saying the actual 'c' word.

"I know, I know," she retorted defensively. "You don't need to go on about it."

In the event, John's fear concerning the fuel situation proved unfounded, because for once the weathermen had got it wrong and a thaw set in with such suddenness there became a real danger of flooding.

However, despite the fact that the arctic conditions seemed to have eased their grip, John still needed to exercise extreme care on the drive south to see his lecturer friend, and, even then, almost twice lost control due to melting ice on the road surface. But at last, the familiar outlines of the university came into sight. Started in the early nineteen fifties, the buildings, which were designed by Sir Basil Spence, had been quite ground-breaking in their day, and John still found them an impressive experience. Part of the charm lay in their location; just north of Brighton, the whole campus nestled at the foot of the South Downs. However, unlike many of its town counterparts, the university buildings had been well spaced out over wide intervening lawns and afforded a very pleasant rural environment – especially during the summer months.

As he drove through the main entrance he couldn't help but notice a huge and rather lop-sided snowman, which despite its terminal state of decline still seemed somehow determined to extend a welcome. Fascinated, John stopped briefly to gaze at the slightly forlorn-looking figure whose once smiley face was now on the verge of collapse along with the rest of its sagging body. Although obviously the work of young students who probably thought it cool to be silly, they had nevertheless managed to impart a certain life to their creation which was slowly fading away. But to where, John idly wondered while putting the car into gear. Or does such vitality just simply cease to exist...?

But his philosophising was suddenly cut short by the impatient sound of a car horn from behind, in response to which he immediately wound down his window in order to facilitate the robust use of two fingers.

Although the thaw was now well underway, the campus still bore mute evidence of its battering by the recent blizzard, and while whole areas of grass were beginning to emerge from the snow, great banks of it remained tenaciously piled up against the eastern side of the buildings. John, however, was faced with the joy of trying to find somewhere to park, but if the facilities at St Richard's Hospital had been irritating, those of Sussex University proved nothing short of a nightmare.

Things had changed dramatically since he'd studied for his Master's Degree – not least being that visitors were now restricted to their own car park with goodness only knows what penalties if they dared to leave their vehicle anywhere else. But, of course, by the time he'd arrived the place was packed to capacity with drivers not only filling every available space but also commandeering the slightest bit of available grass verge.

"Great. Bloody great," John muttered as he repeatedly drove round in search of a vacant space. Utterly frustrated, he felt tempted to just leave his car anywhere on one of the campus roads and to hell with the consequences. However, upon a more careful appraisal of the penalty notices he quickly realised there was a real danger of either being clamped or impounded.

Finally, however, he found himself outside the professor's study.

When his wife had first pointed out Peter's strange birthmark, he'd made light of it. But, despite his normally rational way of thinking, it had left him feeling distinctly uneasy and he fervently hoped his old friend might be able to help. Idly glancing down the corridor as he knocked the lecturer's door, he couldn't help but notice yet another security camera winking down at him.

"Talk about big brother," he murmured under his breath.

The professor was accommodated at the far end of the university as part of a new extension, and he'd seen dozens of these intrusive entities right across the campus.

"Come on in," called a voice which was immediately recognisable as the warm tones of his friend. "Hello, John," welcomed the professor as Peter's father entered the cluttered study. "Long time no see." His visitor reached out and exchanged an affectionate handshake.

"I know, Michael," he observed. "Where does it all go? Time, I mean."

His friend indicated a chair.

"Please do take a seat," he invited while brushing back his long white hair.

Michael's locks had always been a feature in

their own right. Grown inordinately long at the side of his head, John had often suspected they were to compensate for its total absence elsewhere. The problem was it had always been allowed an unruly life of its own. Yet, in a strange way, symbolised the overall sense of disorder which pervaded the entire room.

For a start, Michael's desk was far too large for the actual space available, and literally groaned under the weight of books; some of which were piled three or four high while others lay open or just shoved to one side. In addition, John could count at least three discarded cups, the antiquity of whose contents were probably better not dwelt on. And this was without the folders and numerous scraps of paper depicting various jottings and graphs.

What had always amazed John, was the way his friend totally ignored the facilities offered by the computer, but even so he knew that behind all this apparent chaos lurked a razor-sharp mind that had never ceased in its quest for knowledge.

"I see you haven't changed much, Michael," he observed. "Still always engaged in some sort of research or other."

"Yes, well, I'm virtually retired now, you know," he replied while shuffling some of the loose material to one side. "And it gives me more time to study the things that really interest me. Oh, I do the occasional lecture, of course, but that's about all."

It made Susan's husband wonder just how much

time his friend actually needed, for he only ever remembered him delivering the odd lecture during his own time at the university. Obviously, academia constituted the professor's whole life because he had no family to John's knowledge but, thrusting such thoughts aside, he came straight to the point of his visit.

"Michael, I need your advice."

"Well, you know I'll be pleased to help in any way I can," he volunteered while moving in the direction of a small and cluttered sink. Situated at the corner of the room, it seemed to cry out for a little domestic intervention. "In the meantime," offered his friend, "can I get you a cup of anything?"

But with one eye on his health and the other on the prevailing hygiene, John felt it wiser to decline.

"The fact is," he began as the professor re-joined him, "I've just become a father for the second time."

His friend didn't immediately respond but raised a rather tired and cracked mug of steaming something-or-other to his mouth, but as he did so, John thought he saw a momentary flicker of remorse cross his face.

"Well, congratulations," complimented the academic while lowering his drink to the desk. "I'm afraid that's one of life's joys I've not experienced. And at my age," he added with a ruthless smile, "I doubt whether I ever will."

"Michael," rejoined John hastily, "being a parent is far from the pleasure you might think. I've had nothing but worry over my little girl's health, and the new baby... Well, actually that's what I've come to see you about." And he went on to briefly describe events from the acquisition of Blake's oil painting to the mysterious birthmark on Peter's left shoulder. "But it's the shape, Michael," he stressed, "that concerns me, because it's reminiscent of a runic symbol and you know better than I do that such signs were frequently associated with early Germanic occult practices."

"You think you could draw it for me, John?" asked his silver-haired friend.

"I can do better than that," replied John while reaching for his phone and scrolling to a photograph. "As you can see, it's almost like the modern capital letter B, only it's back-to-front and the normal rounded sections appear pointed."

"Ah. Now that," exclaimed his friend while looking at the photo, "reminds me of a 'Berkanan' and it's pronounced 'Bear.kahn.awn'. It normally signifies rebirth or some sort of fresh start."

"Or reincarnation?" suggested his increasingly alarmed guest.

The professor shook his head while leaning forward to rest his forearms on the desk.

"I can't say I've ever come across any evidence to suggest that sort of interpretation. However, in this case the letter's in reverse, so..." And with that he got up and made for one of the numerous bookshelves which lined his study. After running a finger over the backs of several volumes he seized one entitled *Evolution of the Runes*, then, returning to his desk, he put on his glasses and proceeded to thumb through its pages. "Yes, here you are," he said eventually, after mumbling through an apparently relevant passage. "It seems," he said guardedly, "if the rune we're talking about is rendered in reverse, then it could be indicative that its initial optimistic message might be cancelled out or even foreshadow some sort of impending disaster." He looked at his friend in an attempt at some sort of reassurance. "I should add," he said gently, "that not all scholars agree with this particular exposition, and you know as well as I do that runes, or whatever words we use, are only symbols of our thoughts and have no intrinsic power in themselves."

"Unless," echoed his visitor, "they become a warning of things to come."

His host looked somewhat taken aback as he pulled off his wire-framed spectacles.

"You surprise me, John. I'd always seen you as an out-and-out rationalist and certainly not one given to any sort of superstition."

"That's true," responded the new baby's father. "But you see, it's not a question of superstition but rather a matter of faith in God and a spiritual war against evil. I'm different to you in some respects, Michael, because I think there's more to life than mere objective materialism."

"You mean," replied the academic with a slight smile, "I'm an atheist?"

"No offence, but, yes."

"Oh, don't worry," countered his friend warmly, "because, yes, you're right. That's just what I am – an out-and-out atheist. But at least it has the consolation in that I don't have to worry about evil influences, etcetera."

With that, John got to his feet. While he'd enjoyed renewing acquaintances with his old friend, he sensed it was time to leave – although, as he closed the study door on that musty academic world, he did wonder if he'd come away any the wiser.

Making his way back to the car, he glanced about the campus where it seemed the whole world was alive with young people busily clutching their books and rushing from one lecture to the next. Whether in pairs or animated groups, they seemed utterly oblivious to his presence; almost, as it were, as though he didn't exist. And, wandering along the now slushy campus paths, it made him acutely aware of the divisiveness of age.

Part of the way took him through the university refectory which had been virtually deserted on his arrival, but, with lunchtime fast approaching, was now a hive of activity; everywhere throbbed to the ceaseless clatter of crockery and eating utensils which blended with the vibrant conversations of students all hell-bent, no doubt, on putting the world to rights and conducted with an intensity of which only the young are capable. Again, it all made John feel completely irrelevant as he made his way down the length of the restaurant and out beyond the far exit.

Once in the cooler air, he breathed a deep sigh while muttering to himself, "John, you're nothing more than yesterday's man." He thought briefly of his own student days and the hopes and vitality that had accompanied them, all of which were now but distant memories. It seemed to beg the question whether anticipation was greater than its realisation.

Moving on towards his car, he again came face-to-face with the sad lopsided snowman and in some strange way he couldn't help but identify with the neglected figure, for the milling students seemed as oblivious to its existence as they had been of him. However, even since his first encounter, the dying creation had managed to shed one of its eyes as the thaw took an ever-increasing toll on its very being. Somehow, it seemed as though the lonely entity was winking a final farewell, and despite himself, John impulsively reached out to pat what was left of the snowman's shoulder.

His visit to the university had left the retired teacher in a sombre mood; certainly, his concerns over Peter's birthmark had not been resolved while, in some inexplicable way, the pathos of the snowman had somehow got through to him.

Driving north, he asked himself why should what was, after all, just a heap of snow, have such an emotional effect? Could it be the snowman's demise somehow reflected the human condition of beginnings and ends, together with all that implied? In a strange way it reminded him of his own little sister who had only been granted a mere six weeks of existence and whose death had robbed him of a lifelong companion.

But then, shaking off the morbid thoughts, he concentrated on the journey ahead. Snow still clung to the upper regions of the South Downs, but once clear of the hills, the effects of the recent heavy falls were fast disappearing to herald the early dawn of a new spring.

Chapter 6

AFTER PETER'S BIRTH and its accompanying uncertainties, life at the farmhouse appeared to resume some semblance of normality, and six months after her son's arrival, Susan returned to work in Horsham, thereby leaving the day-to-day care of the two children with John's ex. But, to Jeanette's concern, Miriam's little brother continued to demonstrate peculiar behaviour. During the early days, while still in the pram, he would lay passively inert and stare intently into space. Baby toys such as his rattle and the string of coloured beads across the hood seemed to hold little or no interest for him. It was a pattern that would continue through into his years as a toddler, and although Jeanette undoubtedly had a way with young children and did her utmost to stimulate him, she had very limited success. He would just sit about and stare fixatedly at the nursery floor. It was almost as though behind those unblinking and piercing green eyes, the child was somewhere else.

Miriam, who was almost nine and fast becoming

a mirror image of her mother, gave vent to her feelings one evening.

"Mummy, little Peter's two now but he never says anything. I've tried playing ball with him, but he takes no notice."

Jeanette, who by now virtually constituted part of the family, glanced uneasily across the table at Susan, for she had long since realised Peter was far from normal and wondered how his mother would react.

"Darling," began Susan slowly while carefully aligning her knife and fork on the plate to signify an end to her meal, "the fact is, everybody's different. Peter's just a bit slow and quiet. That's all. I'm sure he'll eventually turn out to be the little companion you've always hoped for."

It had been said with a conviction she certainly didn't feel, and she began to agitatedly gather up everyone's plate, almost, as it were, in an effort to distract her mind. But, as she lowered the soiled crockery into the sink, John appeared at her side.

"Are you all right, love?" he enquired.

"Yes, I'm okay," she whispered. "I'll talk about it later when there's only the two of us."

Finally, with the remainder of the household retired for the night she turned to her husband for comfort and, sitting in the now subdued kitchen light, she reached towards her ever-present packet of cigarettes. For a long time, she simply sat with an unlit cork tip hanging loosely between her lips.

Eventually, without even lighting it, she took the addictive article from her mouth.

"John," she began miserably, "much as we might like to deny it, there's something seriously wrong with little Peter; your ex knows it and now so does Miriam. I tell you, he just sits for hours on end lost in a world of his own. It's almost as though anything outside that inner domain of his doesn't exist." Her eyes misted over and her voice began to break. "Oh, what is to become of him, John? You don't think what Tim was talking about has come true? And our little boy has become overshadowed by some evil?" And she buried her face in her hands.

It was a month later with Susan at work and John busily engaged on business in Brighton, when Jeanette had occasion to leave Peter in the security of his playpen during a visit to the bathroom. Upon her return to the nursery, however, she became horrified to find there was no sign of him. Panic-stricken, she frantically raced from room to room in a desperate search. Again and again, she called out his name without result. But then, after a futile hunt throughout the house, she crossed the hallway for the umpteenth time to try the kitchen. And there he was, just staring fixatedly up at the aquarium.

"Peter, what are you doing? You naughty boy," she said in a simultaneous combination of anger and relief.

Later, during the evening meal, it became obvious that both the women had something on their minds which they were desperate to express.

"Oh, you go first Susan," smiled the ex.

Starters consisted of thick, homemade lentil soup which was one of John's favourites, and while his wife used the handle of her spoon to tap the table for attention he wasted no time in using his implement to savour the contents of a well-filled bowl. However, he paused with it halfway to his mouth when he heard what she was about to say. Susan had obviously been savouring her news for just this moment and made her announcement with a flourish.

"Today," she said, standing up suddenly and triumphantly raising one hand high in the air, "I've been officially promoted to Housing Director for the whole county."

The brief ensuing silence that followed was almost immediately broken by their daughter.

"Mummy, how wonderful," she gasped excitedly, and getting up, rushed round the table to give her mother a long hug. Miriam had been quick off the mark, but her father wasn't far behind and he took Susan in his arms.

"If anyone deserves the position, it's you," he enthused. "Congratulations, darling. Absolute congratulations."

However, their mutual euphoria and display of affection was not entirely shared by everyone, for as Jeanette looked on she couldn't help but sense a touch of envy. Obviously, Susan had that certain something she must have lacked during her marriage, but, nevertheless, she was quick to applaud her new friend's achievement.

"Susan, that's brilliant," she smiled while attempting to hide her true feelings. "I'm so pleased for you." But now it was her turn to speak, and between spoonfuls of soup, John urged her to get on with it.

The pseudo family member placed her spoon slowly and deliberately side of her bowl, then, leaning forward with her elbows on the table, she locked her fingers.

"After your great news, Susan," she began cautiously, "I'm almost loath to say anything. But the fact is – it's about Peter." And at that point she went on to describe the events that led up to his discovery in the kitchen. "And, even when I shouted at him," she stressed, "he took no notice but just continued to stare at the fish tank." Then, pointing at the aquarium, she added, "But it's what happened next that shook me."

"Well, go on," urged a slightly irritated John. "What did happen next?"

"As far as I can remember," she observed hesitantly, "Peter has always been a very quiet and introspective little boy. In fact, up to that point I'd never heard him say anything. Anyway, I was in a bit of a state as you can probably imagine, and I had to shout several times to get his attention. But when

I did, he slowly turned and glared at me with those piercing eyes of his." She glanced apologetically at John's wife. "I'm sorry, but I do sometimes find the way he looks at me a bit scary. Anyway, it was then that I heard him speak for the first time. He only said three words which I think were, 'I like fishes'. Or it might have been, 'I like fishing'. But just at that moment, the grandfather clock in the hallway chimed the quarter so I couldn't be quite sure which it was." She shrugged noncommittally. "But, I suppose that doesn't really matter does it? The important thing is he actually said something."

However, the apparent minor discrepancies actually represented a seismic difference. On the one hand it could have been merely a child's natural interest at the sight of vital and living creatures, while on the other a chilling echo from a past era.

John glanced warily at his wife for her reaction.

"We'll talk about it later, darling," he advised her.

What John couldn't understand was how his young son had managed to escape from the playpen in the first place.

"That!" exclaimed the nanny, "is an absolute mystery."

"I mean," persisted John, "did you leave any toys or boxes that he could have climbed on?"

"Only a few of those picture bricks to amuse him while I was gone," she replied defensively. "But they're far too small to be of any use. I don't know." Jeanette sighed. "Perhaps he just levitated."

It was, of course, a singularly unfortunate expression for her to have used, although at the time she had no knowledge of Tim's dire warning concerning Blake's pact, and in a similar state of ignorance Miriam was quick to pipe up.

"Mummy? What's levi..."

"The word is levitation, darling," explained Susan. "It means rising in the air and hovering. You know, a bit like a helicopter." However, anxious to avoid her young daughter being dragged into the uncertainty over her little brother, she quickly added, "Jeanette was only joking of course, sweetie".

"Anyway," interjected John, keen to restore the upbeat mood of his wife's earlier announcement, "at least our little boy has started to talk."

That night saw John unable to sleep, his mind refusing to switch off. Again and again he agonised over their pastor's warning and faced the question he would never dream of discussing with his wife. Had the acquisition of the fisher boy, in some diabolical way, facilitated the reincarnation of its subject in the form of their son? Only time would tell, and indeed as the months passed into years, Peter's behaviour continued to be far from normal. Almost totally introverted, he only spoke on rare occasions, and apart from the fish tank, all his toys might just have well not existed. Although, with John and his wife being away at work for long hours, they saw very little of this first-hand. However, the ex was never slow to inform them of his latest antics.

The results of their son's abnormal persona came to a head on his initial day at primary school. Susan deemed it unnecessary for him to attend any form of playschool because Jeanette had proved so capable with his early learning. Getting home unusually late that evening, it seemed as though she had barely passed through the front door before it was time for supper. Jeanette had furnished them with an exceptionally delightful meal, and at the very moment Susan pulled up her chair Jeanette chose to break her bad news. Looking apologetic, she began to describe what had happened on their son's first day.

"I arranged to collect Peter from the cloakroom," she began, "to ensure he had his bag and coat etcetera. And of course, I also wanted to see how he'd got on. Anyway, when I found he wasn't there I went straight to reception where I was politely informed that he was in the headteacher's study." She paused for a moment. "Shepherd's pie, John?" she suggested.

But by his wife's expression, she could see this hint of past domesticity had not gone down too well.

"And?" exclaimed Susan with a touch of irritability. "What exactly was Peter doing in the headteacher's room?"

"Unfortunately," confessed John's ex, "the head refused to go into details. But from what I could gather, it seems he was involved in some kind of altercation with another pupil and she wants to see you both at the earliest possible opportunity. In the meantime, Peter's been banned from the school."

"Oh, great!" exclaimed his disgruntled father as he sat back and folded his arms. "Just great."

"And do you know?" added Jeanette disgustedly while serving the last of the main course. "She was a snooty bitch, if you don't mind my saying so. One of those people who's let a little power go to their head. Funny," she observed finally. "The woman reminded me a bit of your last nanny."

But even at the mention of Brenda, John felt a pang of remorse.

Two days later and at 9am sharp, Susan and her husband found themselves outside the door formidably endorsed: 'Miss D Hardy M.A. – Headteacher'. And even after her recent promotion it left John's wife feeling slightly queasy. School day fears of authoritarian figures, it seemed, had never quite faded.

"Go on. You knock," she whispered timorously to her husband.

"Why are you whispering?" he grinned. "You don't get caned anymore, you know."

"Oh, go on. Get on with it, John."

Secretly he was interested to see what the woman looked like and wasted no time in complying.

"Come."

The response to his tap was sharp and immediate, and he pulled a face as he opened the door to reveal the lady herself. Seated at her desk in the tight authoritarian atmosphere of the room, she looked up keenly at the parents, and although it might have been his imagination it seemed for a split second that her gimlet expression faded as their eyes met. And, yes, he thought with a slight feeling of warmth, the lady did bear a passing resemblance to Brenda with her high cheekbones and regular features. However, although probably only in her early forties, she'd allowed the pounds to pile up.

"Ah, Mr and Mrs Grant," she greeted them, rising to her feet. "Please do take a seat." Then, after shaking hands she lowered herself slowly back onto her chair. "I understand congratulations are in order, Mrs Grant. Chief Housing Officer for the county. That's no mean achievement." But then, seeing her visitors' puzzled expressions she hastened to explain along with something approaching a smile. "Oh, my husband's a county councillor so I'm well clued up on most civic matters." During the brief but slightly strained silence that followed, the headteacher picked up her phone. "Angela, would you be kind enough to send Miss Francis to my room? Oh. And Mr Briggs as well, if he's available."

Replacing the handset, she looked straight at John and whatever warmth he thought he might have seen initially certainly wasn't there now. She reached for a pen and balanced it between her two forefingers. "On our first day of term, Mr Grant," she began in clipped tones, "we experienced the most serious incident I've ever occasioned in the whole of my teaching career."

John sighed inaudibly while hooking an arm over the back of his chair and bracing himself for the anticipated verbal onslaught. However, at that moment there came a gentle tap from outside and, glancing round, was in time to see a rather shy and bespectacled female face peering round the edge of the door.

"Come in, Miss Francis. Come in," ordered the head impatiently.

As the woman entered, John found himself looking at the most unattractive female it had ever been his misfortune to clap eyes on. With her freckled face and frizzy auburn hair swept back into a tight bun, together with her rather dowdy midi-length dress, she hardly constituted a man's delight. Or, in his own words later on, a woman totally and utterly bereft of any sexual charm whatsoever.

"Now," continued the head, "allow me to introduce you to Peter's parents, Mr and Mrs Grant." Then, with these formalities complete, the miscreant deeds of their son began to unfold in no uncertain terms, and John had to admit what he'd initially seen as an eternal Miss came across surprisingly well.

"I was in the playground on duty last Thursday lunchtime," she began, "when one of the older girls came and told me there was a fight going on in the hall. Now, I've been teaching here for some three years and until then I'd never once heard of any physical violence between the pupils." Then, turning her attention directly to John, she added, "I immediately rushed back into the building to find your son forcibly holding down another pupil and hitting him about the head with his clenched fist." But as the teacher emphasised what she was saying, her sleeve slipped back to reveal angry looking wheal marks on her forearm. "Anyway," she continued, "I rushed over and ordered him to stop at once, but he just looked round at me defiantly and took no notice, so I had no alternative but to try to physically drag him off the other child."

At that juncture, the headteacher intervened to observe, possibly superfluously, how disgracefully their son had behaved. Although, it tended to make John wonder if perhaps she wasn't taking a certain perverse satisfaction out of the whole situation – a feeling, however, quickly dispelled when Miss Francis described what happened next.

"I couldn't believe it!" she exclaimed in a voice that rose by half an octave. "Because immediately I took hold of Peter's shoulder he turned on me and tried to push me away. He was so incredibly strong, it was frightening. And his face, it was literally twisted in fury. I mean, a child of five? I've never experienced anything like it."

She paused for a moment as if to let what she'd said sink in, and John took the opportunity to ask almost wearily, "And is that how you came by those marks on your arm?"

The primary teacher who had barely taken her eyes off him, nodded and looked down at the back of her wrists.

"The day it happened," she explained, "I was wearing short sleeves, and during the struggle your son tore at me with his fingernails." She rolled up her sleeve and John was horrified to see scratches stretching from her upper arm to her wrist. He glanced across at the headteacher whose facial expression had by now become an essay in its own right. "Do you know," she continued. "I was more upset by what your Peter had done to our little fish tank than what he'd done to me. Because you see, our PTA had clubbed together to provide an aquarium for the hall; not only as a focal point of interest but also as an aid to the pupils' education."

Moved by the woman's obvious distress, John leaned forward in his seat.

"I'm so sorry, but what had my son done to the tank?"

"Well, we kept a number of different kinds of fish which the children had watched develop from the time they were just spawn. Now, apparently your son had been standing on a chair and systematically lifting them out of the water and throwing them on the floor. And when Mark, one of our older pupils, tried to stop him, he turned nasty. So, when I first arrived," she added almost tearfully, "I could see the poor little creatures flopping about on the ground, struggling for breath."

Not for the first time, John wondered whether there was some kind of insidious connection between his boy's obsession with fish and Blake's dead son? But his wife's distressed voice jerked him back to reality.

"Is there anywhere I could have a cigarette?" she enquired tentatively.

The headteacher didn't actually look down her nose, but she came pretty close to it.

"There's a smoking area just off the staffroom – although it's not something we encourage at St Martin's. In any case, don't you think it would be more beneficial to remain here until these proceedings have been completed?"

But John had had enough of the woman's condescending attitude.

"Let me make one thing abundantly clear," he snapped. "My wife does what she wants when she wants, and anyone thinking differently can answer to me."

But, as his wife got up, Miss Francis proved more conciliatory.

"Just turn left out of here, Mrs Grant, and it's the second door on the left. You can't miss it."

However, as Susan was leaving, she almost collided with a newcomer.

"You wanted to see me, Headteacher?" said the man.

"Yes, indeed I do, Mr Briggs," she replied while turning to the still-disgruntled John. "Mr Grant. Allow me to introduce our caretaker." Glancing at the man, Susan's husband summed him up as a bull-necked, pugnacious-looking individual who probably carried a permanent chip on his shoulder. "Now, Mr Briggs," continued the head, "would you be kind enough to tell us what you know of the disturbances in the hall?"

Assuming a folded arms posture, the man began to recite a sorry sequence of events.

"As it happened I was in room two at the time. You see, Miss Grace had asked me to check the roll mechanism of her blackboard."

Dead working-class, thought John. And almost certainly from the west country.

"Anyway," the caretaker continued, "I 'eard this 'ere sound of kids shouting in the 'all but at first I took no notice." He shrugged. "I mean, kids! What do you expect? But then I 'eard this woman scream. It were Miss Francis 'ere," he explained, indicating the teacher. "So, I rushed out in time to see her struggling with this young boy, but before I could get any closer she must have lost her footing and fell over."

"And then what happened?" enquired the obviously disgusted headteacher.

"Well, this 'ere young whippersnapper went on 'itting Miss Francis even though she was still on the ground. And you should have seen the state of her arms. They were scratched and bleeding. The little sod needs a damn good thrashing if you arst me."

"Thank you, Mr Briggs," reproved the senior teacher. "We can do without that. If you would just be kind enough to stick to the facts, please."

At this point, the patient Miss Francis spoke up hesitantly. "Will that be all, Miss Hardy? Only I don't like to leave my classroom assistant on her own for too long."

But her request merely drew a dismissive wave.

Meanwhile, John's mouth had been reduced to a thin line and he was just grateful that his wife had left the room, because he could see from the man's enthusiastic attitude there was more to come.

"Right!" exclaimed the caretaker. "Now, when I went to pull the little wretch away from Miss Francis, he tried to fight me off and I can tell you his strength for a small–"

But he was given no chance to finish by Peter's father.

"I think," observed John slowly and deliberately while looking the speaker up and down, "that I've heard just about enough derogatory superlatives concerning my son." Although, even as he spoke, he seriously wondered if the man was capable of understanding such terminology. However, from the caretaker's expression it quickly became obvious he'd got the drift, and as he aggressively turned in response the roll of fat round the back of his neck looked ready to burst.

"You need to teach that brat of yours how to behave his self, if you ask me."

During this exchange, Susan's husband had remained casually seated with his arm hooked over the back of his chair, but at this verbal onslaught he slowly got to his feet to confront the belligerent close-up.

"I suggest," he began in a quiet baleful voice, "that you mind your mouth, your manners and your own business." With a three inch and two stone advantage, he was quite prepared to mete out the same treatment that had befallen his ex's bullying husband.

Seeing the explosive situation, however, Miss Hardy was quick to intervene.

"Thank you, Mr Briggs. That'll be all."

Her voice carried a ring of authority that demanded immediate compliance, and the caretaker lost no time in leaving. Then, as the door closed, John took a seat adjacent to the head's desk while searching her face for a reaction. To his amazement, however, and for the briefest moment, he caught sight of the look he'd so often seen in Brenda's eyes, for the mask had slipped to reveal the real woman and all that entailed. But the magic was gone in an instant as the head resumed her authoritarian persona.

She leaned back in her chair while studying the pen she'd again picked up from her desk. Finally, after slowly and deliberately placing it down, she observed bluntly, "You were about to assault that man, weren't you?"

John studied the woman carefully before replying, as he again hooked his arm over the back of the chair. He'd put her age at about forty, but the nature of her job had taken its toll on a once-beautiful face. Deep lines were etched into her forehead and round the edges of her mouth.

"I was about to point out," he replied, "that I won't accept that kind of insult from anyone, and that caretaker of yours was in danger of taking on more than he could handle."

"Really, Mr Grant," she retorted tersely. "I know nothing of Peter's home background or the influences which have affected his early years, but from what I've just witnessed it makes me wonder what sort of example you've been setting the child."

Susan had returned in time to hear the head's critical comments, and by her expression she was obviously very angry. "I'll have you know that my son has had the best possible upbringing with love, care and discipline. Unfortunately, Miss Hardy," she continued now completely devoid of her earlier reticence, "as I'm sure you will know, a child is not just a product of its upbringing, but also, and probably more importantly, of past genetic influences."

John felt almost tempted to applaud.

"I'm well aware of the theory, Mrs Grant," said the head icily. "But the point is, where do we go from here? Because I've had to suspend Peter indefinitely, until we receive some assurance of his future good conduct." John looked at his wife and pulled a face.

Meanwhile, their host was warming to her theme. "Tell me, have you experienced difficulties with Peter's behaviour at home?" Her query had been addressed to Susan. "Although I suppose, with the demands of your work, Mrs Grant, you don't get that much time to spend with him."

Susan glanced uneasily at her husband. "That's true to a point," she admitted. "And we employ a nanny for the children. But, having said that, we still spend as much time together as a family as possible."

She again glanced across at her husband for support.

"The fact is," stated John frankly, "ever since his early days Peter has exhibited certain strange behaviours."

"John!" Susan frowned.

"No, let's be fair about this, love," he persisted resolutely. "Some aspects of his conduct have been unusual to say the least."

"And they would be?" interrupted the head, as if sensing blood.

"Well," continued his father. "He's never done anything violent or destructive such as you've described here. It's more, I don't know." John was struggling. "It's more that he's extremely introverted. Almost as though he's searching for something from deep within his mind. I mean, for example he virtually takes no interest in any of his toys and hardly ever plays with his older sister." Once more, John caught a look of disapproval from his wife. "It's no good, love," he insisted again. "We've got to be honest." He turned his attention back to the headteacher. "When I heard about this incident with the fish tank," he continued, "it made me think because we have an aquarium at home. It's much bigger than the one you've got here, and it's actually built into the wall, but for some reason Peter spends hours on end just standing looking at the fish." He shook his head slowly. "And it's more than just a passing interest. It almost amounts to a fixation."

"And you never thought to seek help or advice?" enquired the head, slightly patronisingly. Then, at the parents' lack of response she added, "You do surprise me – especially you, Mr Grant, with all your experience in education. However, under the circumstances, I suggest that your son should be properly assessed by a psychiatrist who may prescribe a series of therapeutic consultations. But whatever the result, I must stress that Peter's return to school will depend very much on a satisfactory medical report. So, I'll leave you to arrange the details with your local GP."

Her final words left John in no doubt that the painful interview was now at an end, and as he got to his feet she began thumbing through her diary before reaching for the phone – a blatant sign that there were other matters that needed attention. And yet, as John and his wife made to leave, she unexpectedly glanced up at him with a smile and mouthed a silent goodbye – a further sign that reflected the instinctual needs of a woman obscured by a facade of authoritarianism.

Once clear of the stifling atmosphere of the head's study, Susan suddenly stopped in the corridor and glanced about before giving her husband a very straight look.

"That woman fancied you."

"Can I help it if the fair sex find me attractive?" he grinned smugly while raising his arms in a token of mock guilt. "I mean, it just goes to show how lucky you are to have me." For which gem he received a clip round the shoulder from his wife's handbag.

"Why, you conceited..."

But further suitable superlatives eluded her. It was, however, a brief moment of fun in an otherwise very stressful morning, well rounded off by John's cryptic observation, "Can you begin to imagine what it would be like to get caught up with a tarantula of that magnitude? No wonder she's still a Miss!"

Peter's referral for psychiatric assessment turned out to be but one of a series of medical problems soon to face the Grant household. Susan had smoked during her entire adult life, and her lungs were beginning to give rise for concern. In her early forties, she'd always been slightly asthmatic. However, she was now becoming increasingly dependent on the use of a nebuliser and John insisted she consult a private specialist.

Her appointment was set for a Monday, but on the preceding Saturday, their son again caused a serious reappraisal of his behaviour. Suspended from primary school, Jeanette had taken over his home education, and although she was very competent, Peter's morose and resentful attitude proved very unrewarding. As a result, she'd decided to keep lesson time to the minimum of half an hour each day, and this included Saturdays; it was a move specifically designed to avoid boredom and Peter's resultant irritability. However, on the occasion in question, they had been exploring a book depicting various ships which ranged from huge sea-going liners to small rowing boats.

At first all seemed well. The boy appeared genuinely interested until they came upon an illustration of an early horse-drawn barge. It was depicted being pulled along one of the canals which formed a network of transport across England during the eighteenth century. The waterway itself was shown winding away towards distant hills, and the sight of it sent Peter into an uncontrollable spiral of anger.

"I don't like picture! I don't like picture!" he repeated again and again in his strangely guttural voice. Then, in a frenzy of temper, he tore the offending page from the book before screwing it into a tight ball and hurling it across the nursery floor.

But worse was to follow, because when Jeanette reached to restrain him, she experienced first-hand the full extent of his fury, for as with Miss Francis, he scored his fingernails deep down the side of her face.

Stunned by the ferocity of this onslaught, John's ex staggered back clutching at the side of her bleeding cheek while Peter, having reached the nursery entrance, screamed back, "I hate you! I hate you!" then slammed the door shut with every ounce of his manic strength.

By the time Jeanette reached the hallway, the boy had vanished while the sound of the crashing door had brought John onto the scene, closely followed by his wife.

"Jeanette! What on earth's going on and what's happened to your face?" Susan exclaimed upon seeing the blood seeping through the nanny's fingers. But, when John's ex moved her hand it revealed the scarlet wheals on her cheek. Susan knew the answer only too well. "Peter! The vicious little sod." Despite him being their son, she felt unable to restrain her gut reaction and turned furiously to her husband. "John, never mind waiting for consultations with psychiatrists. That boy needs a damn good old-fashioned thrashing. Look at the state of Jeanette's face. He's nothing but a little barbarian."

However, the retired teacher looked dubious.

"I'm not sure further violence is necessarily the answer," he responded guardedly.

But this second incident, following so closely on the heels of the school episode, had left his wife completely out of patience.

"John, sort it out!" She then turned to the injured woman. "Come on, Jeanette. Let's get you into the kitchen where I can get a proper look at those scratches." But, once John's ex was seated at the large dining table, light from the bay window revealed just how serious the wounds were. One was especially deep and continued to ooze blood. "I'll do what I can," promised Susan as she applied cotton wool dipped in antiseptic. "But then I'll have to take you to A&E. I'm so sorry," she added. "I can hardly believe he's my own son. There's been absolutely no remorse shown over his behaviour at school, and it's making me wonder if he's not psychotic. But tell me, was there anything in particular that sparked him off?"

Flinching from the sting of the iodine, Jeanette did her best to relate the sequence of events that had culminated in Peter's excessive reaction.

"I don't understand why he should behave like that," she stressed. "It was a pleasant enough picture which just showed a canal and some hills in the background. Up till then, we'd looked at lots of illustrations depicting boats and there'd been no problem at all."

Even as she had listened, a disturbing possibility flashed through Susan's mind. Could there be, she wondered, some sort of eerie connection between the boy fishing along the Arun and the picture of the barge? But she just as quickly dismissed the idea because Peter had never actually seen the canvas. It had been taken down and stored in the basement of the Portakabin some time before his birth, and it had remained there ever since. Even so, as she helped John's ex to her feet, the worries persisted. Was her son really a re-embodiment of the artist's dead son who had carried forward memories of happy times spent fishing with his father?

She shivered slightly and the perceptive nanny was quick to notice.

"Yes, yes. I'm fine," Susan assured her.

Jeanette had never been privy to Pastor Tim's warnings, and Susan had no desire to change the situation, contenting herself to steer the injured woman in the direction of the front door while at the same time advising her to keep the facial pad firmly in place.

With Susan and his ex gone, John was left to contemplate his admonition to 'get it sorted'. He had, of course, always been aware of his wife's practical, no-nonsense approach to life, but he did sometimes wonder if he'd chosen the Brenda option whether she would have spoken to him in quite the same off-hand manner. He felt slightly humiliated, because although Susan was now a senior housing officer, he himself had once held a very responsible post in education. But even so, and with his later success in business, he did slightly envy her rocketing career. Achievement in public life was one thing, while quietly working as a professional landlord from home was quite another.

Be that as it may, he was nevertheless an educational product of his age when one would never normally countenance the corporal punishment of children, and certainly not one of his son's tender years. And where the hell was Peter anyway? The farmhouse was a large property which could afford numerous hiding places for a small child, and John knew he faced an exhaustive search both inside the house and the Portakabin. There were also other outlying buildings to take into account, such as the barn and the stable block.

Susan and Jeanette didn't arrive back from hospital until something after 5pm, and he'd still found no sign of his recalcitrant son while Susan looked almost as vexed as when she'd first left the house.

"John, can I have a word with you in the kitchen?" she asked tersely, almost before getting past the front door.

Oh no. Not more shit, he thought.

But his wife had already turned her attention to Jeanette who was now wearing a surgical pad taped to the side of her face.

"Jeanette," she said gently. "Go and make yourself comfortable in the drawing room and watch the television with Miriam. I'll bring you a cup of coffee shortly." Susan then turned to her husband. "John," she repeated while indicating the kitchen entrance. "We need to talk."

Ensuring he wouldn't be seen, John couldn't resist turning his eyes up.

"Grab a couple of glasses of wine while you're at it," she suggested, "because we're both going to need a drink." Then, once ensconced on the sofa and with the requisite stimulant, she added bluntly, "Your ex-wife could be scarred for life by our son's actions. Well, that's unless we're prepared to pay for some pretty expensive plastic surgery. And even then, the doctor didn't like to say if the damage to her face could be completely rectified." She reached for her cigarettes but started to cough almost immediately after lighting up.

John had always hated tobacco smoke and quickly moved away to the far end of the kitchen.

"Look!" he exclaimed exasperatedly. "You're seeing a specialist on Monday because of your breathing problems, so why the hell don't you cut it out. For goodness sake, think woman. Where would the kids be without you?"

But Susan was too wracked by coughing to give an immediate reply.

"You've always got your ex," she managed finally, after slowly regaining her breath. "I don't think she's likely to be going anywhere soon."

"I have not 'got my ex', as you put it," he frowned

impatiently, "and want no part of her. I only tolerate the situation because she's good with the kids and you seem to like her. Otherwise..."

And so saying, he drew a forefinger across his Adam's apple accompanied by a screeching sound of his tongue.

"And what have you done about Peter?" she enquired while ignoring his crude gesture.

John expelled a long breath of frustration as he returned to the sofa.

"The simple answer to that," he replied, "is nothing. Because although I've searched the damn place from top to bottom, I just can't find a trace of him anywhere."

"Do you know, John," she said with a noticeable drop in her voice, "there are times when I wish he'd never been born? I know that sounds terrible," she added wretchedly, "but I'm afraid it's the truth. He never responds to any affection, never spends any time with Miriam, hardly ever speaks, and when he does it's in that strange deep voice of his." Then, indicating the aquarium, she noted, "The only things he seems interested in are those fish. John," she stressed finally, "you have to admit there appears to be some link between our son and things to do with water life."

Her husband leaned forward while clasping his hands between his knees, but even as he made to agree, he became aware of a slight movement in the kitchen entrance, and swivelling round on the sofa caught sight of the wayward child himself. At the same time, Susan shouted, "And what do you think you're doing in that hat?" John instantly recognised the cause of her anguish, for there, standing in the doorway, was their five-year-old son with his head almost obscured by a large tatty old straw hat. Turning to his wife, they exchanged mutual glances while at the same time he raised a warning finger to his lips.

"Leave this to me, Susan. I'll deal with it. You go and join Jeanette in the drawing room."

However, Peter's mother was unable to contain herself. "When your father's finished with you, I also want a few words."

One question burned in John's brain. How had his son come by the hat?

"Peter," he called out in a voice that precluded any thought of disobedience. "Come over here." His son responded by raising both hands to the hat's brim and pulling it back to reveal a face full of resentment. "Did you hear me, Peter? Come over here at once," he commanded.

Slowly and reluctantly, the child moved across the kitchen to stand looking up at his father. John went to put his hands on the boy's shoulders in an attempt to establish some sort of rapport, but Peter immediately and furiously rejected the affectionate gesture.

"Peter," insisted John. "I need to know why you attacked Jeanette. You've hurt her face terribly. Why would you do such a thing when she's only ever been kind to you? It was very bad and cruel." But the boy just stared back sullenly with the same unblinking eyes and said nothing. "Look!" shouted his father while forcibly grabbing him by the shoulders. "Why did you hurt the nanny? She's never done you any harm."

At this point John began to appreciate something of what Miss Francis had been through, for with a strength beyond his years the miscreant tore at John's wrists in a frantic attempt to break free. It was, of course, futile with such a powerfully built man, and fast running out of patience, John shook him angrily.

"Listen. Tell me. Why are you being so naughty?"

For a brief moment, the child seemed to relax, while the deep baleful look in his eyes began to fade, and as John continued to watch he could almost detect some inner mental turmoil taking place in the boy's mind.

"Daddy," he began in a voice devoid of its normal depth. "I don't know why I was so naughty to Jeanette."

Sensing a breakthrough, John hunkered down to his son's level. "Can you perhaps tell me about the fish at your school?" he asked gently. "And why you took them out of their tank and left them to die on the floor?"

Studying his son's face carefully, it seemed as though two diametrically opposing forces were struggling for supremacy, and as he continued to watch, John was struck by an alarming thought. Could it be that his real son was engaged in a conflict between himself and some other nameless horror or entity that, up until then, had always held the upper hand? However, even as these thoughts flashed across his mind he saw the boy trying to answer his question.

"I don't know, Daddy, why I wanted to kill the fish."

But, even before he could finish John detected the all too familiar gravel sound creep back into Peter's speech, and glancing at his eyes he saw their deep green was also starting to return.

Later that evening, John sat down with his wife for a serious discussion concerning the brief but strange change that had overcome their son earlier on.

"Now," he suggested, "I know you've sometimes feared Peter's peculiarities might in some way be the result of reincarnation, and I must admit that there have been times when I've suspected the same thing. But after what I've witnessed today, I'm all but certain that's not the case."

"And?" queried his better half drawing up her legs and reclining back on the sofa. "What alternative gem did you come up with?"

Her craving for a cigarette and the nicotine comfort it offered was almost overwhelming, but at the same time she was desperately aware that her life was at stake if she persisted.

"I've studied educational psychology," observed

her husband as he moved over to accommodate his wife's legs after having learned the lesson of sofa etiquette. "But I'm no clinical psychologist. However, after what happened today it does make me wonder if perhaps Peter's suffering from what some experts would call a dissociative syndrome. Although, apparently, there's a lot of disagreement as to the exact nature of the disorder."

"But what does dissociative, or whatever you call it, actually mean?" Susan frowned.

"Well," he began, "basically, it's akin to having two minds in the same brain. I know, I know," he stressed while holding up both hands despairingly as he caught her expression. "It's a horrible thought and it's only a theory, but if that's the case then we have to ask ourselves why has it taken some five years before we've caught a glimpse of a second personality?" He sighed wearily, and getting up made for the 'medicinal' cabinet. "It's the only rational explanation for his behaviour that I can come up with," he added over his shoulder.

Then, reaching into the cabinet he bypassed the wine section and grabbed a whisky bottle from which he took a long, grateful swallow. Gasping on the liquid's sting, he nevertheless wasted no time in taking down a second draught.

"And you know," he continued with a touch of sadness while returning to the sofa, "for a few moments back there, Peter was the lovely little boy I'd always imagined he would be. And, what was worse, I could see he genuinely didn't understand why he'd behaved so badly. I doubt whether he even remembered attacking Jeanette at all. In fact, I think it's probable that he's being controlled by some influence too powerful for him to resist."

John stopped and looked far away through their bay window. Far away towards the pale grey clouds which lazily drifted across an azure sky; a tranquil and different world where such problems had no place.

"Whatever's happened to Jeanette's face?" Unnoticed, their daughter had entered the kitchen. Fast approaching fifteen, she was a tall elegant girl and doing well at school, but she was appalled when informed of the afternoon's events. "What's the matter with him?" she exclaimed. "He's only just caused all that trouble at school, and who on earth's going to look after him now? I can't imagine Jeanette will want any more to do with him."

"Fortunately," answered her mother, "she's quite prepared to carry on. Although, I must admit I'm more than a little surprised. But," added John's wife with a slight smile, "she said on the way back from the hospital, 'I'll give the little sod more than he bargained for if he comes it again.' And I tell you what. I believe her."

Returning to the sofa, John stretched luxuriously before contracting back on himself like a rubber band.

"Phew! I needed that," he breathed before turning

to his daughter. "Shouldn't young ladies of your age be in bed and fast asleep? That is," he smiled, "unless you want to become a raddled oldie like us before your time."

"Err, less of your raddled oldies if you don't mind," objected Susan indignantly. "Although, if you're just referring to yourself, of course, be my guest."

Miriam had been standing close enough to catch a whiff of her father's breath. "Daddy, have you been drinking?" she enquired anxiously.

"No poppet. Not in the sense that you're thinking," he hastened to assure her. "As you know, I only rarely share a glass of wine with your mum. But after what's happened recently, I'm afraid I needed something a bit stronger. But don't worry. It won't become a habit." He moved over to drop a kiss on his wife's head. "I'm off to my retreat, love, to listen to a bit of Johnny Cash and try to relax. So, I'll see you later on upstairs."

Entering the small room that in all probability had once been somebody's study, John quietly closed the door and completely surrendered to the atmosphere of his lost youth. Although it was the last word in escapism, he felt no less a man for looking back to a happier and far simpler way of life. However, no sooner had he sat down than he got up and crossed over to the ottoman trunk situated by the side of his desk. He always kept it locked. Not only because it housed one of his most prized possessions, but also for safety reasons. Throwing back the lid, he lifted out a .22 rifle.

A member of the combined army cadet force while at grammar school, he'd been introduced to the weapon in his teens, and although disliking its malign purpose, nevertheless took to it straight away. The beauty of its design and balance had always appealed to the aesthetic side of his nature and he'd determined that, come the day, he'd have one of his own. Indeed, their move to the countryside had seemed an appropriate opportunity, for he had fully intended to join in all the usual pursuits associated with rural living. But the best of hopes...? For the acquisition of the gun had been as far as his dreams were realised. The demands of life and business had allowed for little in the way of self-indulgence.

Returning to his chair, he nostalgically fondled the weapon's shiny walnut butt and savoured the mechanical smoothness of its firing mechanism.

After removing the bolt, he raised the gun up towards the light and peered down the barrel. But never having been fired, it gleamed back as a spotless spiral of polished metal. Replacing the firing mechanism, he leaned the weapon against the side of his chair. Then reaching for one of his desk drawers, he withdrew a small cardboard box. Marked 'Caution .22 ammunition', its seal had never been broken, and, somehow, it held an echo of his relationship with Brenda. Close but never realised. Removing the lid, he loaded one of the small shells into the breech and locked it in place with a crisp movement of the firing bolt. Then, lifting the stock to his shoulder, he squinted along the sights at imaginary targets within the room. However, in the middle of this man's-play, the door suddenly burst open to reveal his wife who was obviously very agitated.

"John! You'll have to come at once. There's been an emergency at 19 Black Street. The sewer cover in the basement has burst open and the whole of the lower ground floor is awash with sewage."

"Call the plumber and Southern Water," he responded urgently. "I'll have to go straightaway." And with that, he dashed from the room.

John's next twenty-four hours were nothing short of a nightmare, and it was late Sunday night before he finally managed to crawl back home. Totally spent after nearly twenty-four hours on the go, he dropped into bed utterly exhausted.

Chapter 7

IT TRANSPIRED THAT appointments with psychiatrists were few and far between, and several months passed before Peter's assessment. In the meantime, things were destined to go from bad to worse for the Grant household. Monday following the horrific weekend saw a very tired John and his wife in the consulting room of a lung specialist – not that the actual consultant was present. He wasn't.

"What do you expect?" grumbled Susan's husband.

He leaned back lazily and crossed his long, outstretched legs before adding superciliously, "Certainly not punctuality. If there's one thing you can be sure of in the world of medicine, it's wait and wait...!"

"Oh, for heaven's sake, stop moaning," objected an equally frustrated Susan. "It's bad enough being here in the first place, without having to listen to your griping all the time."

"Mr Huston will be with you shortly," came a sudden disembodied voice.

Turning, John was just in time to catch sight of a nurse's face disappearing from round the edge of the door. He pulled a grimace and stretched out ever lower in his chair, while folding his arms and looking up at the ceiling.

"Of course," he mimicked. "The question is, just how short is shortly?"

But in the event, 'shortly' meant just that, for no sooner had he spoken than a tall, grey-haired, distinguished looking man entered the room. Although of similar age and height to John, that was about where the similarities ended. Here was a man of immaculate appearance whose collar and tie looked as though they had been made on him while Peter's father couldn't remember the last time he even wore a tie, and his naturally unruly hair had always just been left to its own devices. However, upon the doctor's entry, he mustered just about sufficient respect to at least sit upright.

"Mr and Mrs Grant. I must apologise for being late."

Then, after taking a seat behind his desk, the doctor spent several minutes studying his computer screen before eventually swinging round in his high-backed chair to deliver a verdict.

"Mrs Grant. The good news is that there's no sign of anything malignant in your lungs."

"Thank God for that," breathed Susan with a sigh of relief.

"However," continued the consultant gravely,

"your lungs are nevertheless in a very serious condition. I believe you already rely on a nebuliser and this is because you are showing the early signs of pulmonary disease, or emphysema."

"And in layman's terms?" interjected John.

White coat sat back in his chair and joined the tips of his fingers.

"The lungs, Mr Grant," he explained patiently, "are lined with tiny sacs which transfer the oxygen we breathe into our bloodstream. If, however," he continued, "these filters get damaged, they become less efficient, and the patient struggles to make up the deficit by straining to take in ever more air. In other words, they become breathless."

"Which is what's happened in my wife's case," stated John bluntly.

"I'm afraid so, yes. But, fortunately it's only in the early stages, and provided she no longer smokes her condition should at least stabilise. But," he insisted, "I must stress that this will depend very much upon her total abstinence from tobacco."

"Don't you dare tell me, I told you so," echoed Susan as they returned to the car.

John wisely refrained from comment as he turned the ignition key. Finally, however, as they made their way out onto the main road he observed quietly, "Let's look forward to a long, healthy life together. There's nothing to be gained by going back over old ground."

He'd tried to sound optimistic and it would be desperately needed when they eventually arrived home. It was still early September, and marked the decline of a very indifferent summer. Indeed, as John drove north he was not surprised to see ominous and heavy-looking clouds closing in from the west.

"If that's a storm, I shan't be very pleased," he grumbled. "Especially after the summer we've barely had."

He'd only just spoken however, when a deafening clap of thunder almost rocked the car and driving rain suddenly lashed against the windscreen with such force he was temporarily blinded. Even the wipers at full stretch failed to make much impression, and after switching his headlights on to the main beam he was compelled to reduce speed to a crawl.

"Well," sighed his wife, "I was hoping to get to work this afternoon, but by the look of this lot there'll be a fat chance of that."

Immediately ahead, a blinding jagged flash of lightning tore through the increasing gloom and caused her to duck instinctively, while drumming rain on the roof virtually precluded the possibility of any serious conversation.

However, by the time they turned into the lane at the bottom of their drive, the storm had begun to recede towards the east, although the rain still remained very heavy. But, as John peered ahead, he was stunned to see blue tape stretching across the entrance to their drive.

"What the dickens is going on?" he exclaimed angrily as he got out of the car.

But reaching to rip the obstruction down, he suddenly caught sight of the flashing blue lights of two police cars parked directly in front of the farmhouse. With no coat, he was immediately drenched and wasted no time in getting back behind the wheel. But his wife looked as white as a sheet.

"John, what do you possibly suppose can have happened?" she whispered fearfully.

"I don't know," he frowned. "But I bloody well intend to find out."

And with that, he roared up the drive. John had never had much time for authority. To him, the police were a bit like angels. You believed they probably existed, but never actually saw them. However, as he neared the house, a senior officer clad in a yellow rain-soaked oilskin, held up a restraining hand and approached the driver's window. Drips fell steadily from the peak of his uniform cap as he leaned forward to speak.

"I'm afraid, sir, this is an official crime scene. So, may I ask you to state your business here."

John was finding difficulty in containing his temper.

"My business!" he snapped. "I'm John Grant and my business is that I own the place. Lock stock and bloody barrel."

"There's no need for rudeness, sir," replied the officer. "We're dealing with a very serious firearms offence." On hearing this, John immediately felt his heart sink and his fury melt away to become replaced by apprehension; a shift in attitude that the senior officer was quick to sense. "I think, sir, it would be better if we discussed the matter in the house." Then, turning his attention to Susan, he observed, "I take it this lady is your wife? Mrs Grant? How do you do, madam." His voice carried a gracious ring. "Please allow me to introduce myself. I'm Chief Inspector Hocks; Jim Hocks to be precise." The ghost of a smile flicked across his officially stern features, and despite her agitation, Susan felt a certain warmth for the man. "I'm sorry," he continued, "that we could not have met under happier circumstances."

Despite his authority, he was obviously a consummate gentleman – although that was not exactly how John would have described him. He had his own quite different vocabulary for such men.

"If you could just park to one side, sir," instructed the chief inspector, "it will allow my officers free access to the house."

Closing the window, John mimicked, "'If you could just park to one side, sir!' Who the hell does he think he is, ordering me about on my own land?"

"John," protested his wife. "Don't you think we've got enough trouble on our hands without you throwing a tantrum?"

With the car duly positioned, he pulled on the handbrake.

"You wait here, love, and I'll get your coat.

There's no point in us both getting wet through, and it'll give me a chance to see what it is we're dealing with inside."

Upon entering the house, however, he immediately became horrified to see a large bloodstain on the front doorstep which gradually trailed away across the hallway floor. But, barely had this time to register before he was almost bowled over by his ex who had rushed forward to throw her arms around his neck in a way she'd never done, even during the best days of their marriage. This, though, was no embrace of passion, but rather one of utter relief.

"Oh John!" she exclaimed hysterically while releasing her hold with a sudden rush of embarrassment. "I'm so thankful you're back. It's been an absolute nightmare. Peter managed to get hold of your gun and fired it at the postman!"

"Excuse me, sir," interrupted the senior officer. "But I need to discuss this matter in an orderly manner."

With Susan by his side, John entered the kitchen area which now resembled something like a scene from a Darth Vader movie. Situated either side of the bay window stood two men in full body armour with sub-machine guns across their chests. Totally clad in black with gleaming dark helmets and tinted visors, they could easily have dropped in from a nearby star system. Complementing this dynamic duo were two sour-faced constables standing either side of the kitchen entrance, and never short on sarcasm, John was quick off the mark.

"Bloody hell!" he mumbled. "What are we expecting? An invasion?"

"I'm sorry, sir," explained the chief inspector. "But this is standard procedure in such circumstances." And with that, he dismissed the two armed officers before inviting John and his wife to take a seat at the table.

"What circumstances?" queried John irritably. "What the hell circumstances are we talking about?"

But it was an irrelevant question, for he knew deep down perfectly well what circumstances. His apparently psychotic son had obviously sneaked into the little retreat and found the loaded .22 rifle, which in the emergency of late Saturday night he'd neglected to lock away in the ottoman trunk. The real quandary, of course, was what had Jeanette been up to while Peter was roaming around with a loaded gun?

"Before I discuss the situation," answered the chief inspector, "I want to talk to you about your son who, incidentally, is with a social worker in the drawing room. Because after what's happened, we have to ensure he's being brought up in a safe and secure environment."

If anyone else had made such a suggestion, they would almost certainly have found themselves on the wrong end of John's fist.

"I'll have you know, inspector," he snapped. "My children want for nothing. They're dearly loved by both myself and my wife. In addition to which, they have the fulltime care and attention of a nanny."

"But what about discipline?" retorted the officer. "I understand from this lady that due to his behaviour Peter was suspended from school on the very first day of term."

The officer had a point, but John was in an impossible dilemma, for how could he explain the concept of an evil influence that might have accompanied his son's possible reincarnation of someone long dead? In the event, however, Susan came to the rescue.

"Inspector. Everything my husband has said is perfectly correct, and I can assure you we are both firm and supportive of our son. But having said that, it's true he has displayed some distressing traits; traits which need professional attention, and therefore he's been referred for psychiatric assessment. I can promise you, inspector, even with all their training, your social workers could do no more."

The chief officer didn't respond directly but went on to discuss the situation when he'd first arrived.

"A man, who I later discovered was a Post Office employee, was being loaded into an ambulance. He was obviously in great pain, and when I asked the paramedic the nature of his injury I was informed he'd been shot through the groin and had lost a great deal of blood."

"Urgh! Nasty," muttered John under his breath. "Very nasty."

"Sorry, Mr Grant?"

But Susan's husband merely shook his head.

"Nothing, inspector. Just carry on."

A dubious expression flickered across the officer's face.

"You must realise, before I got here," he continued, "all I knew was that there had been a shooting incident – hence my armed escort. But even when I stepped over that pool of blood at the entrance, I had no idea a child had been involved." While he was speaking, the officer reached down side of his chair to retrieve a plastic-wrapped rifle which he placed on the table. "Is this your property, sir?" he asked bluntly.

"As far as I can see," replied John equally abruptly.

"And may I ask the purpose of you possessing such a weapon?" enquired the officer cautiously. "After all, it's hardly the sort of gun one would normally associate with a country shoot. I also assume you have an appropriate licence!"

After Peter's father had explained his affinity with a .22 rifle, the officer lifted it from the table and hefted it in both hands.

"Rather heavy for a child to hold and fire with any accuracy, wouldn't you say?"

"What are you implying?" retorted John. "That I did the shooting?"

"No, no," the inspector hastened to assure him. "It's not that. I know your son was responsible because the nanny explained what happened." He hesitated. "I don't know her name, I'm afraid."

"Mrs Gately. Jeanette Gately," came the brusque reply.

"Well, Mrs Gately," he continued, "was in a terrible state when I arrived. It seems that while she was called away to the phone, your son somehow or other got hold of the gun and the first she became aware of the fact was the sound of a shot. The question is, Mr Grant," he added, "how was it possible for your son to have access to a firearms weapon in the first place? Because, this sir," he emphasised while pointing to the plastic-wrapped gun, "should have been kept securely under lock and key."

After Susan had intervened in an attempt to explain the emergency situation of Saturday night, the inspector turned to one of the jaundiced faces still stationed by the kitchen entrance.

"Constable, would you be kind enough to ask the nanny to step in here for a moment?" Then while the man was gone, the chief inspector described how he had initially spent a short time with their son and the social worker, and he concluded, "I must say that although I have a certain amount of experience with children of that age, I've never come across anything like it."

John was no lover of other men and his dissatisfaction was clearly reflected in his terse response. "Perhaps my son didn't like the company."

It was rude, and he meant it to be. Although his wife was quick to object. "John, there's no need to be abusive. The inspector's only doing his job. After all, it's we who are in the wrong." She then turned to the officer. "I do apologise, inspector. But please, tell us, what did you find so unusual about our son?"

"Well, basically," he explained, disgusted by her husband's outburst, "your boy just refused to acknowledge anything I said. His only response was to glare at me. But more strangely, I didn't see him blink. Not even once." The officer leaned forward with one elbow on the table. "I mean, how do you manage to deal with a child like that? Anyway, in the end I said, 'Can you just tell me, Peter, where did you get the gun?' And it was then that he spoke for the first time. But it was the way he spoke. It sounded more like the guttural voice of an adult German man than a five-year-old boy."

John got to his feet and stuck his hands in the pockets of his jeans.

"And just exactly what did my son have to say?" But then he almost immediately regretted asking.

"He said," replied the inspector, "'My name's Ralph.' And that was all he said." Susan exchanged a horrified glance with her husband. "Does the name mean anything to you?" enquired the perceptive officer. "I understand your boy's called Peter."

"That's right. But take it from me," asserted a shaken John, "you really don't want to know about the name Ralph."

"Well, that's entirely for me to decide," corrected the officer. But even as he spoke, vinegar-face re-entered the kitchen accompanied by Jeanette. "Ah,

Mrs Gattley!" he exclaimed. "I would appreciate it if you could again go over what happened today."

John's ex was quick to correct him.

"Gately," she asserted. "The name is Mrs Gately." Then she added under her breath, "To my sorrow."

"Oh, I do apologise. But please take a seat." The officer smiled.

The inspector was a handsome man, who obviously knew he had a way with the ladies and Jeanette was quick to succumb to his charm, although the overt exchange of mutual appreciation left John feeling quite nauseous.

"As you may have gathered," she began slowly while looking hesitantly at Susan and her husband, "Peter is not the easiest of children."

But, while speaking she unwittingly touched the side of her face which still bore the fading signs of her ward's attack.

"Would you perhaps care to tell me how you came by those marks on your face?" enquired the officer gently. Again, Jeanette glanced tentatively at her benefactors, but John just nodded while the chief inspector looked increasingly grim as she acquainted him with the facts. "And none of this was ever reported?" he queried.

"I didn't want to make an already difficult situation worse," she explained. But her listener merely nodded.

"Sometimes you know, it's better to nip these things in the bud."

His remark made John increasingly exasperated and he threw caution aside. "All your social workers and psychiatrists on earth can't nip what might be some sort of evil, in the bud," he snapped.

"I'm sorry, Mr Grant, but I only deal with learned patterns of behaviour and inherited traits. Unproven concepts such as evil, play no part in my mandate."

"Narrow-minded intellectual bigot," muttered Susan's husband under his breath. But, nevertheless, it was a put-down and he knew it.

Meanwhile, the inspector had returned his attention to Jeanette. "Please, do continue."

"Well," explained the nanny. "Because of Peter's difficulties, we only ever spend between thirty minutes and an hour on education. But anyway, this morning things seemed to be going quite well. We were looking at letters of the alphabet, and he was copying some of them down onto the blackboard in the nursery. Anyway, in the middle of it all, the drawing room phone rang, and I told Peter to finish the last of his letters while I was away. In hindsight, of course, I should have just let it ring, because while I was away I suddenly heard the crack of a gunshot."

"At about what time would that have been?" enquired the inspector.

"Oh, two-ish or thereabouts. But what really frightened me was that it sounded so close, and when I dropped the phone and rushed out into the hallway the first thing I saw was Peter holding this rifle; and worse, that poor postman lying half way across the doorstep writhing in agony." She shivered involuntarily. "It was horrible. Like something out of a bad dream. There were bloodstained letters scattered everywhere."

"Excuse me for a moment, Mrs Gattley," interrupted the officer. "But why was the front door left open in the first place?"

"Mrs Gately," Jeanette again asserted patiently, although a second apology was obviously not forthcoming. "Well, inspector," she explained, indicating her ex. "John – that is, Mr Grant – usually has a lot of mail and the letterbox is often quite inadequate, so we leave the door on the latch so that the postman can come in and drop any excess mail on the monk's seat. You must realise, inspector, that I was in an impossible situation, because much as I wanted to help the poor man and phone for an ambulance, I had Peter pointing this gun at me and I was absolutely terrified he would shoot me as well. You see, I had no means of knowing the gun only held one bullet."

"So, what actually did you do?" asked John.

"I'd learned from experience that it would have been quite futile to try to persuade him to give me the weapon, so I turned away suddenly and shouted, 'What was that?' at the top of my voice. Then, as he looked, I managed to grab it from him."

The officer nodded.

"A very commendable and brave action."

"I was desperate!" she exclaimed. "Normally, I'm very patient and do all that I can to encourage him, but I was so shaken up I just screamed, 'You naughty, evil boy,' and ordered him into the nursery." She shrugged. "Well, anyway, you know the rest."

"Indeed, I do, and if I'd been in your shoes," observed the officer, "I'd probably have called him a lot worse." He turned his attention back to John and his wife as he rose to leave. "I shall have to place this case with the public prosecutor for his consideration. In the meantime, your gun will be impounded for forensic tests and possible evidence." He reached to shake Jeanette's hand as the ghost of a smile again flickered over his handsome features. "A truly terrifying experience."

And with that, the 'invaders' made their way to the exit while John turned to his wife, "No handshakes for us. We, the great unwashed. The condemned."

Distressful events can often occur in triplicate, and so it transpired that fateful rain-drenched Monday, for as Miriam returned from school she almost bumped into the inspector and his troops on their way out. Squeezing past the last constable, she raced into the kitchen after being horrified at the sight of the bloodstained doorstep.

"Mum! What's going on?" she cried tearfully.

"It's all right darling," replied Susan holding their daughter close in an attempt to comfort her.

"But all that blood in the doorway?" Miriam whispered fearfully.

"There's been a slight accident with your dad's gun," explained her mother gently. "But as you can see, we're all fine."

John held back to look affectionately at the two women who meant so much to him. He was particularly proud of his daughter who always looked so smart in her school uniform with its midi-length, pleated grey skirt and monogrammed dark blue blazer. She was a tall, slim girl who with her long dark hair and glasses gave an air of quiet studiousness. But his fond reflections were suddenly interrupted by his ex.

"Oh, John. In case you're wondering," she began, but then quietly mouthed, "I've put those letters in your little room."

His wave of acknowledgement combined appreciation with dismissal and she quickly took the hint.

Later that evening while Peter was in bed and they were sitting down to supper, Miriam raised a problematic topic. It was problematic because John and his wife had decided early on to say nothing to her of the questionable circumstances surrounding the Barrington's auction house purchase.

Starters that evening again consisted of soup, which despite a busy schedule Susan had managed to concoct herself. But, as John stirred the thick brown oxtail broth in anticipation, Miriam asked suddenly,

"Daddy, why have you put that picture of the boy fishing in the storage area under the Portakabin?"

He looked at his wife.

"Well," her father smiled evasively, "it's been there for some time, so why do you ask now?"

"Oh," she replied. "I realised it had gone and thought perhaps you'd sold it. I know you like pictures in the house and that you buy and sell them from time-to-time. But the thing is," she persisted, "won't it get spoilt out there? It's got mildew over it already."

During this inquisition, John had held a spoonful of soup poised half way to his mouth, and before answering he completed the manoeuvre with a certain appreciation. However, Miriam hadn't finished and adjusted her spectacles as she looked straight at her father. "There's also something else, Dad. Not that it's important I suppose, but I seem to remember the boy in the picture was wearing some sort of hat. You know, a bit like the one in the story of Tom Sawyer, all tatty and frayed. But, the strange thing is it's not there anymore."

"Are you quite sure you've looked properly?" he asked gently while at the same time proffering his empty bowl in the hope of a top up. But his wife just raised her hands in a negative gesture.

"Sorry. It's all gone."

John turned his attention back to his daughter.

"In any case, what were you doing poking about under the Portakabin?"

"Oh. Do pardon me," she objected. "I didn't realise the place was out of bounds, but if you must know I was looking for a tennis racket which disappeared from my room, and I found it out there all covered in mildew as well." At this point, an agitated Susan reiterated her husband's earlier question.

"Mum," Miriam stressed, "I saw that picture every day when it was above the fireplace, so I know the boy wore a hat and the fact is he hasn't got one on now. There's also something else which seems a bit of a coincidence," she continued, "because yesterday I saw the same sort of tatty old hat in the nursery."

John glimpsed both perplexity and a ghost of fear flicker across his daughter's face, and he glanced towards his wife. But from her expression as she got up to clear away the dishes, it was obvious she found their daughter's remarks very disturbing.

"Well, you can't read a lot into that," he tried reassuringly while leaning back and folding his arms. "But I can assure you, the boy's hat didn't just jump out of that picture and turn up in the nursery, if that's what you're worried about."

It was a half-truth, because he knew his wife had thought along similar lines when Peter had showed up wearing something similar a few days previously. Nevertheless, he continued to strive for a more rational explanation.

"You've got to realise," he added, "parts of this house and some of the outbuildings in the small field are very old and were never fully cleared out before we moved in. So, I think Peter probably just found it amongst a lot of other leftover rubbish. Remember, it's the sort of thing farmers would have worn in the old days."

After her father's exposition, the meal progressed in relative quiet, at the end of which Miriam moved round the table to kiss her parents goodnight.

"Goodnight, love," responded her father. "Sleep tight."

Later, as Susan placed steaming hot cups of coffee on the table, she observed dryly, "A polished piece of invention, John, if ever I heard it."

"Well, not really," he replied defensively while slowly stirring his drink. "We don't know for certain where the hat came from. I think it's quite feasible that Peter might have found it somewhere. I mean, honestly," John shrugged, "what's the alternative? It jumped out of the picture straight onto his head?"

"There's no need to be facetious," she objected while taking her seat at the far end of the table. "You tell me, how did our five-year-old son manage to come up with the name Ralph? It must be a million to one chance against. Not only that, but according to the inspector he was adamant that was his name. No," she insisted while leaning forward with her elbows on the table and lifting her drink in both hands. "It's too much of a coincidence, and the more I think about it the more I think we're dealing with something beyond our understanding." She lowered her cup. Then, raising her eyebrows, she added, "Tell me. Have you seen that picture lately? Because if not, I suggest you get out there and check it, for if what Miriam said is right then it's time we got some serious spiritual help."

"I hope you're not suggesting I go out there now. It's pouring with rain and absolutely pitch black," he objected.

"Well, if you don't I will," she stated adamantly. She was, of course, bluffing, but, nevertheless, it called his manhood into question. So, with little alternative he crossed the kitchen and began rummaging in one of the drawers. "If you're looking for the flashlight, you'll find it in the cabinet, side of the 'medical section'."

And so, grabbing an oilskin he plunged out into the rain-soaked night. But, even with the assistance of the portable light, it was hard going. The grassy surface of the big field had become little more than a saturated swamp, and several times he nearly slipped headlong on patches of treacherous mud. Driving rain beating into his face made it difficult to even maintain a sense of direction and he wondered why on earth Susan couldn't have waited until the morning.

Finally, however, the beam of his torch pierced the gloom sufficiently for him to catch sight of his objective. But with torrents of water pouring off his oilskin and saturating his trousers, it all seemed a very different world from the one they'd shared with Pastor Tim earlier that autumn.

The storage area of the Portakabin lay immediately beneath the main structure, and although John ducked as he thankfully entered he nevertheless cursed as his head still caught the low doorway. Once inside the musty interior, he slowly ranged the beam of his torch over its various contents – much of which spoke of past memories; things that had once played a part in their lives, but, with the passage of time, had now become redundant.

Covered in thick layers of dust and laced with the work of spiders, they seemed to convey an almost intangible air of neglect and sadness. But perhaps the most poignant of all was the sight of two bicycles lying intertwined on the floor, as if in an attempt to comfort each other in their hour of neglect. Long gone was the original shine of their paintwork, while thick mildew strove to conceal the once brilliant chrome of their wheels and handlebars.

More than that though, like John's gun they represented a dream that had never been realised. And standing there in the gloom, he recalled the enthusiasm with which he and his wife had originally acquired them. At first, thrilled with the prospect of country life they'd determined to spend time together cycling round the rural lanes. However, complexities of life and the demands of work combined with parenthood had long since precluded any such hopes – although John had been loath to totally abandon the idea and stored them away in the hope that one day perhaps...

But the might-have-beens of yesterday had averted his attention from the true purpose of his visit, and he somewhat reluctantly swept the torchlight back across the floor where it picked out the now tarnished gilt frame. Originally propped against the wall, vibrations from activity overhead had caused the canvas to slip down onto the floor and become victim to the same corrosive effects suffered by its fellow inmates.

Although a smothering of dust and mildew obscured much of the picture, enough of it remained visible for him to feel a sick feeling of shock, for as his daughter had said, there in the dim light he could see no trace of the subject wearing any form of hat.

Scarcely able to believe his eyes – in fact, not wanting to believe them – John knelt down and desperately wiped away at the grime covering the area around the fisher boy's head. But it made no difference and only enabled him to see the subject's thick, dark hair more clearly. Numbed, he straightened up as far as the low oak-beamed ceiling would allow. Powerfully built, he'd never really been afraid of anything, and although of artistic temperament he possessed a well-balanced and logical mind. But now faced with the apparently inexplicable, he felt his reason momentarily stagger knowing there was no possible physical explanation for what he was witnessing.

John's faith had always prohibited anything to do with the occult. In his opinion, there was enough evil in the world already.

The incessant tattoo of rain against the Portakabin, however, jerked his mind back to the reality of the waterlogged slog he now faced on the way back to the house, and closing the door behind him he struck out into the torrential downpour.

Having changed his rain-sodden trousers, a rather dejected John traced his wife to the main drawing room. It had been a long, taxing day and he wearily sank down beside her on their Chesterfield couch, where, surprisingly, of all things, she was sitting holding the straw hat, while opposite, and with her legs drawn up, Jeanette reclined on a matching leather armchair. Deep in conversation, Susan broke off as he entered.

"It's all right, John," she exclaimed, seeing her husband's face. "I've told Jeanette everything. After all, she's been good enough to take the main responsibility for Peter, so if you'll pardon the expression, it's only fair to put her in the picture."

"Hmm. Very droll, I'm sure" he muttered. Then added, "It's not a question of who's in the picture. It's more a case of what's not in it."

Susan turned sharply in her seat.

"Why? What did you find out there? Was...?"

"Well!" he exclaimed before she could finish. "Apart from a lot of rain and a nearly broken neck, Miriam was right. There's not a sign that the boy ever wore a hat."

At this point, Jeanette spoke up. "From what Susan has told me, John," she ventured, "intangible influences are one thing, but if physical objects such as that hat are beginning to materialise then it does make you wonder where it'll all end. It seems to me," she continued hesitantly, "although I suppose, arguably, it's not for me to advise. But if I were you, I'd burn that picture before it brings about some disaster on the whole family."

Well, I'm not you, he thought irritably. And I'm damned if I'm going to incinerate a six-thousand-pound antique.

But seeing her husband's expression, Susan hastened to reinforce his ex.

"John, Jeanette's right," and she emphasised the point by fingering the ragged edges of the hat.

Peter's father, however, responded with his favourite trick of stretching out his long frame prior to heaving a massive sigh.

"I'll certainly think about it," he replied, casually getting to his feet. But it was a blasé attitude that only annoyed his wife.

"You'll do it, John. I mean it."

And from experience he knew she meant it.

"By the way, changing the subject," he asked while preparing to leave the room. "Has there been any news about that postman?"

"I've been in touch with the hospital," ventured Jeanette again who seemed to have an unusual amount to say for herself.

"You've been in touch, and...?"

"He's in the Princess Royal at Haywards Heath!" she exclaimed. "I'm not a relative so they'd only tell me that he's comfortable. But in any case, I'm going to visit him tomorrow evening after Susan gets back from work."

"Hmm. Very laudable, I'm sure," John muttered ungraciously before turning to his wife. "I'll be in the retreat for a bit, love. So, I'll see you upstairs later."

Sinking down into the comfort of his old armchair, John put his feet up and mulled over the traumatic events of the day – a day so different from that beautiful, sunny Easter bank holiday spent with Miriam and her nanny on Henfield common. The sheer joy on Brenda's face as she'd ridden the carousel stood in such stark contrast to the rain-soaked and blood-spattered threshold he'd returned to earlier on.

All in all, he concluded as he got to his feet, it had been a hellish twenty-four hours and he was glad to see the back of it. But what hopes he might have entertained for anything better the following day, were destined to be dashed by yet another disaster from a totally unexpected quarter.

Chapter 8

NORMALLY JOHN WAS a sound sleeper, but that night following the shooting incident he found any slumber very evasive while his restless tossing and turning finally proved too much for Susan.

"John, for goodness sake, I've got work tomorrow. If you must tango all night, go and do it outside Jeanette's room. Or better still, at the far end of the lake. Perhaps then you might fall in and give us all a decent rest."

"Gee. Thanks a bunch," he mouthed under his breath. "I love you too." Which was quite different to what Susan actually heard. "Sorry, love, I'll go up and sleep in Brenda's old room. Goodnight."

Even several years after her departure, John still felt a surge of nostalgia as he climbed the final set of stairs that led to the nanny's old room. Closing the door and switching on the light, he could once again sense her feminine presence which still seemed to pervade the atmosphere with a faint fragrance. He paused to gently run a finger round the brim of her hat which he'd left on the corner post of the bed during his last visit.

Putting out the light, he collapsed onto the single bed with a long, heavy sigh before pulling up the duvet and attempting to sleep. Knowing that the forever unavailable love of his life had slept there so many times, somehow seemed to offer a certain comfort, and gradually the outer fringes of slumber began to envelop him. But the grey zone between wakefulness and deep sleep can be a place haunted by unmentionable horrors.

And as John slowly drifted off, he found himself somewhere in their small field. It was twilight, with an atmosphere that seemed heavy and oppressive. In his dream-like state, he felt totally disorientated while, to his utter confusion and distress the farmhouse seemed to no longer exist. Moreover, as what little light remained slowly began to fade, childhood terrors of being isolated and alone closed in with a vengeance.

Bad dreams can often seem devoid of normal sequence and reason, for suddenly he became aware of Blake's picture under his arm and the desperate need to burn it. But the question was, how? And he frantically went to search his pockets for a match. But, to his horror, he found he was stark naked. Naked and alone. It was his ultimate and subliminal terror, and as he tossed in bed his mind squirmed agonisingly. Yet the nightmare persisted as he then, inexplicably, found himself gazing at a roaring bonfire.

And, still vaguely aware of a mental pressure to incinerate the painting, he took the offending artwork and hurled it into the heart of the blazing inferno. But as the gilt wooden frame succumbed to the flames and the canvas began to curl, he heard the most protracted blood-curdling scream, while to the chagrin of his already tortured mind he saw reflected in the flames the fisher boy in his straw hat, who turned to look directly at him and mouth just one word, "Why?"

Worse, the next thing he knew the boy had somehow transmuted into a full-grown man who, with a face twisted into a mask of hate, was screeching, "Why? Why?" How the gardening fork appeared in John's hand was an anathema. All he knew, it was suddenly there, and in desperation he brought it down brutally and repeatedly onto the entity's head. But it made no difference. Again and again he struck out with the heavy metal end of the fork, but the nightmare image just refused to die.

"John! John! He's had enough."

Turning, he inexplicably found Brenda by his side with her long flowing hair and arms wide open as if pleading to be embraced. Dreams, however, are devoid of inhibitions, and he finally fulfilled years of longing by clasping her tight. Then, as if to savour the moment, he closed his eyes and slowly lowered his head to kiss her, but only to immediately draw back in horror, for the sensual and soft warmth of her mouth he'd so anticipated was now nothing more than cold unyielding bone. Opening his eyes, he found himself staring into the two empty sockets of a skull. Although the hair was still long and luxurious, it flowed from a naked skeletal head. Then, just as suddenly as she had appeared, the whole apparition collapsed at his feet in a rattling heap of bones. At which point, he started screaming and screaming, before jerking up in bed drenched in sweat as his mind fought to restore some semblance of mental normality.

Swinging his legs over the edge of the bed, he buried his face in his hands.

For a long time, he just sat there to let the horrors of the night gradually seep away. Finally, feeling chilled, he lay back under the duvet, but fearing a resumption of the nightmare he fought off any encroachment of sleep until, through the small dormer window, he could see the dawn slowly beginning to streak the eastern sky.

"What on earth's the matter with you, John?" cried his wife when he entered the kitchen. "You're as white as a sheet. You'd think you'd seen a ghost."

"I'm not sure I didn't!" he exclaimed in an exhausted voice before slumping down at the far end of the table. "I'll spare you the details, but I've just had the worst nightmare it's possible to imagine."

"Get this down you," sympathised Susan as she passed him a steaming black coffee. "I'll also do your porridge. Then I must be off to work."

He leaned forward and buried his head on his folded arms while expending a long drawn-out sigh.

"If I only do one thing today," he vowed, "it'll be to burn that picture."

"I can't hear a word you're saying with your face in the table," protested his wife while irritably slapping a bowl of porridge by his elbow.

"Sorry," he muttered. "I actually said I'm destroying that painting first thing."

"About time. Perhaps then we can all get some peace." At which point she reached for her handbag on the settee. "Anyway, I'm off." And after dropping a swift kiss on the top of his head, she was gone.

He dipped his spoon languidly into the hot porridge while wondering briefly how the postman was faring and what charges the public prosecutor might decide to bring after his 'sins' with the gun.

"Morning, Daddy."

He looked up and smiled as his mood soared at the sight of his daughter in her smart school uniform. She was one of the good things in life.

"Hello, love. All set for today's studies? Your mum's left your porridge ready for you in the oven."

"Hmm," she muttered settling down to her breakfast. "No sugar. Mum always forgets."

"She doesn't forget. It's not good for you," retorted her dad, emphasising the point with his spoon. He got up and crossed the kitchen to put his bowl in the sink. "Thought any more about what you might like to do when you leave school?" he asked idly as he turned back to his daughter.

"Well, Dad. As you know, I did think of being an

accountant, but I'd really like to be an artist or art teacher like you."

"You could always come and work with me in the property business," he suggested with a half smile.

"Much as I love you, Dad," she replied, getting up and swinging her school bag over her shoulder, "I can't see you as my boss. I just want you to stay as my dad." She rushed over to kiss him on the cheek. "Must fly or I'll be late for 'brain improvement'. Have a good day, Dad."

He smiled again as he lovingly watched her go, little knowing their short time together would prove to be the best part of his day. Determined to incinerate Blake's canvas, he strode purposefully towards the nursery where he found his ex already involved with her Peter duties. His son was squatting on the floor at the far side of the room indolently flicking through an illustrated book of various fish, while Jeanette looked up in surprise.

"Hello, John. Don't often see you here this early."

Not wishing his son to hear, he turned his back and spoke quietly.

"I've come for that wretched straw hat Peter was wearing the other day. Where is it?"

"Well," she replied hesitantly, "I know it's virtually falling to bits." But then, pointing in Peter's direction, she added, "You realise it's the apple of his eye? So, I don't think you'll get any thanks if you take it away."

"I'm not after any thanks," snapped John irritably. "Just tell me where it is."

She indicated a cupboard that held some of the toys.

"Right! Keep him amused until I'm gone."

Standing outside the back of the farmhouse with the headgear in one hand and a jerrycan of fuel in the other, he assessed the weather. The heavy rain had ceased during the early hours, and although still cloudy he decided any further downpour was unlikely. Their small field which he had in mind lay to the west of the farmhouse. There were several barns and horseboxes situated on this part of his land, and although he'd never explored them, he did know his predecessors had run horses and he hoped perhaps they might have left behind the odd bale of hay. He was in luck, for the smaller of the buildings revealed half a dozen rather tired and mouldy-looking bales.

To burn another artist's work went very much against the grain, because being creative himself, he knew only too well the skill and patience that must have gone into its execution, and this was without the pleasure which normally would accompany such a detailed piece of work. He was also aware that despite the agonies surrounding it, Blake had done the painting not only for the benefit of his wife, but perhaps more importantly for the enjoyment of posterity: further generations that stretched far into the future and who, by its destruction, would forever be robbed of a small part of their rightful heritage. Therefore, in a strange way he felt that to destroy it was a form of robbery, and with a heavy heart, he turned his footsteps in the direction of the Portakabin.

Once in the storage area, he lovingly wiped away the encrustations of mould and grime from the picture's surface to again reveal the sheen of oil paint and sheer brilliance of Blake's workmanship. It was, by any standard, a skilful rendition of a beautiful setting, with the artist using bright sunlight to stunning effect. The dappling rays on the boy's shirt and the riverside path alone were nothing short of breathtaking.

"I'm sorry, George," he murmured, "but it's something I've got to do. I just can't risk the chance of the hell you've been through affecting my family any longer. I only hope you'd understand and forgive me."

Finally, with the bales of hay in place and duly soaked in petrol, it was time for John to reluctantly commit the canvas to oblivion, although even as he went to strike the fatal match he hesitated. But the memories of Mrs Shawcross' warnings and the admonitions of Pastor Tim finally tipped his elbow, and with an instant roar the ancient horse fodder erupted into an inferno; ferocious heat that beat

John back with his eyes stinging from the sudden exposure to the acrid smoke.

At first, the weight of the picture momentarily subdued the flames' raw hunger, but gradually, as the precious artwork fed their appetite, they roared their appreciation all the more furiously. Initially the canvas curled as it succumbed to the intense heat, but then, as the gilt frame turned black, it reminded John of his nightmare and made him half expect to hear some tormented shriek. But this was reality, and the only sound to be heard was the crackling of the flames as Blake's picture entered its final death throes. Lastly, the straw hat was sacrificed to the god of fire, which responded with a shower of sparks as if in gratitude for the offering.

Feeling like a murderer, John turned away and headed back to the farmhouse where, after the previous day's traumas, he fully intended to relax for the rest of the day. However, this was not to be, for no sooner had he stepped indoors than his ex informed him of a missed phone call.

"Did they happen to say what it concerned?" he enquired, but then added wearily, "No. Don't tell me. I bet it was the police on about that gun incident."

"No, nothing like that," Jeanette hastened to assure him. "It was a funny sounding bloke. He had a strange high-pitched voice for a man. In fact, if you'll forgive me for saying so, but I think he was probably the sort who swings the other way. If you know what I mean."

“I know exactly what you mean,” asserted John bluntly.

“The politically correct term, of course, is ‘gay’, John,” she advised him, knowing only too well how crude and sarcastic he could be.

And her advice was timely, because the previous day’s episodes combined with a bad night had left him in a foul mood.

“I couldn’t give a monkeys about what’s politically correct or not,” he retorted irritably. “I know what I call such men, and as far as I’m concerned, that’s how it bloody well stays.” She didn’t pursue the subject. Then, turning towards the kitchen for a coffee, he called back, “I’ll be in my retreat for a bit. So, if that individual calls again give me a shout.” In the event, the individual did call again in the early afternoon, and Jeanette pulled a cautionary face as she handed him the receiver. “John Grant,” he snapped. “What can I do for you?”

“John Grant? Father of Peter Grant?” queried a rather effeminate voice.

“Yes, for whatever business that is of yours.”

“Really, Mr Grant. There’s no need for rudeness, because believe me I’ve only phoned to tell you something you should know about.”

“Well?” questioned John a little more soberly.

“Well,” echoed the caller. “If you think back, I’ll warrant it was your wife’s idea to call your son Peter.”

“So?” exclaimed John.

"So, ask her if she knows anything about a man called Peter Witherspoon."

John felt the hair on the back of his neck begin to stir as an horrific suspicion entered his mind.

"Look, whoever you are. What the hell are you trying to say?"

"Hmm. You might well ask," replied the evasive caller. "But I will say this: if I'm correct, your son was born about the twenty-ninth of October 2012, and I think if you count back nine months you'll find it coincides with the date of Mrs Grant's office party."

And with that, the line clicked and assumed the normal dialling tone. But completely devastated, John repeatedly tapped the top of the phone.

"Hello? Hello?" he shouted. But to no avail. The unknown troublemaker had hung up, and sick to the stomach John replaced the receiver.

Numb with shock and momentarily unable to move, his tortured mind went over and over what he'd just heard. Was it even conceivable that Susan, whom he'd always trusted, had also betrayed him.

"John. Are you quite all right?"

And there was Jeanette, the first traitor, who after her treachery now had the audacity to enquire after his welfare. Choked with fury and bitter disillusionment, he snarled, "All right? You might well ask, because I've just been informed that my wife could have been up to some of your old tricks."

Shocked by the sheer ferocity of his anger, Jeanette drew back.

"John, I'm sure that's not the case. She loves you far too much."

"So did you," he retorted. "And a fat lot of difference that made."

Knowing what he could be like, she nevertheless managed to screw up sufficient courage to defend her actions.

"John, that was altogether different, as I suspect you must know." But he might as well have not heard, for snatching his coat from the hall stand and with a murderous look he made for the front door.

However, with the last dregs of her courage, Jeanettte placed herself between him and the exit. "John, please don't do anything stupid. Something you'll later regret."

But her ex was beside himself and her interference only fuelled his anger.

"Get out of my way, woman!" he shouted, pushing her to one side. "There's a weasel in that Horsham housing department that needs his neck broken."

Jeanette staggered back, yet still somehow managed to persist.

"John, if you go and do something violent the chances are you'll be arrested – especially after yesterday's episode. And for what? You don't even know if what that man said is true. At least give Susan the chance to explain. It's probably all just a pack of lies anyway."

Her logic finally pierced the red mist and he hesitated before driving his fist into the heavy oak front door. It relieved his feelings but did precious little for his knuckles.

"Thanks," he said grudgingly. "You may well be right."

"Look," she replied gently, "I'll just check on Peter in the nursery, then if you go into the kitchen I'll have a look at your hand." It was probably the most sympathetic exchange between the two since her unexpected arrival several years previously.

But, as she applied a gauze dressing to his hand, Peter appeared in the kitchen entrance.

"Where's my hat? Where's my hat?" he shouted repeatedly in his usual truncated speech.

Jeanette glanced up at her ex while securing the bandage with Elastoplast.

"That's what I was going to mention, John!" she exclaimed uneasily. "So, I'm afraid, on that score it's over to you."

John turned firmly to his recalcitrant son. "That hat was falling to pieces," he said bluntly. "So, I got rid of it."

It was straight and to the point, but the boy's face darkened and he scowled back with his piercing green eyes. "Want that hat. Ralph's hat."

For once, John found it difficult to contain the anger he felt towards his son. "The hat's gone and that's an end to it. Now go back to the nursery before I spank your backside."

His aggressive reaction, however, was a mistake, for Peter then rushed across the kitchen before either of them could intervene and with a violent sweep of his arm sent the vase of flowers on the table crashing to the floor. Seeing the wilful destruction proved the final straw, and despite all his educational philosophising, John lunged forward and grabbed his son's arm. Then, sitting down, he administered the kind of punishment originally advocated by Mr Briggs, the school caretaker. Squirming on his father's knee, Peter hissed back in evil fury before finally being frogmarched upstairs to his bedroom.

"You'll stay there till tomorrow, and don't you dare break anything else or there'll be another thrashing!" John shouted while closing and locking the bedroom door.

Downstairs, Jeanette raised her eyebrows. "Don't you think that was a bit heavy, John?"

But John, who couldn't care less, just stood at the foot of the stairs with his hands on his hips.

"I'm at the end of my tether with that boy. He may have some sort of psychological problem, or worse, but I'm damned certain of one thing: he'll understand pain. Anyway, make sure he stays in his room and if you hear him causing any more damage, just call me."

And having said that, he made his way off in the direction of his retreat. But even there he found it difficult to relax and was conscious of his heart thudding against his ribs. Leaning back in his old armchair, he found it almost impossible to dismiss the pernicious phone call from his mind and he sighed, knowing there was no alternative but to have it out with Susan. Although, how on earth, he agonised, did you ask your wife whether you're really the father of their child, without bringing yet another divorce down about your ears? However, the sanctity of his refuge was suddenly dispelled at the sound of Susan's unexpected early return from work. Even so, for a while he didn't move. Nevertheless, snatches of conversation between his wife and his ex were just about audible, and from what he could gather, his wife was enquiring after the whereabouts of little Peter. Deeming it better for her to hear a rendition of events from himself rather than Jeanette, he reluctantly got to his feet and made for the hallway.

"Oh, there you are!" she exclaimed while turning at the sound of his door. "You seem to spend more and more time lately hiding away in that bolthole of yours."

"Believe it or not," he replied, "I'm attempting to hang on to the few shreds of sanity I've got left."

"Oh. Lucky old you," she retorted. "I have to face the stark facts of reality all the time – both in this menagerie and at work." But then, relenting slightly, she asked, "Tell me, what's gone wrong this time and why is Peter confined to his bedroom?"

John glanced over to his ex who immediately got the point and lost no time in doing a disappearing act. Then, by way of answering his wife, he gestured towards the kitchen.

"Notice anything missing?" he enquired as they entered the multi-purpose room.

"My Doulton vase!" she exclaimed after a cursory look around. "The one you bought me for the Christmas just after we got married. Where is it?"

"That son of yours," he replied blunty, "took it upon himself to smash it. I actually saw the little wretch do it, and I tell you his bottom suffered as a result."

Later that evening, during supper, Susan turned to her husband. "Have you heard any more from the police, John?" she asked while passing him a plate containing the main course. "Oh, and by the way, that's shepherd's pie – one of your favourites – courtesy of Jeanette's own fair hand."

But he was in no real mood for food. In fact, it might as well have been strips of cardboard for all he cared, and his wife sensed something was seriously wrong. "John, what's the matter with you? You were in a funny mood when I got home. If it's that vase you're upset about, it's no problem because we can always buy another one."

He looked up and glanced around the table at his ex and their daughter Miriam.

"Yes, there is something that's bothering me; bothering me very much. But I can't discuss it here. I'll talk to you about it later, when we're on our own."

In the privacy of their bedroom while Susan was comfortably settled down and preparing for sleep, her husband just remained standing by the window with his hands clasped behind his back as he wrestled with the thorny problem of how to broach the subject of the phone call – thoughts that stood in sharp contrast to the peaceful ambience of the room: a spacious place where subdued lighting reflected a mellow warmth from the lofty oak-beamed ceiling.

"John," came his wife's voice abruptly, "if you've got anything to tell me, please make it quick or I shall be asleep."

Her husband half turned to glance across at the bed, but then observed, almost as if he had heard nothing, "It's an incredibly beautiful night." He nodded towards the view beyond the mullion windows. And indeed it was, for the crescent-shaped silver moon had bathed the whole countryside in a gentle half-light to create a scene of absolute serenity. "There're no problems or troubles out there," he murmured wistfully.

"I'm sure it's absolutely delightful," she retorted slightly irritably. "But if that's all you've got to talk about then I'm off to sleep."

But in response, John came straight to the point. "When you were based in Horsham, was there some gay guy working with you in the office?"

At this sudden abrupt remark, any hope Susan had of sleep instantly evaporated. "What makes you ask?" she exclaimed, sitting up on her pillow.

"I mean what I've said," he asserted. "Did you know a man in your office who had the effrontery to call himself Mister, you know..."

"John, I really find that sort of vulgar talk very offensive," she objected.

"Well," he retorted crossing the room and leaning on the bed with out-stretched arms and fists that dug deep into the duvet cover, "that's nothing to the offence some poofter poured down the phone at me this afternoon, and I've reason to suspect that he works in your old office."

"What offence? What phone call? You haven't mentioned any phone call, but now perhaps you'll be good enough to tell me what's bothering you because, honestly, you've been nothing but a miserable old sod ever since I got back."

He turned and sat on the bed with his back to her.

"Who is Peter Witherspoon?" he asked, with no attempt to respond to her objections.

"And why do you wish to know?" she replied in a similarly abrupt tone.

"Because," he said, suddenly swivelling round to face his wife, "the guy who phoned as good as said that man's Peter's real father."

It had not been John's intention to handle the situation quite so indelicately. Nor had it been his desire to make it sound such a blunt accusation, but with his pent-up emotions at boiling point, that's how it had come over. His wife, who had gone as white as a sheet, just stared at him in total disbelief. Then, getting up, she reached for her dressing gown and strode round the bed to have it out face-to-face.

"John Grant," she hissed furiously. "The only carnal relations I've ever had have been with you, and well you know it." Then, with her voice approaching a scream, she added, "How dare you accuse me of committing adultery or even think me capable of such betrayal?"

And so, the fury and thunder he'd so dreaded continued to crash and roll about his ears. Finally, however, she became exhausted and he was able to mutter, "I never accused you of anything. All I was trying to do was tell you what I'd heard over the phone, and," he added defensively, "it was something which would have made any man feel upset. Surely," he pleaded, "you must understand that."

But there was no 'must' about it.

"I don't know how you've got the gall," she continued, "to even mention the subject. Especially after the years you've spent flirting with that Brenda bitch right under my nose. I'm not Jeanette you know."

"I know that," John shouted back. "I've just told you what I heard, and I fully intend to sort the bastard out."

But his wife was beyond reason and, realising the futility of pursuing the subject any further, he got up and reached for his own dressing gown before leaving the room. Determined to spend the rest of the night in the peace of his little retreat, he made for the head of the stairs.

For a long time, John just sat in semi-darkness and the comfort of his faithful old armchair, while his troubled mind wondered if he could have handled the problem any differently. Was there, perhaps, he thought, sometimes no real solution to life's difficulties, no matter how hard one tried? Was it better, in fact, to just let the shit of existence roll on and not bother?

The central heating had been off for a while and he shivered slightly in the late-night chill. Reaching for a blanket he kept for such an occasion, he wrapped it around himself and tried to settle down for some sleep. But with the cold and a restless mind, he found himself still struggling to drift off as the first rays of light began to relieve the darkness of night.

Abandoning any further attempt at sleep, John finally got to his feet and tied the cord of his dressing gown. At least the aroma of hot coffee emanating from the kitchen seemed inviting.

"Good morning, John," greeted Jeanette as she lifted a steaming pot from the stove. "Coffee?"

"Hot and strong please," he just about managed while collapsing wearily on a chair at the end of the kitchen table. "You're up and about early," he mumbled while rubbing his tired eyes.

"Try that, John," she suggested while handing him a cup of the near-black stimulant. "You look as though you need it." Then, after an uncertain pause she asked cautiously, "Bad night?"

"Don't ask!" he muttered. "Because I found out there's no easy way to ask your wife..."

But he just about stopped in time as Susan entered the kitchen.

"No easy way to ask your wife what, John?" she asked tersely.

But in the tense and potentially explosive atmosphere that followed, Jeanette had the courage and presence of mind to try to explain his difficulty.

"Susan, I took the phone call yesterday and it's obviously caused a lot of problems. I'd inadvertently left it on speaker when I handed it to John, so I couldn't help overhearing some of what was said and, believe me, it was extremely suggestive and unpleasant. Especially after what John had been through with me, and it took all my persuasion to stop him from storming off up to your old office."

Sharply dressed in her dark-blue tailored suit and matching high-heeled shoes, Susan looked every inch the competent and professional woman she was. Nevertheless, she listened graciously as Jeanette continued. "John didn't actually say much for the rest of the day, but I sensed he was fretting about broaching the subject with you."

"And part of his frustration," observed Susan acidly, "was obviously taken out on Peter's backside." And from her expression, it was clear she wished to be left alone with her husband.

"I'll just pop up and check on Peter!" exclaimed Jeanette diplomatically while disappearing in the direction of the stairs.

Satisfied she was out of earshot, Susan then turned and apologised for her reaction the previous night.

"I'm sorry, John. Instead of being understanding, I just dwelt on my own feelings and how it made me look." With no trace of the professional persona normally demonstrated to the outside world, she dropped her gaze in a display of embarrassment. "As you know," she continued, "it's a subject I'm particularly sensitive about. Probably more so because I'd always saved myself for the man I'd eventually marry. I know, I know," she stressed, "it's not fashionable in these 'enlightened' times, but that's how it is and that's how I am."

"And I'm grateful for it," rejoined John warmly while taking her in his arms.

Finally, she pulled back briefly to look up at him.

"I'm sorry about the phone call, but if I'm honest I suspect it might have been partly my fault, because when I was in charge at Horsham I had to push through a lot of modernisation on the computer system and it was very unpopular with some of the older staff. You might recall I mentioned some particularly difficult days at the time. I also think," she added, "my recent promotion probably caused a certain amount of jealousy in some quarters. Anyway, if I'm not mistaken I suspect the man responsible was someone called Adam Stanley. He's a vindictive individual at the best of times and just the sort to bear a grudge. And bent... You wouldn't believe it. However, what I don't want," she asserted, "is for you to go round to my old workplace and iron out his creases – which I believe is a favourite phrase of yours."

"Or straighten out his wrist," he replied dryly.

"That," she smiled, "would be something beyond even you." And so saying, his wife moved in the direction of the kitchen table.

"Cornflakes again," he observed, joining her for breakfast.

"Tradition," she responded while shaking the light brown flakes from their packet and watching them bounce around the bowl. "Either that," she asserted while reaching for the milk jug, "or sheer lack of imagination."

"You know what?" smiled her husband who obviously had nothing better to talk about. "Why don't you enjoy the crisp texture of those flakes instead of saturating them with milk and beating them into a pulp?"

"Early morning intellectual conversation was never a strong point with you, was it?" she observed dryly after savouring the first spoonful of her tormented cereal.

However, even as she spoke, Jeanette re-entered the kitchen accompanied by their very subdued and sulky-looking son. Approaching the table, she spoke directly to Susan.

"Peter has something he wants to say to you," she said quietly.

"He's taken my hat and won't give it back," accused the boy sullenly while pointing to his father.

Although the accusation amounted to more words than the child had yet strung together, it nevertheless brought an animated response from his nanny.

"Peter!" she exclaimed angrily crouching down on one knee. "That was not what we agreed to talk about when I let you out of your room, now was it?"

But then, as John stared into his son's almost alien-looking eyes, he became surprised to see their deep green slowly give way to the semi-pale blue he'd witnessed once before, and, riveted, he could only watch as the subordinate personality in his son's life began a desperate struggle for supremacy. It was an amazing transformation to witness as Peter's normally aggressive look slowly became one of childlike innocence.

It was the first time Jeanette had experienced the conflict, and as the unrecognisable boy emerged, she was rendered virtually speechless.

Finally, the child looked at his mother.

"Mummy, I'm sorry about your flowers and your vase," he said gently, in a voice bereft of its normal resentful tone.

However, intelligent woman though she was, Susan found it all but impossible to know how to react.

"That's all right, darling," she managed finally while taking him into her arms. "But why do you do such things?"

Watching her child's face, it became obvious that his young mind was virtually incapable of dealing with the two opposing forces vying for control of his thoughts and actions. In the end, however, he came out with a staggering remark.

"It was Ralph who made me do it. He's very naughty, Mummy, isn't he?"

"Yes," replied Susan gently if uncomprehendingly. "Very naughty." Then, looking at her husband and Jeanette, she added, "If you don't mind, I'll hand this bundle of enigmas over to you because I'm off to work."

"I'll have to leave you to do your best, Jeanette, because I've also got a busy day," added John.

But, a busy day meant going strictly against his wife's wishes and a trip to her old office in Horsham. Several miles north of the Grant family home, the ancient rural town hosted a variety of historic buildings; a lot of which dated back to the fifteenth and sixteenth centuries and contributed a rich mellow charm to the overall environment. The Carfax, as it was called, or town square, with its bandstand, bustling open market and continental-style coffee bars offered an almost carnival-like atmosphere and was especially popular at weekends.

Moving on through the square, John finally located his goal; a rectangular block of soulless concrete and glass which stood in stark contrast to its harmonious counterparts. How such a monstrosity had been perpetrated on the townscape beggared his imagination. But a critique of local planning was not his agenda, and feeling slightly downbeat he pushed back the heavy glass door of the main entrance to his wife's old workplace.

Bereft of all but basic necessities, the endless labyrinth of corridors was an even more soulless spectacle than the building's exterior. While with the reception area festooned by arrows indicating the direction of various local government offices, John decided to take the easy option and enquire the whereabouts of the housing department from the first official who looked as though he knew half of what he was talking about.

Finally, he found himself standing in front of a dingy counter which cordoned off the equally dreary area that had once been his wife's domain. The resident attendant had his head down busily sifting through various papers and gave scant attention to his arrival.

"Excuse me!" snapped John irritably. "But is there any chance of service here?"

"Oh, I'm sorry," came the rather effeminate reply, as the official removed his wire-framed spectacles and minced over to where the newcomer was standing. "Is there anything I can do to help?"

On the surface the offer was innocent enough, although the man's dapper movements and tone made it sound more like an indecent proposition.

"By the way," enquired John, "your name wouldn't happen to be Adam Stanley, would it?"

"Oh, no," replied the speaker while making a deft hand movement to the back of his head, as if checking some non-existent hairpiece. "Adam works in the back office."

Blimey, thought John.

"Well! Would you be so kind as to tell him that I want a word in his shell-like."

"Very well," replied the attendant, who, with an almost dismissive wrist action, turned and headed for the rear area.

Adam Stanley turned out to be a bigger man than John might have expected, although size seemed in no way to affect the effeminate way he sashayed up to the counter.

"I've just been told there's a strange man who wants to see me; which is nice!" he exclaimed in the same high-pitched voice John remembered on the phone.

"You obviously don't know who I am," Peter's father retorted, glaring straight into the man's eyes.

"No, but I'd be quite happy to find out," offered the Stanley character almost suggestively.

John paused for a moment to study the individual's

flighty and fidgety persona. Here was a man very much gone to seed and yet who dressed in the most blatant bright colours to broadcast his sexual orientation – as if it weren't blatant enough already.

"Perhaps when I tell you I'm Peter Grant, then you may not be quite so happy to make my acquaintance," snapped John. "Because, let me make it abundantly clear. If you ever do anything else to cast aspersions on the legitimacy of my son, then there won't be enough left of you to scrape up off the floor." And with that, John reached forward and grabbed the man's shirt front before lifting him halfway over the counter. "Do you fully understand me?" he muttered darkly before shoving him back across the reception desk.

"Perfectly," responded the shaken, effeminate voice.

"One other thing before I go. Make absolutely sure my wife never hears about this visit. Got it?"

"Got it. Completely understood," winced the offender.

During the drive back, John wondered briefly if he'd rammed the message home quite hard enough or whether perhaps he should have reinforced the point with the end of his fist. But in the light of all the other uncertainties rumbling about, he decided that caution had probably been the better part of valour.

With his mission complete, John faced a fairly quiet day ahead and upon arriving home made his way out through the back of the house with the intention of a relaxing stroll around the grounds.

However, upon reaching the small field he was surprised to see a thin eddy of smoke still drifting up from the funerary pyre of Blake's painting. Finding it strange that it should still be smouldering, John wandered over for a closer look where, unbelievably despite the fierce heat of the previous day's fire, it still remained possible to discern an outline of the picture's frame. It almost seemed as though the strange life which had appeared embodied in the canvas was loath to die, but as he turned away with a slightly uneasy feeling he noticed Jeanette by the field gate frantically waving to get his attention.

"John!" she called out urgently. "There's another phone call for you." Then she added, tactfully, "I think it's something to do with Miriam's previous nanny."

Filled with anticipation, John raced for the field entrance and eagerly took the cordless phone from her hand.

"Hello, Brenda!" he exclaimed excitedly, but then only to be bitterly disappointed by the sound of a man's voice.

"No, I'm sorry. I'm not Brenda," apologised the caller. "But I do believe she's a mutual friend and I'm afraid it's my unpleasant duty to tell you that she's seriously ill in hospital." At these words John felt a sudden numbness spread through his entire body. "I know," continued the speaker, "she was nanny to your little girl but returned home to nurse her sick father, who incidentally passed away several years ago." The man paused. "Anyway, up until recently, she's been helping out with my three daughters, but now, as I say, she's very ill and as far as I know has no living family since her father's death. She's a beautiful and lovely person," he added gently. "And when I asked if there was anyone she would like me to contact, she immediately mentioned your name. In fact," he stressed, "she often spoke very fondly about you during her time with my girls."

"But what's actually wrong with her?" asked John in a stricken voice.

"I'm afraid it's cancer," came the chilling reply. "She's been diagnosed with a malignant growth on the pancreas. I'm very sorry. She's currently in the cancer department of the Royal Manchester Infirmary. I might also add, there's been some talk of moving her to an American clinic where I understand there are several new experimental treatments available."

Finally, after again conveying his sympathy, the speaker gave John the details of his home address and telephone number. And then he was gone. Slowly, John handed the phone back to his ex before sinking dejectedly down onto the still wet grass.

"Bad news?" she enquired quietly.

And sitting there with his hands clasped round his drawn-up knees, he responded barely above a whisper. "Brenda's seriously ill."

Then, with a surprising sensitivity, Jeanette

squatted down beside her ex-husband and gently touched his forearm. "I'm sorry," she murmured. "It was none of my business of course, but during the short time I knew her I sensed there was some kind of bond between you both."

A brief moment of apprehension flashed across his features.

"I hope it wasn't that obvious," he observed wearily.

But she shook her head.

"No, John," she assured him quietly. "But sometimes it's possible for us women to pick up on things like that. Certainly, I could see Brenda was carrying a torch for you. Incidentally, I wouldn't sit too long on that wet grass. Anyway, I must be off to check Peter's not on one of his destructive forays. Although, he seems to have been surprisingly good today."

Despite her well-meant advice, John remained where he was. Even with the damp rising up through his clothes and with a steady drizzle beating into his face, he seemed frozen to the spot as memories of the girl on the carousel flooded back: memories of the chiming music and the brightly-coloured carved horses as they continued on their never-ending journey to nowhere.

Finally, notwithstanding the possible dilemma of upsetting his wife, he determined to make the journey to Manchester. In a sense, Brenda's resignation had been a relief, for his wife had voiced her feelings about her flirtation on more than one occasion. But faced with the stark reality that the love of his life might die...

Once back in the house, he lost no time in approaching his ex.

"Jeanette. When Susan gets in from work, tell her that I've been called away to Manchester to visit a sick friend and that I may not be back until tomorrow." His ex looked up from the nursery table that she'd been sharing with Peter and nodded. "By the way," he added, "there's no need to say who..."

"I understand, John," she responded quietly. "I fully understand. Just be careful what you're getting into, that's all."

It surprised him that she even cared enough to show concern. But then he wondered, perhaps, whether her feelings for him had never completely died. However, with no time to dwell on pointless speculation, he made for his car.

From his home in Mid-Sussex to the northern outskirts of Manchester proved a long and tiring drive, which was made no less easy by the blinding headlights of oncoming cars as they reflected from the rain-drenched road ahead.

By the time of his arrival, it had been dark for several hours, and as he looked up at the high-rise hospital blocks with their myriad of brightly lit windows, he wondered where on earth to start the search for the girl he loved. Ironically, it was almost a repetition of his experience earlier in the day as he asked one nurse after another for directions to the cancer department. At last, however, he found himself outside the ward marked 'Green Timbers', which somehow seemed a little perverse in the midst of such a sea of concrete and glass. However, the quest to see Brenda was brought to an abrupt halt at the reception desk, where, after an extensive perusal of her computer screen, the monstrosity of a matron politely informed him that Miss Brenda Hawsworth was now on her way to a clinic somewhere in Florida.

"And would you by any chance have a contact number for the place?" he asked in a tired, frustrated voice.

"Well, that would depend on who's asking and whether you're related to the patient in some way," replied the stony-faced woman. "Because, as far as our records show, Miss Hawsworth has no living next of kin and we can't just hand out any details without some proof of relationship."

Convention and practicalities inhibited the urge to lift the grossly overweight matron across the counter and shake the facts out of her. However, with no other option, he had to be content with a surly grunt of thanks for nothing before making his way to the exit.

It had been a long hard drive in increasingly torrential weather. And for what? And it was well past midnight as he finally turned his car back onto the soaking road home.

Thoughts of Brenda were never far from his

mind, and he kept wondering if she'd reached her destination. He longed to be with her, knowing full well that no matter how excellent the medical care, there was no substitute for having someone close to you in times of ill-health.

Feeling exhausted, John eventually arrived back at the bottom of the farmhouse drive while a glance at his watch told him it was approaching 4am. Rather than disturb his wife, he decided to spend the remainder of the night in his little retreat. But, as he pulled up wearily on the forecourt and reached for the handbrake, he became surprised to notice a chink of light seeping from under the kitchen blinds. Mystified as to who could still be up and about at such an hour, he quickly secured the car and took the front steps in a bound.

Quietly entering the kitchen, he was shocked to see his ex clad in her floral dressing gown and matching slippers sitting slumped dejectedly over the kitchen table.

"What are you doing up?" he enquired in hushed tones.

She straightened slowly and turned with a tired expression. "Oh, I don't know," she replied in an equally subdued voice. "I just couldn't sleep for wondering how you were getting on and thinking about that poor woman with cancer. I mean, what has a young person like that done to deserve such a fate while the real monsters of this life seem to go unscathed?" She paused and reached for a very obviously empty cup, and in doing so caused a clump of her greying hair to fall across her face. Sweeping it back, she got up and made for the stove. "Coffee, John?"

"Black and strong as it comes," he replied shortly.

"By the way," she added. "Did you manage to see Brenda?"

He sat down slowly at the table with a suppressed sigh.

"Would you believe it? I drove all the way to Manchester only to be told she's been airlifted to some clinic in Florida." He paused to accept the welcome coffee. "Do you know, the hospital up there wouldn't even give me the American contact number?" He shrugged resignedly. "So, I'll probably never know what became of her or even where she'll be buried."

Jeanette gazed at him sympathetically. Deep down, if she were honest she was still quite fond of the man who had originally so captivated her. But then, life... She shrugged imperceptibly over the apparent futility of it all. However, seeing John's stricken expression, she moved to sit beside him.

"Modern medicine can achieve a lot these days, you know, John. So, I shouldn't entirely give up hope." And then, imparting a reassuring squeeze to his hand, she rose to leave but then paused to observe, "It's strange, but after you left earlier I found it difficult to believe that Peter was the same boy."

John nodded grimly. "I know. It's as though he's two different people."

"But that's terrible, John," she protested. "Can you even begin to imagine what goes on in that poor boy's head? In any case, what could have caused such a condition?"

John expelled a long slow breath.

"The honest answer to that is I don't know! And that's mainly because there's been virtually no research on the subject; at least, that I'm aware of." At this point he glanced at the kitchen clock. "Blimey! 5am. I'm off for a bit of shut-eye before the rest of the menagerie wakes up."

But Jeanette's curiosity had been aroused and he was not to escape so lightly as she pressed him for more details.

John paused for a moment trying to collect his thoughts. "Well," he explained, "it's only my idea and it's pure speculation, but if you notice, from time-to-time we get unbidden thoughts and ideas that seem to come from nowhere. However, it's my opinion they don't just come from nowhere but consist of vague memories from previous generations – although, usually, they're not strong enough to cause a problem. But," he went on, "in Peter's case, I believe they do. In fact, I think they resonate from one ancestor in particular and are so powerful they dominate the poor boy – hence his split personality." He tapped his empty cup. "Any chance of more coffee?" His ex smiled briefly before reaching to give him a refill. "More to the point," he continued, "you might even have heard Peter mention a specific name."

Jeanette thought for a moment. "Yes, now you come to mention it. I have. Ralph, I believe."

"Well," John declared after a grateful sip of his drink, "here's the strange coincidence, because that was the name of Blake's only son, and, incidentally, Blake was the man who painted the picture that used to hang in the hallway."

"Surely if what you say is correct," reasoned his ex, "then it's possible that Peter could be related to that family in some way."

He nodded. "Yes – now you come to mention it, that may well be the case."

"And what is it that may be the case?" came the unexpected and slightly suspicious voice of Susan.

"Hello, love. I hope I haven't disturbed you, but I was just trying to explain to Jeanette what I think causes Peter's apparent swings of mood and changes of personality."

"At this hour?" his wife retorted while struggling to re-tie her dressing gown cord. "And I understood that you weren't supposed to be back before tomorrow."

John responded by glancing at the time. "Well," he observed ruefully, "according to my watch it is tomorrow; early, but definitely tomorrow."

Seeing them both crouched convivially over

the kitchen table during the small hours and obviously engaged in animated conversation had understandably aroused her curiosity. So, John hastened to put her mind at rest. "You see, love, I didn't want to trouble you at work, but yesterday I heard that Miriam's old nanny has been diagnosed with terminal cancer and I felt morally bound to visit her after her years of faithful service. There was also the fact that she has no family and probably not long to live." He paused and took a deep breath. "Anyway, as it happened, by the time I reached Manchester Infirmary it was too late, because she'd already been moved to an American clinic. And so," he emphasised, "that is why I'm back earlier than anticipated. I saw Jeanette was up and she kindly offered to make me a coffee, which I can tell you, after such a long tiring drive, was very acceptable."

His wife responded by sitting down slowly.

"Oh, I'm sorry to hear about that, John. I knew Brenda was sweet on you, but... cancer. How awful. I mean, she can only be about thirty or so. It's terribly sad." She shook her head. "However, I've got a demanding day ahead, so with what little time's left, I'm off back to bed."

And being the wise man that he was, John wasted no time in following suit, which left the odd member of the trio to dwell on her sombre thoughts alone.

Although Susan's husband tried to continue life as

normal – or as close to normal as possible – he was nevertheless devastated by the news of the nanny's terminal illness and would often find himself sitting alone in his little retreat, thinking about her and the occasion of the Easter bank holiday carousel. It was an image destined to increasingly haunt him over the years, knowing there was now virtually no chance of ever seeing her again. And it seemed to hurt all the more, because if he were honest he'd always cherished the impossible dream that, despite the odds, somehow, some way, they might yet have still got together. But now...

After the shock over Brenda, several uneventful weeks were to pass, during which time late spring finally burst into full summer with all its colourful upbeat glory. But upbeat glory was an elusive quality at the farmhouse, especially early one morning when John awoke to the sound of frenzied screaming.

"What is going on?" exclaimed his wife, foisting herself up on her elbows. But then, throwing back the duvet, she cried, "That's our Miriam." And grabbing her dressing gown, Susan made a dash for the bedroom door closely followed by John who was still in his pyjamas. Then, having raced down the stairs, she headed straight for the kitchen; but quick as they'd been, Jeanette had got there first, and as they entered they found her striving to comfort a desperately distraught Miriam.

Sensing rather than seeing their arrival, the nanny pointed mutely towards the wall-mounted aquarium. Mortified, John became transfixed to see the normally crystal-clear water with its brightly coloured inhabitants now an opaque mass of soap suds; a froth which was oozing up out of the feed aperture to form an ever-expanding puddle on the kitchen tiles. Stunned beyond belief at the sight of such wilful destruction, he could only watch as the tide of lather threatened to engulf a half-empty packet of washing powder which the perpetrator had obviously left lying discarded on the floor.

Final proof of the culprit's identity, if it were needed, was provided by a soaking wet chair which stood propped up just beneath the tank itself. It was impossible to see any fish – but they would almost certainly have succumbed to the noxious conditions. It was an act of extreme sadism which proved too much for Susan and she screamed hysterically.

"How could he? The beastly little swine! How could he do such an evil thing?"

Shocked though he was, John immediately put a reassuring arm round her shoulders while indicating for his ex to get Miriam out of the kitchen as quickly as possible.

Arriving in the hallway and while still trying to comfort Susan, he added, "Take Miriam into the drawing room and do what you can. I'll join you in a few minutes."

It was a fraught moment and he felt torn between the two distraught women but knew his first duty lay with his wife, and once in their second reception room he just held her for several moments before she pulled back to look up at him with a tear-stained face.

"John, he's evil," she sobbed brokenly. "He's my own son but he's absolutely evil. What are we going to do? It's getting so that I don't even feel safe in my own bed."

A disciplinarian by nature and someone who'd had thousands of children pass through his hands, John had to admit he'd never occasioned anything like it, and, similar to his wife he felt at a loss.

"I think," he observed eventually as they relaxed on the chaise longue, "what we have to decide is whether to call in the authorities or try to deal with the problem ourselves."

"But, John," she objected. "We're just not qualified. I mean we don't even know what we're really dealing with."

"No," he agreed, gazing about the room. But then, turning to face his wife, he added assertively, "Neither, I suspect, would anyone else – although, as I explained to Jeanette the night I got back from Manchester, I've a pretty fair idea. Anyway, if we call in the authorities and say our son is beyond control and a danger to the rest of the family, then he'll either be removed to a safe house or certified and incarcerated in some mental institution." He leaned forward with his elbows on his knees while clenching both hands together. “And we have to ask ourselves, is that something we really want for our son?”

“It’s not a question of what we want,” cried his wife, desperate for the comfort of a cigarette. “It’s how the hell are we going to manage in the future. If he’s like this now, what’s he going to be like as a teenager? Don’t forget, you’re nearly sixty. You might be able to handle him at the moment, but what about in ten years time?”

John nodded knowing that his strength would ebb with the years. However, shelving the problem temporarily he heard himself wonder out loud.

“What I don’t understand is when the hell did the little sod do it and why? He must have crept down in the middle of the night while we were all asleep.” And with that, he got up and went into the next room to see how Miriam was getting on, but he found her still tearful and sitting close to Jeanette. “Don’t be too upset, love,” he said comfortingly. “We can soon clean out the tank and get some more fish.”

“But, Daddy,” she protested, “I loved those fish. We’ve had some of them for years and that big black one – you know, with the bulgy eyes – we’ve had him right from the beginning.”

Gutted himself, John turned to his ex.

“Where is his lordship? Still in bed?”

She nodded. “Yes, I usually let him sleep in until about 9am, because it makes for a shorter day in which to keep him amused.”

"I can well imagine," replied Peter's thoroughly disgruntled father. "But perhaps you'd be kind enough to drag him out of his cosy zone, so I can have a word in his ear?"

Jeanette went to object, but then thinking the better of it left the room without further comment.

After she'd gone, Miriam said quietly, "You'd hardly think that Peter was my brother, would you Daddy? I mean, how could he do such a cruel thing to those poor fishes. They must have died a terrible death."

"I know, and it makes you wonder if he's even got a conscience at all." Susan had just entered the room in time to hear Miriam's remark, but her husband was more circumspect.

"I don't think it's quite as simple as that," he observed, while indicating the need for a quiet word in the hallway. Then, after assuring his daughter he'd be back in a moment, he closed the reception room door. Sitting down on the monk's seat, he looked up at his wife. "I've been giving Peter's condition a great deal of thought lately. I've told you before that I think he's probably suffering from a severe case of split personality, and one of them, I believe, is very dominant. I also believe this influence or persona is struggling desperately to remember its true identity and the possible details of a previous existence. It may be," he continued, "that it feels totally disorientated. And the result..." John shrugged. "Frustration and aggressive behaviour like we've just witnessed."

"You mean," she asserted, "we're faced with a case of evil reincarnation? Which Blake's wife tried to warn us about and what I've feared all along, which you've always pooh-poohed as rubbish."

"I have," he admitted, leaning back and folding his arms. "And I'll tell you why, and that's because the whole concept of reincarnation implies the regeneration of just one individual, whereas, in this case, we appear to be dealing with two: our own boy, Peter, and something or someone else."

What neither of them could possibly have known was that the final solution to their dilemma would eventually come from the boy himself. However, his wife had moved on to the immediacies of the day.

"I must get ready for the office, because unlike you people of comparative leisure I have to work to a set pattern of hours."

"I don't think," objected John, "that I'd exactly call the property business, a leisure-time activity."

"Oh, and by the way!" she exclaimed, "while I'm on the subject of work, I understand that some undesirable recently visited my old office in Horsham and roughed up one of the officials. Namely, Mr Stanley. Obviously, you wouldn't happen to know anything about that I suppose?"

John raised his eyebrows with a blank expression and shook his head.

"Er, no. It's news to me. Why? What happened?"

"What happened?" she shouted. "You know damn well what happened. How could you? Especially after

I expressly told you to stay away from the man! Do you realise that in my position I have a reputation to maintain? How do you think the councillors would react if they thought I was married to a thug?"

"I wouldn't actually call myself 'thug'," muttered John. Theirs was an almost comic confrontation between a slightly built woman of barely five-foot-three and a six-foot-two man... and he was on the sharp end. "Well," he protested sheepishly, "I only lifted the guy over the counter and warned him to mind his mouth."

"You what?" she cried furiously. "You only lifted him over...? Uh!" she almost screeched, while clawing at the air in frustration.

However, upon reaching the front door the sound of voices caused her to turn.

"And what kept you so long?" she heard John call up the stairs.

Jeanette and Peter were at last on their way down from his bedroom, and in the way of a reply, she repeatedly pointed her forefinger down at the top of their son's head. "This refused to leave its comfort zone."

And by the disgruntled look on the boy's face, his father could well believe her.

"John," called his wife from the doorway, "I'm off – I'm late already. I'll, er, leave you to sort out that circus in the kitchen with his lordship. Oh, and good luck," she added, closing the door on the pending storm.

"Gee, thanks a bunch," he muttered. "Where would I be without you?"

Jeanette's hearing, it seemed, was well above average. "I'll tell you where you'd be, John – in one word. And that's, lost!" she exclaimed.

He nodded while making a slight click of agreement with his tongue. At the same time, he had no idea how to handle the catastrophe they'd once called a kitchen. Finally, however, he indicated that his ex should take the boy through to the scene of devastation. Then, pointing to the wanton destruction, John stooped down to look in his son's face. But realising that his behaviour might have sprung from a sense of frustration, he decided on a more gentle approach.

"Peter. Tell me. Why would you want to do such a horrible thing to the fish tank?" But one look at the expression in the boy's deep-set eyes told John the aggressive persona that so dominated his son was very angry.

"You took my hat and wouldn't give it back!" he shouted insolently. "And I hate you." Then, casting around the room, he added, for the first time, "And I hate this place. I don't belong in this place."

Hearing this, John felt sure his assessment of his son's condition had been pretty well correct. On the other hand, however, the boy's rudeness only incensed his ex.

"Peter. Don't you dare speak to your father like that!"

"He's not my father!" the boy shouted back furiously.

Had John not some idea of the forces at work, it would have been very hurtful, and while the utterly disgusted nanny would have said more, he held up a restraining hand before asking the boy quietly, "Tell me, Peter. Who is your father?"

Watching the youngster carefully, John saw the resentment and anger gradually become replaced by a look of uncertainty. Indeed, as he searched the boy's face, it seemed the alien side of his son was desperately trying to recall some vague and distant memory; a memory of something or someone that John suspected lay hidden deep in the past. Slowly, however, it became obvious that, despite the child's efforts, it remained tantalisingly beyond his reach. Peter's green eyes took on an uncharacteristic sadness which quite touched his father, and he was briefly tempted to take the boy in his arms, but mindful of how he'd been recently rebuffed, he kept his distance and instead contented himself with a continued kindness.

"Never mind," he said softly. "I understand. I'm sure you'll remember all you need to one day." Then, standing up, he looked at his ex, and lost for words just shook his head. "I've got business in Brighton all day so perhaps you could give Mrs Oldfield a ring to clear up the kitchen. She's the woman who comes in from time-to-time to help with the cleaning. You must have seen her about the place." Then, as his son left the kitchen, John mouthed silently, "Look after him. He needs it."

"I know, John." She nodded. "I know. Leave it to me."

A few weeks later, and after a number of visits to the psychiatrist, Peter had been allowed back at St Martin's primary school where, at first, everything appeared to go reasonably well, and it seemed the therapist's treatment had at least been marginally effective. Although, his father suspected the real cause of Peter's improved attitude was a direct result of his own sympathetic understanding of the boy's condition, for until the fish tank incident he hadn't fully appreciated how his son had been engaged in a lone struggle. And a lone struggle can be a bleak experience – especially when no-one seems to know or care.

St Martin's was the infant section of a much bigger junior school, with the two buildings being separated by a main road; movement between which was facilitated by a zebra crossing controlled by the local lollipop lady. The whole school catered for a very mixed social catchment area, and rougher elements of the junior section had not been above suggesting she stick her lollipop in questionable locations. In fact, several of her predecessors had resigned over their rudeness. However, the present incumbent – built more like a chieftain tank than a woman – was quite happy to clip the odd ear if the occasion called for it. One mid-week lunchtime, she found herself shepherding half a dozen or so of the older, more unruly boys, over to the primary side. It was unusual, and she wasted no time in saying so.

"And where do you think you scallywags are off to at this time of the day?" she demanded.

One of the bigger lads with long floppy hair and a stained pullover went to be cheeky. But, fearing a clump from the woman's lollipop, decided caution was probably the wiser option.

"Er, we're just orf to see Miss 'ardy," he replied with a ring of insolence.

It was, of course, a lie, for they had something far more malevolent in mind, and reaching the other side, one of them with hair shorn virtually to the top of his head, turned and shouted, "You daft old bat. Get a life!"

And the suggestion was quickly accompanied by the judicious use of two fingers before the group fled to the comparative safety of the primary school playground. With the weather being mild, most of the four to seven-year-olds were outside and the air was filled with their noisy chatter and laughter. Some were running about just having fun, while others were playing on various constructions like the stationary wooden steam engine and its two brightly coloured trucks – all this happy activity being set against a background of school classrooms, many of whose windows were festooned with great swathes of colourful artwork.

Miss Francis was again on lunchtime supervision, but she'd been called away to the school office in response to an urgent phone call. This had left a rather inexperienced teaching assistant in charge, but she had stepped outside the immediate play area to speak to one of the passing parents. It was unfortunate, but it presented an ideal opportunity for the roughneck visitors to carry out their malicious intent.

Bad news travels fast, and it hadn't taken long for the struggle Miss Francis and the caretaker had experienced with Peter over the fish tank, to reach the ears of the junior school bully. Rejoicing in the name of Josh Lang, he and his cohort had become determined to see just how tough this primary school kid really was. Lang was a strapping boy for his age and a burgeoning thug if ever there was one. He also took a wanton delight in intimidating his fellow pupils. Worse, such individuals, it seemed, had no trouble in attracting characters of their own ilk, and now this group of miscreants were on the lookout for Peter.

"Oi!" shouted Lang to one of the infants. "Come 'ere a minute." Sensing trouble, the poor little fellow wandered over and looked up in terror at the towering eleven-year-old. "Where's Peter Grant?" demanded the bully.

"Over there," replied the child timorously, while

pointing to Peter who was sitting quietly alone on one of several log seats.

His father's greater sense of understanding had left Peter in a mellow mood, and never one to join in with the other children's games, he had been quite content to just sit and watch as they amused themselves. Suddenly, however, a shadow fell across where he was sitting, and hearing the crunch of footsteps he turned to be confronted by the menacing junior school group.

"Is your name Grant?" hissed Lang. Then, turning to his toadies he sneered, "He ain't so tough looking, is he?" And so saying, he sent the off-guard Peter spinning from his seat with a single shove; a shove which caused the youngster to fall heavily and strike the right side of his head, whereupon Lang's shorn-haired friend, Mickey Shannon, who emanated from a large family of like-minded undesirables, led a chorus of approval and kicked Peter as he lay on the ground; thus causing the victim's blue eyes to look scared and puzzled as he winced with pain.

"Why did you do that?"

"Why did I do that?" mocked Lang. "Did I hurt Mummy's baby boy then?" He really was a thoroughly nasty piece of work. "I did it," he jeered, "because you're supposed to be tough, and you're not, are you? You're still just a baby." Then, turning to the group, he added, "Come on. Let's get out of here, before some of the staff show up."

Many of the other younger children, terrified by

what was going on, had fled towards the shelter of the school buildings. But, as Peter got to his feet, his pale blue eyes darkened and he called out after the retreating Lang. In response, the aggressor turned and slowly swaggered back.

"Yes, baby? What does Mummy's boy want?" The rest of his group paused to watch as Lang poked his forefinger repeatedly into Peter's chest. "I said baby, what does baby want?"

Peter had originally been sitting close to the boundary, and at Lang's continued provocation he grabbed the bully's wrist and hurled him against the wall. The invader was finding out the hard way just how tough Peter could be.

Meanwhile, Mickey Shannon, who had detached himself from the rest of the gang and been on his way back to watch the fun, stopped dead at the sight of the thrashing being meted out to his fellow troublemaker.

But, as fate would have it, Miss Hardy, the headteacher, chose that very instant to step out into the playground. Her blood pressure, under normal circumstances, would probably have been quite stable, although what its reading was at that particular moment would have been anyone's guess.

"Mickey Shannon!" she barked, with a face like stone. "Get yourself and those other boys over to my office immediately." Then, while he and his sullen-faced accomplices slunk off towards the administrative block, she turned her attention to the activities of 'David and his Goliath'. Goliath, who by this time was on the playground floor having been the recipient of the same treatment Miss Francis had experienced during the school fish incident. "Get up at once, the pair of you," ordered the head furiously. "And you, Josh Lang, go and join the other boys outside my room." The junior, however, looked the worse for wear after his 'fun with the baby', and seeing the bruise on the side of his lip, the senior teacher added, "But first you'd better report to the school nurse and let her look at your mouth." Then, after he'd slouched away, the 'tarantula', as John had once described her, began to remonstrate with his son. "No sooner do I have you back in school than this is how you behave," she snapped. "Come with me while I phone your parents."

But, even as she spoke, Peter's salvation was at hand in the form of the nervous little infant who had first pointed him out.

"Miss," he ventured hesitantly. "Peter didn't do anything."

Sensing the sincerity in the brave little boy, the head's ferocious expression momentarily softened.

"What do you mean, Peter didn't do anything?" she asked gently while crouching down on one knee.

"It was him," replied the diminutive speaker, pointing after Lang. "I saw him. He pushed Peter over first. It's not fair."

The head studied the shy-looking infant with a certain admiration.

"That was very good of you to tell me," she smiled approvingly. "You did absolutely the right thing. Well done. I'll see your teacher gives you two extra stars."

His small round face beamed as he turned to go, and as the senior teacher watched him race happily across the playground to join the other pupils she couldn't help but feel a certain brief stab of pathos. It was not new and something she'd experienced on many previous occasions during her long haul up the educational ladder. With her whole life devoted to study, there had seemed little time for any thought of marriage and having a family; or was it, she sometimes wondered, that the right man had just never seemed to come along? She glanced down at Peter and a picture of his father flashed across her mind. His shock of dark blond hair, his obvious physical strength and talent, combined to make him a desirable proposition for any woman, but where, she wondered forlornly, had the John Grants of this world been in her life?

Later that same evening, there was another remonstration, only on this occasion it was Miriam's father on the receiving end for fiddling about with his laptop at the supper table.

"John, must you do that? I find it very irritating," complained Susan.

Jeanette who was also present along with Miriam, perhaps wisely endeavoured to look as though she'd heard nothing.

"Right," he nodded, in an attempt to keep his wife quiet while juggling the keyboard with one hand and a spoonful of soup in the other.

"John," she persisted. "It really is very anti-social, and I'm sure your mother would have agreed with me."

Finally, he gave her his full attention.

"I'm not sure that's a strictly valid observation," he smiled, "bearing in mind that my mother would probably have thought this laptop was a small TV with a lid. Anyway," he exclaimed, "remember, we were discussing Peter's condition that morning after the fish tank incident and how he insisted his real name was Ralph? Well," he nodded towards his ex, "after my discussion with Jeanette, she suggested Peter's problem might arise from some genetic link with the Blakes. So, I've been checking my ancestral tree on one of the heritage websites. After all, I must have got my artistic talent, such as it is, from somewhere." And tapping the laptop with a touch of satisfaction, he added, "Believe it or not, I've found a connection. I didn't know it, but Blake's sister was married to my great-great-grandfather, Isaac Grant."

"Hmm. Very interesting," she observed vacantly, while gathering up the dirty dishes. Then, after depositing them in the sink, she turned to ask, "And where exactly does that painting fit in with all your high-blown theories? And the uneasy feeling it gave Mrs Shawcross? Not to mention my dream of walking along the river bank and meeting that poor wretched woman."

"I think," he responded slowly. "There's a good chance that the woman in your dream was probably Blake's wife. And after her husband's pact with evil, she felt driven to warn anyone of the possible consequences if they owned the picture. And this was particularly true if one of them should become pregnant, and if there was some family genetic link then the danger became even greater." He shrugged. "It's only guesswork of course, but that's my honest opinion – for what it's worth."

At this point, Jeanette interrupted.

"Can I help with those dishes, Susan?"

"That's very kind," she smiled back. "But if perhaps you could make the tea, I'd be more than grateful." Mundane life, it seemed, persisted in the very teeth of philosophical debate. "Also," Susan exclaimed, "it's time for bed young Miriam. Remember, early to bed and early to rise makes a man healthy, wealthy and wise. So, off you go now."

"Goodnight everyone," their daughter chorused, while dutifully getting up to leave the room.

"A lovely girl," complimented Jeanette after she'd gone. "You must be very proud of her."

John smiled in agreement before his wife added, "You know, none of what you're saying accounts for how that hat disappeared from the picture, which," she shivered, "really gives me the horrors."

He didn't respond immediately, but instead just nodded while staring vacantly straight ahead. Then, tilting his chair back on two legs, he took a deep breath.

"That," he confessed, without refocusing his fixed gaze, "is a complete mystery, and probably something that we'll never understand."

A brief silence fell over the supper table, during which time John looked at his ex and pointedly indicated his empty cup; a mute hint which brought an immediate response whilst, at that point, he decided to deliver the final 'joy' of the evening.

"By the way, I didn't tell you, love!" he exclaimed, turning to his wife. "But I had a phone call today from that spider woman at Peter's school. "You know," he grinned, "the tarantula one."

"Go on then – tell me. Now, what's the trouble?" She sighed wearily before adding, "Oh, I do sometimes long for a cigarette."

Her husband then proceeded to describe the playground debacle, before adding with a smirk of satisfaction, "From all accounts, Peter gave the wretch a right trouncing. And I say, good for him. It almost makes me proud of the boy."

"Well, it would, wouldn't it?" retorted his wife tersely. "It's just the sort of reaction I'd expect." She paused reflectively. "You know, it's something I've often wondered about you – you're a strange mixture of artistic refinement, and, if I'm honest, downright thuggery."

And so the evening drew to a close – although, after all the philosophising there seemed to have been precious little achieved in the way of any solution to their son's problem.

Chapter 9

SLOWLY THE YEARS passed over the Grant household, but even as John's landmark sixtieth birthday approached, his poignant memory of Brenda remained as undimmed as ever. Repeated efforts to ascertain her fate had only ever drawn a blank, and more and more he bitterly regretted having let her slip away without declaring his feelings. It was a poignant example of the eternally sad words: too late. However, often there seemed little time for regret as ever-fresh problems loomed, albeit one in particular being of his own making.

Well-educated and financially successful, he had nevertheless been brought up in a rough working-class neighbourhood where violence had often proved a ready currency; this and a naturally aggressive disposition combined to make John a force to be reckoned with – although, as his wife had observed, it was a trait she found offensive and something she'd taken exception to on a number of occasions. One Saturday morning, however, the consequences of his latent hostility finally came to a head.

Miriam was out visiting a college friend while Jeanette had taken Peter to the local village. This had left John and his wife sharing a coffee at the kitchen table where her husband gazed idly out of the big bay window. Beads of water chased each other down the glass, and although not heavy, the drizzle-like rain had the capacity to quickly soak anyone who ventured out. Falling from a low grey sky, it epitomised the classic dreariness normally only found gracing the English countryside.

"Lovely day," he muttered as he continued to stare out over their bleak and uninviting-looking lake. "Oh, to be in England, eh?"

"Don't be so miserable," objected his wife. "If you've nothing better to think about, go and book seats for us tonight at the Theatre Royal in Brighton. I understand there's a good play on there by Arthur Miller."

But even while she was speaking, her husband suddenly cocked his head.

"Shush," he interrupted while holding up his hand. "Did you hear that?"

But Susan shook her head.

"No, I can't hear anything," she responded while reaching for her cup.

"There it goes again. Surely you can hear it now!" he exclaimed, getting to his feet. "It's one of those bloody hunting horns. But I tell you what. They're not churning their way across our ground again after that last episode."

And, with that, he raced from the kitchen.

"John," she called after him desperately. "Please don't do anything silly." But then sighed resignedly doubting whether in his impetuosity he'd even heard.

But she was not entirely unsympathetic, especially when recalling their early days at the farmhouse when, upon returning from a holiday abroad, they had found a huge area of the big field reduced to a virtual sea of mud, which, from the numerous imprints, had obviously been the result of horses milling about after a kill. However, what really sickened her was the shredded remains of some poor, unidentifiable animal which had obviously been torn to pieces by the dogs.

By this stage, John had emerged from the rear of the house and was briskly making his way towards the big field where he could hear the baying of hounds and see huntsmen in their bright red jackets and black riding helmets. Thundering over the neighbour's land, they were obviously heading straight towards his own property; although even as he absorbed this approaching circus, he caught sight of a large and beautiful fawn-coloured fox as the terrified animal struggled desperately to squeeze its way through the boundary fence. With its luxurious full pale beige tail, it was probably the most striking example of its kind Miriam's father had ever seen and fuelled his anger against what he saw as barbarity.

The leading horse took the boundary obstacle in its stride, but found John waiting on the far side to grab the animal's bridle almost as it landed. Obviously a snob of the first order, the rider immediately tried to snatch back control of the reins.

"Unhand my horse at once, sir!" he shouted with the colour rising in his face. "Don't you know I'm master of the hunt?"

"I don't care if you're King Kong!" shouted back John. "You and your type can bloody well keep off my land."

Seeing the confrontation, the remaining riders hesitated on the opposite side of the fence and even the hounds ceased their howling as if sensing the uncertainty – all of which gave the magnificent fox a chance to make good its escape. The saga was over for the frightened animal, but it certainly wasn't for John.

"Did you hear me?" rasped the purple-faced huntsman as he threateningly wielded his riding crop. But, if he'd aimed to intimidate he was sadly wrong, for his kind only brought out the worst in the retired art teacher who didn't mince his words.

"You can carry out your shit activities where you like, old son. But you're not doing it here. Got it?"

Whether the intruder 'got it' or not was questionable, but as John continued to restrain the increasingly restless horse, its rider made the fatal mistake of bringing his riding crop down hard across the back of John's hand; for mistake it was, because John immediately grabbed the man's arm and wrenched him from the saddle with such force that it sent his helmet flying and brought him crashing heavily to the ground. But the farmhouse owner's anger knew no bounds and the offender found himself being hauled upright to face the business end of his assailant's fist. However, seconds before the impact, John felt a restraining tug on his arm, and turning found his anxious-faced wife had followed him across the field in time to witness the whole sorry confrontation.

"John, what on earth do you think you're doing?" she cried frantically. "Do you want to end up in prison?"

"Prison or not," exclaimed her husband furiously while indicating the dishevelled huntsman, "I'm not having that lead a pack of bloodthirsty vultures all over our property."

Ignoring his anger, Susan turned her attention to the stricken-looking pack leader in an attempt to make amends. But the man would have none of it and dismissed her out of hand.

"You'll be hearing more of this. That husband of yours – that's if he is your husband – has assaulted me in front of all these witnesses."

"Don't you dare threaten me or my wife!" John shouted back. "Now take yourself and your horse and clear off."

On the way back to the house, however, Susan voiced her serious concern. "We haven't heard the last of that, John. You can bank on it. You'll probably end up being prosecuted for assault." She stopped for a moment and looked straight at her husband. "I know what you're like. If I hadn't turned up, you'd have punched that man, wouldn't you? And it would have been all over the local newspapers, which would have done nothing for my official capacity in the county.

"That man, as you call him," John protested, "attacked me first." And with that, he showed her the vivid weal on the back of his hand.

Nevertheless, his wife was proved right because several weeks later saw him facing the local magistrates' court in Horsham where his previous sins with the .22 rifle and the more recent charge of assault were duly trotted out and well and truly chewed over. The upshot was a two thousand pound fine combined with a six-months suspended sentence, and as his wife emphasised while leaving the building, "Any more incidents like that, John, and you'll find yourself inside. So, for goodness sake try to keep your nose clean from now on."

"John Frederick Grant," mimicked her husband, imitating the magistrate's squeaky voice. "On the tenth of February of this year, you've been charged with affray and assault. How do you plead? De da de da de da... Silly old fluff," he added derisively. "Should have been put out to grass years ago; long since passed it. Passed anything if you ask me."

"Well!" exclaimed Susan. "I didn't ask, but just remember what I said. Keep those fists and that temper of yours under control in future."

"What I can't understand," quibbled her husband, "is why the court made no mention of how the man was trespassing on my land."

"And that," countered his wife, "is because there's no law against it. That's something I *do* know. It's a civil matter, and if you want to keep them off our property you'd have to obtain a court injunction, and I can tell you it wouldn't come cheap."

But despite the drama of the moment, life moved on quickly for the Grants, and as Peter's tenth birthday approached it heralded yet a fresh disaster. Again, it was a Saturday morning with John and his wife relaxing in the kitchen after a late breakfast. But, although long since past any withdrawal symptoms, Susan still desperately missed her cigarettes and was giving vent to the fact when their daughter burst into the room.

"Can you smell something burning?" she asked anxiously.

"Well," retorted her mother, a touch caustically, "I can assure you it's not cigarette smoke."

However, her husband was less reactive. "No. I can't smell anything."

"Come into the hall then," urged Miriam. "Then see what you think."

And indeed, as John and his wife reluctantly vacated the comfort of their post-breakfast retreat, the smell of burning became undeniable.

"It's wood smoke," agreed her father after inhaling deeply. "And it's coming from outside." So saying, he led a dash to the rear of the house.

Then, to their horror, as they stepped from the back door, they could see a great pall of black smoke rising from the stable block in the small field. Built almost entirely of wood, the structure provided ready fodder for the hungry flames as they darted their way up through the dark rolling clouds of smoke.

"Miriam. Phone the fire brigade!" John shouted urgently.

But even as he turned back to collect an extinguisher from the house, he caught sight of his son emerging from the end stable.

"Peter!" screamed his mother in desperation. "Come over here this instant."

However, the wayward child gave no sign of hearing her, but instead just casually wandered away from the inferno before turning to watch the buildings as they burned. It was an incredible display of defiance – although, as Susan prepared to rush forward and remonstrate with him, a terrible suspicion flashed through her mind and she briefly wondered if it was he who had been responsible for starting the blaze.

"What's happened?" came the sudden voice of John's ex.

"What's happened," Susan echoed irritably. "Can't you see our stable block is being burned to the ground and I've a dreadful feeling my son might be responsible." But then, turning to their unorthodox guest she added sharply, "In any case, I thought you were in charge of him on Saturdays?"

"I am normally," confessed a contrite Jeanette. "But I'm afraid this morning I just over-slept."

"You can say that again!" exclaimed the exasperated Susan looking down at her watch. "Peter. Get over here this minute. Do you hear me?" she shouted out again at the top of her voice.

By the time the fire brigade had extinguished the blaze, half of the block had been reduced to ashes, and on the following Monday morning – which happened to be a bank holiday – the chief fire officer stopped by with some very disturbing news.

"Come in," invited Susan as she answered the door to their unexpected visitor.

"Thank you," replied the official while taking care to wipe his shoes on the doormat. "It's not very nice out there. I don't know what's the matter with this country. It never seems to stop raining. In fact, I sometimes wonder why our ancestors settled over here in the first place."

Once in the kitchen, Susan offered him a seat and a cup of tea. "Now," she smiled, "to what do we owe the honour of this visit?"

The fire chief was a tall, though slim, man with greying hair and obviously somewhere in his early fifties. He seemed a pleasant enough individual – although, unlike John, he was far from good-looking and nowhere near as well built. However, once seated he reached into the breast pocket of his tunic and withdrew a small blackened and twisted object which he placed on the kitchen table.

"Does this look at all familiar?" he asked quietly.

"Well, it might if I knew what it was supposed to be," she exclaimed.

"One of my men found it at the scene of the fire," explained the officer. "It's a cigarette lighter – or what's left of it – and I think it might have been used to start the blaze." He looked grim. "In other words, we could well be dealing with a case of arson."

Susan quietly took a deep breath, for while suspecting the lighter might be hers she was nevertheless in an extremely difficult situation knowing that any admission of ownership could well implicate her son. Worse, if she found her lighter missing from the kitchen drawer she would know for certain that Peter had been the culprit. But, despite the dilemma, her maternal instincts prevailed and left her with no option but to lie.

Immediately after seeing the fire chief out, she raced to the kitchen drawer and frantically snatched it open in a desperate hope that her lighter would still be there. Even when seeing Peter watch the stables burn, she had decided to give him the benefit of the doubt – having no wish to fuel his ever-present resentful and aggressive attitude. But, if the lighter was missing...? She frenziedly rummaged amongst the neatly folded tea towels, and although her abandoned packet of cigarettes was still there, she could find no trace of the lighter. And with a sinking heart, she knew that its charred remains were now in the custody of the fire chief.

Bank holidays in her husband's business held little significance and he'd left the house at first light to inspect a recently acquired property, while although she expected him back at any moment, she nevertheless, perhaps unwisely, decided to tackle Peter on her own.

Crossing the hallway, she entered the nursery, which by that stage had effectively become a recreation room complete with its own billiard table, and she found John's ex busily occupying the ten-year-old with a game of pool. Jeanette had been, and was, an ongoing huge bonus in the upbringing of their volatile son; someone who didn't intrude into family affairs and who just got on with what was needed – which made John, and more especially herself, eternally grateful to have her.

"Sorry to interrupt," apologised Susan, "but I need Peter for a quick word."

Back in the kitchen, she lost no time in indicating the open drawer.

"Peter, I want you to tell me the truth. Did you take my cigarette lighter?" At first, her son failed to respond but just stood staring back at his mother with darkening eyes – eyes which fleetingly expressed a flicker of guilt. "Peter!" repeated his exasperated mother. "Did you take my lighter? Yes or no?"

"Yes," he echoed suddenly after a further delay.

For several seconds, Susan just studied the boy in disbelief, and fearful of the answer she hesitated to ask the next obvious question.

"And why did you take it?" she managed finally.

By this time, Jeanette had followed in from the nursery. Experience with the boy over the years had taught them both to recognise the danger signals, but in her frustration and anger Susan failed to heed the warning, and despite the nanny's apprehensive expression she nevertheless insisted.

"Peter. Are you going to tell me if you stole my cigarette lighter and used it to set fire to the stables?"

The pseudo-nanny winced covertly anticipating a volatile reaction, and her fears proved well-founded.

"Why do you keep calling me Peter?" screamed back Susan's deranged offspring. "I'm not Peter. I'm not. I'm, I'm..."

But words failed the boy, and for a moment, his mother thought he might be caught up in some kind of psychotic fit. But clearly lacking John's appreciation of their son's difficulties, she made the fatal mistake of kneeling down to take a firm grip on the boy's upper arms.

"Peter. Control yourself," she ordered. "What do you mean that's not your name? Of course it is."

But any form of self-control was now out of the question as the dominant persona became ever-more aggressive. And like the reaction John had experienced, she felt her restraining hold violently dislodged as he continued to scream.

"It's not. It's not. My name's not Peter. It's... it's..."

And this time the name was forthcoming.

"It's Ralph."

Again, the concept of reincarnation flashed through Susan's mind as her son repeatedly insisted that was his name. Then, as she exchanged alarmed glances with Jeanette, Peter shouted defiantly, "And, yes. I did steal your lighter and burned the stables because I don't belong here! I belong... I belong..."

However, the struggle to identify his origins again became too much, and, lost for words, he broke down into uncontrollable sobbing. Susan only ever had a vague recollection of what happened next for events suddenly seemed to spiral out of control and assume an unreal quality, as though everything was happening in the slow-moving action of a nightmare: one second her son was shaking and crying hysterically, the next he was violently flinging himself at her with a kitchen knife. She also had a brief impression of Jeanette desperately trying to restrain him before feeling a searing hot pain tear down the side of her forearm as the blade slashed into her flesh. Fortunately, however, at that moment the sudden appearance of her husband almost certainly saved her life.

Absorbing the crisis in an instant, John immediately grabbed the raging boy away from his wife, but then only to be confronted by the frenzied knife-wielding fury himself. At this point, sheer instinct took over, and seizing the lad's collar and one leg John lifted him off his feet and hurled him across the kitchen table – an action so violent that Peter was sent flying over to the far side where he fell off to land head first on the flagstone floor. There he struck the left side of his temple and remained in a crumpled inert heap.

Jeanette looked paralysed and as white as a sheet, but John had no time for niceties.

"Get my wife to A&E immediately," he commanded, tossing over his car keys. "And wrap her arm in a towel while I attend to Peter."

It was as though time had gone into overdrive during John's dramatic action, but now it seemed to return to a normal pace as he rounded the table and stooped down by his stricken son. Lying on his side and even with the bloodstained knife not far from his hand, the boy appeared strangely vulnerable and at peace. Choking with emotion, John reached down to stroke his hair. Ridden with guilt for not pressing harder to get further professional help, he felt the tears run freely down his face, because despite all that had happened the boy was still his son. A vicious blue-looking bruise on the left side of the youngster's forehead spoke of the violent impact there had been with the stone floor. However, as John reached for his mobile phone to contact an ambulance, he became relieved to see the boy's eyes flicker open.

"Daddy. What happened?" he asked in a gentle but feeble voice. And as John went to answer, he immediately realised how the pale blue of his eyes had once again replaced their normally brooding quality. But as Peter slowly sat up, the memory of the previous few violent moments were obviously flooding back. "I hurt Mummy, didn't I?" he exclaimed anxiously, but then shook his head. "But it wasn't me, Daddy. I would never hurt Mummy."

"It's all right, Peter. I know that," replied his father while lifting him up. Once again, John knew he was dealing with his true son. "But right now, I'm taking you to hospital to have that bruise checked out."

In response, the boy put his arms round his father's neck and hugged him tight. However, he then said something that, on the surface, sounded very strange. And yet, as John carried him out to his wife's car he realised it might well make a weird kind of sense.

"Daddy," murmured Peter. "We've got to take Ralph back to the riverbank, because it's the only way that I'll ever be happy."

Gently pulling his son away, John asked curiously, "What makes you say that?"

"I just know, Daddy," he replied in a very subdued voice. "Believe me. I just know."

Fortunately, although the cut on Susan's arm looked horrendous at the time, it did, in fact, only require a few stitches, and ever-mindful of the need to protect her family, she made no mention at the hospital of how she'd come to be hurt. That would be a subject reserved for major discussion later that evening when Peter and Miriam were in bed.

John and his wife together with his ex, lingered in the kitchen long after supper. Dirty dishes lay neglected in view of the seriousness of the day's events.

"One bloody thing after another," John growled as he shoved his empty bowl aside and finally broke the heavy silence.

"Much as I hate to interfere with family discussions," ventured Jeanette hesitantly, "I do think that after what happened this morning, Peter needs sectioning. I mean, you could have been killed, Susan."

It was said with genuine concern and John nodded with tightly compressed lips.

"I know you're right, and under normal circumstances I would agree. However, before we do anything radical and make a decision we might regret later on, I want to try something Peter suggested while you were on the way to A&E."

But both women looked askance.

"To be frank, John," retorted his wife, "I wouldn't take anything that boy said seriously. And I'll tell you something else. I need a bloody cigarette! Anyway," she added wearily, "just for the record. What sort of gem did his lordship come up with?"

"I know this will sound bizarre," John ventured, "but his actual words were, 'We need to take Ralph back to the riverbank.'" He raised his hands to quell a chorus of incredulity. "I know. I know how it sounds. But think about it for a moment," he pleaded, "and everything that's happened since we first acquired that painting. Anyway, next Saturday, I'm determined to give it a try." He turned to Jeanette. "You've played a big part in Peter's life, so if you'd like to come along you'd be more than welcome."

The following Saturday morning, therefore, found the four of them working their way along the edge of the River Arun. They were not far from the town of Arundel and John had a pretty good idea of the setting that Blake originally chose to paint – although, weather-wise, the day was a far cry from the one he had depicted. Leaden overcast skies and a stiff breeze had left the water both choppy and looking very uninviting, while a slight haze hung over the entire area. The river itself was situated on a fertile flood plain and either side lay open fields where groups of sheep grazed lazily on the lush grass with no apparent thought for tomorrow – which, under the circumstances, was probably just as well.

Rounding a bend, John almost instantly recognised the location he was seeking. With its inclining tree and a mist-enshrouded view of the distant hills, it was unmistakable.

"Right ladies!" he exclaimed. "The moment has arrived. That's the spot straight ahead."

For a moment he paused reflectively. "Strange," he murmured almost to himself, "how nothing here seems to have changed in over a hundred and fifty years. It's as though time's just stood still." But he quickly thrust the nostalgia to one side in the immediacy of the moment and turned to the two women. "I want you both to stay here while I go ahead with Peter." Susan started to protest, but he was adamant. "Look, I don't know what's going to happen once we get up there. So, will you please just remain here?"

"But, John," she cried tearfully. "You're taking my son."

"I know. I know," he responded gently in an attempt to placate her dread. "But remember, he's my son too and I'm doing what I think is the best for all of us. So please, please trust me and wish us well." And with that, he took Peter's hand. "Are you ready?"

The boy looked back at his father with brooding eyes which nevertheless showed appreciation, and he nodded. "I'm ready."

Slowly, step-by-step, father and son approached the bend of destiny until, finally, they stood beneath the tree that had spread its branches out over the river for so many years. The path they took had been tightly compacted by the passage of many feet; people who had passed that way yet been totally ignorant of the tragic human drama once played out there so long ago. But John knew, and it gave him an eerie sensation to be standing on the very ground where Blake must have originally set up his easel to portray his dead son.

He could almost sense the man's abject sorrow as he executed his melancholy task with such unremitting dedication. And yet, ironically, it had all been set against the most breathtakingly beautiful landscape. But for what, John wondered bitterly, knowing the artist's wife had been about to desert him. And standing there for a brief moment, it seemed as though the heart-rending emotions that had been involved somehow still hung hauntingly in the very atmosphere.

For a fleeting instant, John and his son just looked at each other in a way that made words irrelevant. Finally, however, Miriam's brother gradually sank down onto the grassy slope and leaned back against the tree trunk.

John had dedicated the last two days scouring charity shops in nearby Horsham in an attempt to secure a replacement for the straw hat he'd originally destroyed. And after an exhaustive search, he'd eventually been lucky enough to find one with the same frayed edges as the original. Reaching into the plastic bag he'd been carrying, he said softly, "Ralph. I bought this especially for you."

Slowly and reverently, the boy took the straw hat and placed it on his head.

"Thank you, John. Thank you for your understanding. I'll always remember you and your kindness."

It sounded strange to hear the boy use his first name, but John knew it held an echo of a distinction. A distinction between his own boy, Peter, and the influence that was Blake's son. Goodbyes are invariably sad. A fact which John knew only too well, and with tears at the edge of his vision, he bade the boy a last farewell.

"I hope you find the peace you've sought for so long, Ralph. And may God bless you."

Then, turning away and without a backward glance, he made to re-join the waiting women.

Finally, all three of them stood watching the river bend where a re-enactment of Blake's composition was now taking place, for the boy had slumped forward as if in a deep sleep. The only factor differing from the original scene was the slight but persistent haze. Being an artist, it was a fascinating experience for John as he glanced down the tunnel of time to see the setting just as it must have first appeared to Blake. Susan, however, understandably was only concerned about their son.

"What happens now, John?" she asked anxiously. "Surely we're not just leaving Peter there."

"The honest answer," he replied guardedly, "is that I just don't know. And as I said before, I'm only going on instinct that things will work out for the best."

But even as he spoke, two figures to the far side of Peter slowly emerged from the mist, and although still a long way off, he watched in fascination as they made their way to stand by the recumbent boy. From what John could see, the first appeared to be a tall graceful-looking woman with an abundance of copper-coloured hair that reached way down past her unbelievably small waist, while her full-length dark-velvet dress topped by a white lacework stole served to accentuate an already impressive elegance.

"One of the Pre-Raphaelite stunners," exclaimed John.

Her gentleman companion was of similar height and wore a high-set, raffia-work, white cravat with a waistcoat that was complemented by a black cutaway frock-coat. Altogether, in fact, they represented a classical example of middle-class Victorian England.

Unable to believe what he saw, John could only murmur incredulously, "Blake and his wife, Suzette."

"You mean they're ghosts?" cried Susan hysterically, clutching her hands over her face.

But as the three of them continued to watch, they saw the woman reach down to the prostrate boy and gently nudge his shoulder. In response, he immediately looked up and flew into her arms. Almost mesmerised, Jeanette uttered just three words, "Mother and son."

Peter's equally fascinated father nodded. "Yes, mother and son. Together again at last."

The sheer joy emanating from the trio ahead was almost tangible, and obviously overcome with happiness the woman playfully snatched the boy's straw hat before putting it on and then holding it in place against the stiff breeze; a movement for John so reminiscent of Brenda riding the carousel all those years ago. But the impression was gone in an instant as he saw the woman put her arms up round her companion's neck and hug him in an expression of absolute joy and relief.

"Reconciled at last," he exclaimed. "Remember," John reminded his wife, "Tim said Blake was afraid Suzette would desert him?"

However, if Susan heard him she gave no sign, for she had spontaneously raised her hand and was rigorously waving to the trio from the past.

And so it was, the two families greeted each other across the vicissitude of time. But then, slowly, almost reluctantly it seemed, the images of a previous era turned and, along with their son, gradually began to fade away back into the mists of history.

Jeanette turned to her ex. “Now what’s happening, John?” she asked tersely.

“Well, I sincerely hope,” he replied, “that all three are returning to their rightful place in the past and to the peace that has eluded them for so long.”

The riverside drama, however, was far from over.

“But what about my son?” cried Susan. “Where is my son?”

And then, almost as if to amplify the mother’s desperation, the already substantial breeze suddenly picked up to become a full-blown gale; a fury that tore along the river way and whipped up the water into deep angry troughs, while at the same time the tree where Peter had sat creaked and swayed under the sudden onslaught. Moreover, at first unnoticed, the dark clouds that had been piling up in the west suddenly unleashed driving sheets of torrential rain which caused droves of terrified sheep in the adjoining fields to flee and seek shelter or huddle together in protective groups.

Unprepared and without adequate clothing, John and the two women rapidly became drenched, although, despite the chill and wet, Susan still stubbornly refused to move an inch without her son.

“I don’t care, John!” she shouted above the sound

of the vicious wind. "I'm not going anywhere unless Peter comes with me."

Like the sheep, all three had turned their backs to the foul weather. But, thinking he'd heard a voice, John looked back, and grimacing against the beating rain, he could just make out the figure of his son racing towards them from the direction of the tree.

"Daddy! Daddy!" he cried out. "Wait for me. He's gone, Daddy. Ralph's gone."

And as Peter flew into his father's arms, John knew for certain that the long nightmare was finally over – not only for them, but also for the family of the mid-nineteenth century artist who went by the name of George Blake.

"Home then, John?" suggested his wife.

"Home," he agreed. "Home it is."

Chapter 10

THE BIBLICAL TERM 'carmel', when translated means 'place of refreshing'; a suitable title to describe a care home for the elderly and one adopted by a centre situated in the south-coast port of Shoreham-by-Sea. Not far from the beautiful mellow cairn-stone Norman church of St Mary's, it offered spacious and airy accommodation with each resident enjoying their own personal reception room along with a separate bedroom and an en-suite bathroom. In addition, trained staff ensured they were provided with the best possible attention twenty-four hours a day. It was very expensive, but then John had worked hard all his life and both his children had agreed that he deserved the finest care in his waning years.

Fast approaching his late nineties, the strength and health he'd enjoyed for so many years had ebbed away, and now crippled with arthritis he was virtually confined to his room and an armchair.

There were, of course, no bars at the windows nor were the doors ever locked, but he knew they might just as well have been for he was now effectively a prisoner of age and infirmity. Often, he would quietly long to reach for his keys and stride out of the main entrance; to get in his car and drive back to his old farmhouse home, as he would have done in his younger days – back to the place he loved and had shared with his wife; back to his little retreat and all that it had meant, but which were now gone forever. Not that he complained, knowing there was much to be grateful for. Never a day would pass without a visit from either of his children, and he was still able to enjoy painting. After an eventful and dramatic life, he'd become content to see out his last days quietly in the belief that nothing could ever really surprise him again. But in this respect, he would prove to be wrong, and it took the form of an unexpected visitor.

It was Christmas Eve and festivity filled the air with bright colourful lights adorning the outside of the home, while the entry vestibule housed a huge tree that groaned under the weight of multiple decorations and holly. In fact, the whole reception area was a virtual grotto of colour and imagination; symbols of rejoicing to mark Christ's birth; yet ironically, despite all of this outward show of joy, one had to wonder whether it wasn't somehow inappropriate to celebrate in a place where the inmates' only hope of escape was one of grim finality.

However, even without its festive makeover, the reception area was an impressive experience with its wide curving counter and palms, together with bow-shaped windows that afforded extensive views over the English Channel. In fact, it could well have been a vestibule in one of the finest hotels in the country. Additionally, there were two smartly-uniformed receptionists in constant attendance day and night, but in the late afternoon of the day in question both assistants were deeply involved with their computer screens as an elderly but elegant lady entered the foyer.

Finally hearing the newcomer, one of them looked up.

"Can I be of help, madam?" asked the young receptionist politely.

The visitor slowly eased the slim patent leather gloves from her hands and snapped them shut in her handbag before replying. "I phoned yesterday concerning one of your residents; a Mr John Grant to be precise. And if it's possible, I'd like to see him."

"I think he's already got a visitor," replied the younger woman while turning to her colleague for confirmation.

"He has," asserted the second girl, "although he should be about finished by now." But then, addressing the lady directly she recommended caution. "Mr Grant is elderly and quite frail, so if you do see him I think it would be advisable to make it as brief as possible. He's in room 102, so I'll see if I can get someone to show you the way." And with that, she turned to the intercom. "May we have an attendant in reception please?" It was all very professional and within minutes a uniformed porter duly appeared. "Oh, Andros. Would you be kind enough to show this lady to room 102?"

Andros turned out to be a pleasant-faced man who, by his accent, obviously originated from somewhere in Eastern Europe. The lady visitor smiled as they made their way through a maze of spacious and beautifully appointed corridors lined with quality oak-panelled doors on either side.

"Dare I ask what part of the world you come from?" she enquired.

Obviously happy to talk to such an attractive woman, he was quick to reply.

"Greece, madam. About 45km from Athens. A little place called Saronida."

"Ah," she replied, "the land of culture and classical splendour; the land to which we owe so much of our way of life. You must be very proud."

"Indeed, madam," he smiled. "Indeed, I am."

For several moments they walked on in companionable silence before curiosity again got the better of the visitor. "And what, may I ask, brought you to England of all places?"

"It's the work, madam. Greece is now a very poor country and its almost impossible to find employment."

By this time, they had arrived at the door marked '102', and the visitor expressed her gratitude for his courtesy.

"It's been a pleasure, madam," he assured

her, before turning away and heading back to the reception area.

However, as the lady reached for the handle the door suddenly swung back unexpectedly to reveal a tall, handsome man in his middle to late thirties and who was obviously just about to leave.

"Ah," exclaimed the new female arrival. "That was good timing."

"Absolutely," he agreed, but then paused to study the newcomer more carefully as he noticed her beautifully groomed and luxurious shoulder-length silver hair and high cheek bones; which together with a figure most women half her age would have envied, combined to make for a very attractive proposition indeed.

Stunned beyond measure, a sudden unbelievable thought flashed through the young man's mind.

"Admittedly I'm only guessing," he confessed guardedly, "but if I didn't know it was impossible, I'd say you were Brenda Hawsworth."

The woman returned his look of approval with thinly veiled admiration.

"And I'd say you'd be right," she smiled. "But tell me. Why do you think it's impossible?" But then, without waiting for an explanation, she suddenly gasped. "And you can only be John's boy. There's no other way you could be so like him without being his son."

The man slowly nodded while at the same time being unable to take his eyes off his father's fashionable visitor, and he held out his hand which she immediately grasped warmly.

"The name's Peter," he explained. "But I just can't believe I'm actually talking to the girl who once so famously rode the fairground horse." And as they stood there in the doorway with their hands locked, they became momentarily lost in a capsule of poignancy totally divorced from time and space.

Finally, John's son broke the spell. "I don't understand!" he exclaimed, excited yet puzzled. "I mean, we all thought you had died years ago. But look, we can't talk here. There's a lounge down the corridor. We've so much to catch up on." For a moment he hesitated before adding, "Well, that's supposing you've got the time."

Like the rest of the care home, the lounge was lavishly appointed with expensive designer furniture and beautifully arranged displays of flowers that received constant daily attention. Coffee and light refreshments were also available, while, like the reception area, the room also afforded spectacular views over the Channel.

"Expensive," observed Brenda as she took a seat and crossed her still-shapely legs.

"You can't begin to imagine how expensive," he assured her, handing over a coffee while still scarcely able to believe how little she'd been affected by the passage of time. "But what I can't understand," he managed, albeit a trifle bluntly, "is how you're still alive... I mean, according to my father you were flown to a clinic somewhere in Florida purportedly dying of pancreatic cancer."

Brenda took a first sip from her cup and then looked disconcertingly straight into his eyes. "And that's what the doctors over here believed at the time," she admitted. "What's more, so did I, and it was an horrific experience. But, fortunately, a biopsy in the States showed it was benign. So..." she smiled with an emphatic tilt of her head, "I lived to tell the tale as they say." She replaced her cup in its saucer. "But tell me, you mentioned the girl who rode the fairground horse. How did you know about that? It happened long before you were even born."

Peter shifted slightly uncomfortably in his seat. "My mother's been dead now for a number of years," he began with a touch of sadness.

"I'm sorry to hear that," sympathised his listener gently. "I knew her well. She was a lovely and very intelligent woman."

"Indeed, she was." He nodded. "But be that as it may, her death had the effect of drawing my dad and I much closer, and in the latter years he tended to confide in me a great deal." Peter paused as if uncertain whether to continue. "I hope I'm not talking out of turn when I say he often discussed you at some length. And, I might add, his deep feelings for you." He shook his head slowly and dropped his gaze as sadness deepened and dimmed his eyes.

Slowly, however, he looked up. "Dad told me on a number of occasions how he'd always bitterly regretted having turned down your invitation to join him on the carousel." Peter again shook his head and compressed his lips. "You can't go back and change things in life like that, can you? No matter how desperately you'd like to."

For a long time, Miriam's old nanny just gazed at him with a look of absolute regret.

"No, Peter. You can't. And it's something I've lived with virtually my entire adult life. Because, you see, I loved your father with all my heart, but I knew we could never be together because he was loyal and too fond of your mother. And strangely," Brenda added wistfully, "it was just the sort of loyalty that caused me to feel the way I did, and for that matter, still do."

"And you never got married to anyone...?"

But she gave him no chance to finish.

"To anyone else? No, it would have been totally unfair because there was, and could only ever be, one man in my life. And that," she added with a conclusive note of finality, "was your father." She gazed down briefly at her empty cup before asking suddenly, "What became of the picture that used to hang in the hallway? I don't know if it was still there by the time you came along, but it depicted a boy fishing. Anyway," she continued idly, toying with her cup, "there was something about the thing that always left me feeling distinctly uneasy. In fact, I used to have the most disturbing dreams about it."

The muscles around Peter's angular jaw tightened. "I never actually saw it myself," he admitted. "But that painting caused me and the family more hell than you can imagine, and it contributed to an unrelenting misery that I had to endure until I was well gone ten years old."

He'd said it with such obvious feeling that Brenda began to wish she hadn't mentioned the subject.

"I'm sorry," she apologised. "I didn't mean to..."

But he hastened to put her at ease. "No, no. That's fine. In the end," he explained, "my father burned it. And not before time, because I'm sure it mediated some sort of distress from the past which was affecting everyone." Peter shrugged. "Anyway, it's all over and done with now, long ago."

"Could you not have at least sold it?" enquired the nanny curiously.

Peter emulated one of his father's old foibles by stretching his long frame before contracting with a pleasurable sigh. "From what Dad told me," he explained, "it seems that previous owners suffered similar difficulties and even a suicide. So, I don't think he wanted to perpetrate the same sort of disaster on other people. Anyway," he added, getting to his feet with a certain finality. "As I say, that's what my father told me. Six thousand pounds gone up in smoke."

In response, his elegant companion extended her hand. "It's been my great pleasure to meet you, Peter. We should try to stay in touch. Now, I must go and see your dad."

Miriam's nanny had always carried a mental picture of John as vitally strong; a powerful man who would stand no nonsense – and yet someone who possessed a raw sense of humour and artistic sensitivity capable of rivalling anyone. Therefore, when finally entering his room, she became appalled by what met her gaze, for there slumped in an armchair sat a frail old man. Gone was the shock of dark blond hair she remembered so well. All that remained were a few strands of white, while with his head down and eyes closed he was obviously in a deep sleep.

At first, Brenda hesitated about disturbing him, wondering perhaps whether it wouldn't be better to remember him in his heyday. But having waited so long for this moment, she became determined to see it though and carefully crossing the floor drew up a chair to sit quietly by the man she'd always loved. There was no means of knowing how long John would sleep, but it really didn't matter because she was where she'd always belonged.

With little else to do, her gaze wandered over the beautifully appointed apartment. John had obviously attempted to eat his lunch earlier, for the plate containing the remains of a meal still lay on a table nearby. But then, through a partly open door leading into the bedroom she caught sight of something that made her heart lurch. For there, unbelievably, on the corner of the bed was the hat she had worn all those years earlier at the Henfield fair. Slowly getting to her feet, she made her way through to the sleeping accommodation where, with a lump rising in her throat, she stared nostalgically at what was, after all, a symbol; a symbol of love and a relationship that could never have been realised.

Then, just as John had done before her, she slowly and reverently lifted the hat from its resting place and gently fingered the artificial flower adorning its brim.

Finally, moving over to the mirror she carefully put it on. Although the deep auburn colour of her hair had long since given way to a sheen-like silver, she nevertheless somehow felt young again. Twirling about and admiring her reflection, it was, for a brief instant, that long ago beautiful Easter bank holiday once more.

"Brenda?" gasped a sudden unexpected voice.

And spinning around, she found herself face-to-face with the man of her memories. For there he was. Leaning up against the doorframe with folded arms and a look of absolute incredulity. Knowing sadly that his wife was dead and how Peter had confirmed his feelings, Brenda knew there were now no longer any barriers or inhibitions to keep them apart, and she immediately flew into his arms. Enfeebled by the weight of years, however, her enthusiastic rush almost bowled him off his feet, but he quickly recovered to hold her close.

"At last. At last," he murmured almost to himself as the sensation of their so longed-for physical contact flowed through his entire being. Then, as they kissed it was everything he'd ever imagined and more, for her warm and yielding lips were a far cry from the skeletal nightmare he'd experienced back at the farmhouse. A nightmare he'd never forgotten.

Slowly, he pulled gently away to gaze fondly into her eyes.

"I can't believe it!" he exclaimed tenderly. "I mean, I thought you'd died years ago, and I tried so desperately hard to contact you when I heard of your illness."

"I'm sorry, John," she whispered as he gently held her head against his chest. "I'm so sorry. It's my fault. I should have had the courage to keep in touch and let you know what was happening. But you were married and never actually told me how you felt, and... and..." She hesitated brokenly. "I just couldn't bear living with false hope."

"You know," observed the aging John, "when I just saw you in that hat, it was how I've always remembered you. So lovely, and yet so forever beyond my reach." But the emotional reaction of Brenda's shock visit had begun to tell, and John started to look tired. "You'll have to excuse an old man," he smiled, "but I need to sit down. Come back into the lounge though because there's something I want to show you." Then, making his way towards the armchair, he reached for the inside pocket of his jacket and extracted a crumpled-looking envelope; an envelope she instantly recognised. "Ah!" he exclaimed obviously relieved to take the weight of his feet. "I see it looks familiar. It's the letter you sent, I don't know how many years ago. But I've always carried it with me." He patted his chest. "Near my heart."

Taking his hand, she reached down to kiss his cheek while words somehow seemed irrelevant.

Slightly unsteadily, he removed the poem he'd written and always kept with her letter; the poem he'd forever intended to send but somehow never did.

"Here. This is for you," he said softly. "Keep it and remember me. Because in it I've tried to say something of how I've always felt." He paused. "I so intended to post it to you," he confessed. "But with the rush of life..."

Gently taking the folded and tired-looking sheet of paper, Brenda reached for the glasses in her handbag before moving across to the window where the light was better and where she carefully opened it out. Then, through misting eyes, she started to read. There were just four lines, but they told her everything:

'It is but once we travel this life
Although fate dictates the path we tread
But whether it's the way we choose
Is often quite another thing'

"Oh, John," she cried crouching down beside his chair. "They're lovely words. I just wish I'd had them over the years. They'd have told me everything I needed to know." She took his hand and pressed it up against her moist cheek. "I'm so sorry. We could have had at least a few years together, but now..."

Approaching late afternoon, the light was beginning to fade while from somewhere in the distance could be heard the faint strains of 'God Rest Ye Merry Gentlemen'. By then, however, John's head had again fallen to his chest in sleep and Brenda contented herself just holding his hand.

Like the rest of the care home, a real effort had been made to incorporate the festive spirit with a small tree in the far corner and an array of greetings cards on a nearby casual table. Yet, for all the tinsel associated with Christmas, it failed to mask an inner ring of bitter poignancy knowing she had finally been reunited with her true love but too late; oh, so too late.

The far-off sound of a carol faded away to be replaced by 'Hark the Herald Angels Sing'. But she made no effort to move preferring instead to just sit by John's chair while he slumbered on. Even as the room gradually became dim, she remained by his side with minutes having to take the place of lost years.

"Oh, are you sitting in the dark?" came a sudden surprised-sounding voice which was accompanied by the click of the light switch.

Lost in thought, Miriam's old nanny had failed to hear the door open and admit a smartly-uniformed nursing assistant.

"Yes, I was keeping Mr Grant company while he's asleep," replied Brenda feeling slightly embarrassed as she blinked against the unexpected glare.

"Well, it's just to let you know that we usually settle residents down for the night between 8.30pm and 9pm."

It was said politely enough, although the implication was clear. Brenda smiled briefly to herself as she wondered what John's reaction would have been... 'So, get out!' The assistant, however, quickly sensed the intimate atmosphere and hastily withdrew. The aging nanny glanced down at her watch which told her it was fast approaching 9pm; little enough time left to enjoy their brief reunion – although she consoled herself with the thought that at least there would be lots of future opportunities.

However, as she continued to sit with John in a companionable silence, the warmth of his hand gradually began to fade and became quite cold. Thinking perhaps he needed some extra cover, she collected a blanket from the bedroom. But as she proceeded to wrap it round the man she loved, it suddenly became abundantly clear that no amount of blankets would make any difference and that, once again, she had lost the focus of her life. Only this time, it was absolutely final.

Slowly and reluctantly, she released his icy hand before crossing the room to gaze sadly out of the window. Although she had no means of knowing, it was a ploy often adopted by John in times of stress or sorrow; to just stare at the endless vista of sky and lose himself in an eternity of space and peace. That night, however, there was only an intense velvet black punctuated by tiny pinpoints of light – stars too numerous to imagine. Looking to her right, Brenda could see the perfect and brilliant orb of the moon as it cast a crystal pathway across the distant sea; a timeless skyscape of perpetuity and tranquillity where everything remained constant; so different, she thought bitterly, to the transitory duration of life on earth.

But in this, of course, she was wrong. For even the stars are not immortal and have an allotted span because this is reality and not eternity; they too eventually fade away.

Destined now to forever ride the carousel of life alone, she slowly turned to look at John for the last time before blowing him a kiss.

“Sleep well, my darling. Sleep well until we meet again.”

And with those words, she left the room and gently closed the door before making her way back to the reception area to report her sad news.

The End

If this earth were to pass away into the origins of its dust, then surely the resultant vacuum would forever echo with the silent screams of those who had once called it home: and whose collective agony would endure for eternity – a cry which, if, translated would surely read... **If only!**

Epilogue

Whether a life spent in hope and expectation of one's dreams can be a more intense experience than their actual realisation, is perhaps an open question. While, on the other hand, some might ask whether it be better to have loved and lost than never loved at all. But, in either case, I will leave it to the readers to make up their own minds.